T0382007

Helen Monks Takhar has been working as a journalist, copywriter and magazine editor since 1999. Originally from Southport, Merseyside, she lives in North London with her husband and two children. *The Marriage Rule* is her fourth novel.

Also by Helen Monks Takhar:

*That Woman**
Such a Good Mother
Nothing Without Me

* Previously published as *Precious You*.

THE MARRIAGE RULE

HELEN MONKS TAKHAR

ONE PLACE. MANY STORIES

HQ
An imprint of HarperCollins*Publishers* Ltd
1 London Bridge Street
London SE1 9GF

www.harpercollins.co.uk

HarperCollins*Publishers*
Macken House, 39/40 Mayor Street Upper
Dublin 1, D01 C9W8, Ireland
This edition 2025

1
First published in Great Britain by HQ,
an imprint of HarperCollins*Publishers* Ltd 2025

ISBN (HB): 9780008566432
ISBN (TPB): 9780008566418

Set in Bembo by HarperCollins*Publishers* India

Printed and bound in the UK using 100% Renewable
Electricity at CPI Group (UK) Ltd

MIX
Paper
FSC™ C007454

For more information visit: www.harpercollins.co.uk/green

Strong and beautiful.
For Caroline

Day twenty-one, Saturday morning

It feels like the middle of the night. I've just woken. Probably a combination of dehydration, my throbbing head and early-onset guilt. I look over at Gabriel. It's pretty dark in here and he has his back to me, but he seems sound asleep. I really wish he'd wake up too, let me enjoy the next few precious hours we have left together in this hotel room; stop me from thinking about the world beyond it and what's left of my soul after what I did last night.

Oh my god. I did it. I had sex with someone who wasn't my husband, crossed a point of no return. I'm so scared of what my future may hold now, a danger I can feel all about my body, in my bones, but somewhere inside me, I'm thrilled too. Because nothing, surely, can ever be the same again. I know I should be wishing I could go back to the point where I might not have let it happen, the way I always feel when I wake up like this, cloudy-headed and disorientated after drinking so much I can't really remember everything. I don't know exactly how Gabriel and I finally gave in to the desire that's been building up since we started working together; my memories aren't much more than hot smears of flesh and heat. All I know is that last night, I must

1

have finally taken the path that turned the Marriage Rule my best friend Sal shared with me a few weeks ago on its head, and shattered the actual vows I made to Dom.

With his clothes off, Gabriel's shoulders seem almost as broad as my husband's; my lover's real body is different from the one I've spent hours imagining naked. I peer beyond his frame to the seam of space above the curtains to check for morning's creep. It's June. Whatever time it is now, the night won't last for too much longer. I need to surround myself with Gabriel quickly, give myself a chance to remember what we did last night. While there's so much I'll have to face later, right now Gabriel can still distract me from the guilt I can feel wanting to settle on me, that and the post-coital aches and pains now making themselves known throughout my body; between my legs, around my shoulders; a curious heat across my scalp. Whatever Gabriel and I did, it must have been fiercely passionate. Now I'm properly awake, my body feels like it could have been in a fight.

I glance about the gloom to assess the scene where battle commenced: on my bedside table, I can make out dregs of red wine in a plastic sink-side tumbler; I assume we must have brought a bottle of last night's free wine back here whenever we made our excuses. Next to me, in between the bedside table and a wastepaper basket, I spy a condom on the carpet. From here, it looks tacky-dry; abandoned. Thank god I started taking the pill again after I stopped breastfeeding, something I haven't told Dom about, but haven't *not* told him either.

I can't let myself think about the baby now. I'm so far from her, so distant from where and who she needs me to be. And now, it's all really starting to hurt. Right in my chest, guilt blooming, threatening to explode. It wants to power me out of here, away from Gabriel and into another hotel room where I might run cold shower water through my hair and wherever else I throb, so I can return to the house anyone would say is beautiful, the husband most would describe as attentive and adoring, and my indisputably adorable baby, and act as though I'm innocent. I can't be alone in my head with these thoughts. I focus again on Gabriel. He has to wake up, right now.

I let the back of my fingers trace a line near the top of his spine. Gabriel doesn't stir. I touch his shoulder, saying his name softly into his ear, but Gabriel remains unresponsive. Everything feels tepid. The energy between us has slowed, the cool of his skin suggesting the heat of lustful expectation has been serviced and discharged. Gabriel seems so emphatically asleep I even wonder if he could be faking it. I steel myself to make one final attempt at rousing him, at having something exquisite for myself, maybe one last time before I have to return to the crushing reality of my life with Dom.

I stroke a stretch of Gabriel's neck. Wetness between my fingertips. I couldn't feel it before, couldn't see it; didn't want to. My fingers are sticky with blood. I push myself away, sit up and cross my arms over my nakedness, only to feel the same blood-adhesive on my left shoulder.

Oh god. Oh Jesus.

Gabriel is dead.

My lover is stone-still and cold next to me in this locked hotel room.

In one motion, I kick myself away from him, twisting my upper half so I'm hanging off my side of the bed, snatch the wastepaper basket from the floor and dry-heave into it. I drop it back down, wipe my mouth and flop back onto the bed, panting. What the hell am I doing here? How am I ever going to get out? How will I get back to the life I never should have taken for granted?

I know it straightaway: there's only one person I can call, the one person who can offer me any hope of saving me from where I've put myself; the person I've failed so badly, even before tonight.

I need to call my husband.

Chapter One

Day zero, Saturday morning

Today, I'm starting a boozer's log. The odd thing, well, a few too many things, like barely remembering getting in last night or going to bed the Friday night before it, have made me think it's probably time I kept a record of my alcohol intake and those bits of my life I suspect are making me drink: disturbed nights with the baby, my waking life with my so-called manager, my dreadful mother-in-law. But it's not like any of these things are particularly new, so why start logging them today? I suppose I'm getting bored of thinking the same thing over and over, things like: *I wish I hadn't drunk so much* and *I wish I remembered more.* I've also recognised recently how not everyone jumps in, two-footed, at any opportunity to drink until they're over their head in wine, drowning in regret and their own stomach acid the next day. It's making me feel not completely normal. It's making me wonder whether if I get to understand this, then maybe I can figure out some other things too.

This morning wasn't anything particularly exceptional in that I didn't immediately feel the dreaded weight of hangxiety on my chest. But my throat was a bit sore. That got me worrying.

Was it because of alcohol-induced acid reflux or me bleating on to Sal about all Anton had put me through this particular working week? Again. Since he was promoted over me, that man has made the charity I work for no longer somewhere I can score the minor joys of being a competent copywriter or the more significant victories when I can see the impact of my work, but a warzone where the weapons of choice are Teams, Outlook and Word Tracked Changes. But Sal has heard it all before and my continued moaning must be deeply boring to her by now; frustrating too because it's not like it ever changes a thing.

If I hadn't been bitching about Anton, then I had, perhaps, exhausted my vocal cords unloading about Dom's mother, Patience, for whom I can do nothing right and whom Sal hates because of this. But she's my husband's mother, so most of the time I make sure I keep these things to myself. That leaves me with another option. Worse than the possibility of being awful about Patience, had I been spewing mean, wholly uncalled-for things about my lovely, caring, forgiving husband; feelings I've no business having, let alone sharing with Sal? This is who I think I am when I drink, and it doesn't feel like the person I want to be, especially because my recall of last night only really kicked in when the baby was gearing up for her second night feed, sometime between three and four thirty.

'It's OK, you relax,' Dom told me. He'd already retrieved the bottle and was feeding the baby, shushing her gently as she guzzled, just as he always does. I watched, quietly astonished, as I still am after three eventful years together, at the scale of him, and also of her in comparison. Dom's older brother Ol calls his 'little' brother 'The Norseman' and it feels appropriate. All six and a half foot of my husband looks as though it arrived at these shores via a long lineage of Nordic ancestry, genetically fine-tuned for rowing across oceans. His lean frame is heavy with fatless stretches and mounds of muscle; his eyes are sea-blue, his hair a salty dark blond. How overwhelmed by him I was when I first met him and he bombarded me with the kind of romance I'd only ever read about happening to the stunning and the alpha Amal Clooney sort of women, not accessibly average women like me. I'm so normal I had no idea, and still really don't know, why someone as impressive as Dom, physically and, OK, financially, would see anything in ordinary me. And yet he did; he does. In me, my husband seems to see something exceptional; everything he apparently wants in a woman.

The baby was, in that moment, immune to Dom's charms. She kept stopping her feed to cry. I assumed she could be teething, or perhaps some small part of her wanted to be held by her mum, as I'd not seen her since I'd left for work after eight the previous morning.

'I could try,' I said, craving the sweet warmth of her next to me.

'It's OK, you go back to sleep,' Dom said, turning his frame and the baby away from me, as though shielding me from her noise. He's probably the stuff of most women's fantasies: the ultimate 'doesband' who shoulders the lion's share of the childcare, cooking and any and all domestic tasks. Before I knew him, Ol tells me, Dom did as much caring for my late sister-in-law, his poor wife

Flic, when she became gravely ill. Taking care of everything and everyone, it's what Dom does. I am, I realise, a very lucky woman.

But watching the baby's tiny body stiffen with an escalated rage she could only articulate through even louder wailing, I didn't feel nearly fortunate enough. In fact, I found myself hearing a far-from-grateful voice needling me: *It's Saturday. You deserve a drink.* Yes, the Drinking Devil Elle prodded her pitchfork into my mind right there and then, my first drink trigger of the day, spiking its way through the burgeoning headache, bittersweet mouth, scratchy throat and the sound of my baby needing to be soothed. Devil Elle wanted to tell me a crying baby plus the weekend equated to a reason to drink. She wanted to make my blameless baby my enabler. Angel Elle wanted to swear blind she'd drink only water and eat clean throughout the day ahead, but the rest of me said I deserved, no *needed* the promise of hair of the dog to look forward to, to sustain me through baby swim that afternoon, and even more drink to get me through the birthday lunch for our niece Cora at Patience's house tomorrow. But it's not what I, real Elle, the person at the core of me wants. Is it? Because, I asked myself, there's no reason that person needs to be so afraid of her life if there isn't drink in it, is there? Once Dom had quietened the baby, I could hear a better me, the one that decided to start my drinking log.

Dom put the baby back in her cot and went to use our en-suite bathroom. I positioned myself on my pillows so I could watch her through the darkness, the smudged rise and doubtful fall of her chest as she settled back into sleep. My drink-shrivelled brain started to torment me with the idea that if I didn't see her next breath, it might not happen, the faint shame and regret of hangover already staining my softer thoughts. When I could hear Dom switch off the bathroom light, I turned over and closed my eyes.

'Hopefully that's that,' he whispered as he climbed back into bed. 'She should be out until sevenish.'

'Hopefully.' I brought my pillows deep into the crook of my neck, indicating my own readiness for rest. I didn't particularly want Dom to get the idea I was in the mood for anything else but sleep. Because my husband needs very little in the way of encouragement, something else I know I should probably be much more grateful for than I ever am these days.

Dom ran a hand over my hip, the same palm then slipping over my belly, a part of me he seems all but obsessed by, though I hate my postpartum stomach. Next, he reached for my still-enormous boobs. Truthfully, whenever I feel pieces of my flesh drooping off my core or creasing into each other, like when I'm in bed, I feel a total state. But when Dom looks at me, touches me, it's as though he interprets my lumps and bumps as precious gifts. I knew him touching those messy pieces of me would have left him wanting more; an intimacy I equally realised he'd pretty much earned through all his efforts with the baby. But what he wanted from me I was too tired, too hungover and too full of self-loathing to give. Dom deserves so much more of me than he generally gets.

'You must be exhausted,' I told him, doing everything I could to sound like sex wasn't the absolute last thing I wanted to do in that moment, but that I cared for him deeply anyway. Dom shuffled in closer to me, his leg coming over my squashy thighs, his lips on my neck, his hand roaming over me to reach between my legs. 'I'd love to,' I whispered, guiltily trying to keep my body from clenching, from outwardly resisting his touch. 'But do you think we could try to get back to sleep? She'll be awake again before we know it.' I hoped he could hear only exhaustion in my voice, not the buzzing of every other emotion inside my mind. I was desperate not to have to ask him to out-and-out leave me alone. Not giving Dom what he continues to want from me really feels like not keeping up my end of the bargain of our marriage. That sounds dreadfully transactional, now I've written it down. That doesn't mean to say it isn't true.

'You're just too beautiful,' Dom said into my ear before delivering a soft kiss to my neck and then the cheek nearest to him. After a beat, though, he withdrew and moved to lie on his back. 'Too beautiful for me.' He said it half-laughing at the ceiling. 'Sorry.'

'Don't say sorry,' I told him quietly, turning to face him, stealing a glance at the baby as I reached for the least erogenous zone I could think of, which was the top of Dom's shoulder. 'I really would love to; I could just do with a couple more hours, that's all.'

'It's OK. I understand.'

Dom's face is never more boyish than when he feels he's not wanted. Right then, he looked as though he'd been told Santa Claus had skipped his chimney.

'Tomorrow,' I said, knowing we had things to do in the day. 'We'll find a moment, OK?' I kissed him quickly on the mouth before I turned my back once more. There was silence for perhaps half a minute.

'Do you remember giving Agatha her bottle when you got in?' Dom whispered.

A thump of panic. I gave the baby her first feed last night? Could I remember doing that? Yes? When I thought about it, didn't I hear her stir just after I'd got in and was about to head to the bathroom? But yes, I'd decided not to wait for her to wake Dom with her louder cries but have a little cuddle and some quiet time with her myself. That's right, I ran back downstairs with her in my arms to heat her bottle. Shit, did I drop her? Did I scald her? It's Dom who usually heats her bottles – I don't even know how long you should heat them for, do I? Was that what Dom was getting at? Was the baby so upset, not because she is teething, but because her drunk mother burnt her with boiling milk? *I will not drink today.*

'Yes, I remember feeding her. Thought I'd save you a job, for a change.' *I cannot drink today.* 'Why do you ask?'

'No reason.'

I swallowed before deciding to speak through a sleepy sigh. 'Sorry if I seemed a bit drunk.'

'Don't say sorry. Get back to sleep. Love you.'

'Love you too.'

I didn't go back to sleep, all my brain wanted to do was send itself on tortuous circuits over and over. *Dom was seriously worried I could have hurt the baby, wasn't he? Is that why he does everything for her, because I can't be trusted? Could I have hurt the baby? Even if I didn't*

11

hurt her last night, will I the next time? Was last night another lucky escape for her? For me? When I exhausted that stream of self-hate, I shifted onto the flow of Anton's humiliations last week at work and what he might be planning for the week ahead. When Dom lets me lie in on Saturday while he preps the baby's breakfast and food for the day, all I generally end up doing is rehearsing Monday's horrors. This is not healthy. Neither is how I typically need to go over how much I drank the night before, *again*. My mind fell over itself on repeat.

I was still awake when the baby woke for the day, by then, my pulse loud and painful in my temples. I knew Dom would be unhappy at me being in this kind of state on a Saturday, in his very quiet sort of way, in that I know he's unimpressed even if he doesn't say anything. I couldn't face that yet, so pretended to be asleep, listening to Dom picking up the baby, the rustle of her blanket as he freed her from her cot, then the faint creak of floorboards under the carpet when he turned to watch me for a second, as though he was wondering whether to say something. I froze, considered turning around, telling *him* to lie in, telling him I was so sorry, telling him I'd be better. I *could* be better than this, but that morning, I couldn't. Eventually, I heard Dom leave, whispering into the baby's ear, 'Let's leave Mummy now.'

When he left the room, and I eventually went back to sleep, I dreamt I arrived late for work on Monday. Anton marched me straight into a leadership team meeting to present the new campaign messaging I've been working on but haven't yet finished. Anton was smirking from the corner as the leadership team read with horror the PowerPoint slide he'd forced me to present. It was filled with unintelligible prose. At that point, I realised I was wearing the corset that had held me together on my wedding day, the white satin heels that I remembered felt faintly ridiculous and straight out of the dressing-up box, even on my wedding day, and nothing else. No words came out of my moving mouth; I tried and failed to explain the nonsense copy on the screen and hide my naked lower half behind a conference room chair.

I finally dragged myself from the glue of my second sleep and out of bed after nine. I found the tightest vest I could to keep my boobs broadly stable without having to wear a bra; big, sensible underwear and some supportive leggings, pulling the cord of my dressing gown as tightly around my middle as I could. I didn't want to feel any piece of me wobble when I moved. As well as everything else, alcohol was adding thousands of calories to the already chaotic state of my post-pregnancy body. The baby would be one in a couple of months. I'm leaving the zone where I can attribute any bit of me that I'm not in control of, to her. But it's not her, it's me, it's the drink. I know it is. I just don't yet know *why* it is.

When I reached the kitchen, there she was, at the far end of the extension, lit by morning sun under the skylight, angelic in the Scandinavian beechwood highchair Dom chose for her maximum comfort and safety. She looked perfectly secure, and not at all like the lesser of her parents had damaged her. A wash of relief; I'd been given another chance; I was being totally ridiculous, over-dramatic.

'Morning, you.' I brought my head to hers and kissed her cap of white-blonde hair. There were mushed chunks of pear and bread everywhere, in her hair, in the creases of her clammy little neck, a strand of short pale-yellow hair also trapped in the damp crevice below her chin. I went to pull it free. My booze-poisoned stomach turned despite the smile I gave her when I did, roiling some more when she proffered the squidge of food squeezing through her fist. 'No, thank you, lovely.'

Dom startled me when he came up behind to hug me around my middle.

'Oh. Morning.' My pulse quickened from his unexpected embrace. 'Thanks for the lie-in.' I placed my hands over his in a gesture I hoped felt affectionate but also worked to stop his fingers from entering my dressing gown and the bands of flesh above and below the waistband of my leggings.

'I was just about to bring you this.' Dom released me to fetch a freshly made cappuccino from the coffee machine on the kitchen island.

'Thank you.' My chest tightened when I took a sip; Dom had clearly loaded it with brown sugar, suspecting correctly I could do with an extra boost to get my hungover morning going. I sat myself at the long kitchen table I knew he'd like to line with more children and tried to cheer myself up by making silly faces at the baby, who duly started to giggle. I had to face baby swim later that day, but at least I'd have her all to myself for a bit, give me a chance to make amends for last night's near-miss, and all of the other ones I bet I've put her through in her short, blameless life. This has to stop.

'Thought we'd FaceTime Cora when you're ready,' said Dom, sitting himself at the other side of the table.

'We're seeing her tomorrow, aren't we?' I said, sticking my

14

tongue out at the baby, not really thinking about what I was saying before throwing down another mouthful of my sweet coffee. Dom left his seat to retrieve the elements required for the next round of the baby's morning snack, returning to carefully distribute slices of strawberry on the tray of her highchair.

'Birthdays without her mum, they're pretty tough on Cora, and Ol. And today's her actual birthday. Given we're not seeing them until tomorrow, I thought it'd be nice if we did what we could to make her morning feel a bit special.' Dom said it so calmly and slowly, you would barely be able to hear the seeds of guilt being scattered in the spaces between the words, but I could. Dom is a great dad, brilliant brother and an amazing uncle too. I know he went over and above for Cora and Ol when Flic was ill, staying with Flic through the long nights towards the end to give Ol a break so he had something left to give his tiny daughter at the time. I'm sure Dom isn't completely caring and perfect all the time just to show up how thoughtless and rubbish I am, but sometimes, it can really feel that way.

'Oh god, yes. Of course, yes,' I said, prompting Dom to lay a heavy, reassuring palm on my shoulder as he passed me to rinse his fingers in the sink, a patient smile on his face.

Poor Flic, the sister-in-law who sounded wonderful and whom I never got to meet. She died after a short and cruelly unbalanced run-in with breast cancer and now, the uncaring world had orbited the sun once more as though she'd never existed. Poor Cora. Poor Ol, a widower in his forties. And pity the poor baby who has me as her mother, a woman who doesn't appreciate how lucky she is, who doesn't live her gratitude for her baby, for her

15

baby's amazing dad and our beautiful life every second of it. I left my seat and leant towards the baby's head again, this time, inviting her to rub her little wet fingers all the way from my forehead to my lips, which I shut tight, lest I breathe my booze fumes on her. *I don't need to drink today. I don't want to drink today.*

'Let me finish my coffee –' I turned to Dom '– you hose down this one down, then we'll call Cora and Ol together.'

'Great idea,' Dom said. It sounds a bit sarcastic now I'm writing it down, but I'm sure it wasn't. A second later, the baby swiped Dom's meticulously chopped strawberries onto the floor.

'Here, let me,' I said.

'It's alright.' Dom immediately dropped his huge frame into a crouch to collect small pieces of red detritus from the tiles. It seemed like a task that should be so below him. I wondered what Dom's employees would make of seeing him like this, as keen to lead on the smallest domestic task as he is on the next phase of his business's relentless expansion. Dom is the founder of an artificial intelligence company that specialises in facial recognition technology, helping companies do things like understand when their warehouse staff are bored or tired and therefore might be at risk of making mistakes, or, I believe, may be more likely to steal. It's made him, and therefore me, very comfortable, but in truth, it's not the sort of thing I shout about, especially not at work, a charity providing housing for vulnerable women where I'm a copywriter. I bet a lot of our service users are probably trying to catch a break at the kind of companies Dom is helping squeeze the last drops out of their workers.

'I know you've not been feeling great about yourself recently,'

Dom said, seemingly out of nowhere, picking up another small sliver of strawberry and dropping it into his wide palm.

'Oh,' I said, thinking what I might say to this, berating myself for not trying harder to hide my feelings of inadequacy that probably only added to Dom's already heavy emotional load. 'If I am, it's nothing to do with you,' I said. 'It's completely me.'

'You know you're gorgeous to me, right?'

My throat stiffened. Perhaps I was about to cry. I'd had so little sleep, been so worried about hurting the baby, my emotions were all over the place. I don't know why else this sort of kindness from Dom would make me feel this way.

'I do. Thank you. I don't . . . Stupid baby weight; stupid hangover; stupid me,' I said, struggling to come up with something to excuse the tears sneaking into my eyes.

'Don't talk about yourself like that, Elle. Please.' Dom rose to his feet and moved to the sink where he slapped the smears of strawberry into the food recycling bin. 'I don't know if you're going to like it, but I bought you a new dress, something for tomorrow at Mum's, maybe.' Dom rinsed his hands once more, his back to me.

'That's so thoughtful. You needn't have done that but thank you.'

'It's hanging up in my wardrobe. I hope you love it.' Dom held onto the sides of the sink.

'I'm sure I will.'

'Would you go and try it on?' He turned around. 'I'm dying to know if I screwed up and got you something you actually hate.' He wanted me to love it so much I already felt guilty: my reaction

17

was almost guaranteed to fall short of what he needs to see to feel reassured.

'Of course I won't hate it. I'll love it.' I got up, happy at least to have an excuse to take my ridiculous tears and blotchy face away from Dom. I headed back to our bedroom.

The dress was gorgeous and probably designer, not that I would know much of a difference between that and regular clothes. Dom has such great taste and a discerning eye for quality, something I'm still struggling to learn after a life spent, quite happily, in Primark's best until I met him. I viewed the navy midi-length shift with capped sleeves and a wide, black satin belt. The whole thing looked a little narrow, but the label showed only European sizing, so I couldn't immediately tell if it was the size I'm currently wearing. I slipped it off the heavy wooden hanger and on over my head, shuffling to manoeuvre it past my arms, the struggle already telling me it was going to be tight. I yanked the fabric down over my boobs, the edging of the sleeves biting into my upper arms. The dress fell unflatteringly a little above the knee. After I'd strained to get the zip up at the back, my breasts and general width transformed the tailored front of the dress into an untidy creased band. There were pockets of pale fat visible under my arms. I stepped back and viewed myself in the mirrored wardrobe door and wanted to cry all over again.

'Isn't Mummy beautiful?'

I hadn't heard Dom come up the stairs with the baby. He was standing in the doorway, his blue eyes shining with appreciation.

'Thank you so much, darling,' I said, hoping he might mistake my wet eyes for grateful sentimentality.

'You promise you love it?'

'I do,' I said, forcing a wide smile as I watched him lay the baby down for her morning nap, the one sleep of the day she's guaranteed to accept without a peep. Sure enough, she didn't protest, her eyes closing almost before Dom pressed the button on the musical mobile, the familiar, stalled notes of 'London Bridge Is Falling Down' accompanying the ring of angelic little girls eerily circumnavigating the air above the baby's head. Dom waited for a moment while sleep took her before walking over to me.

'And you love me?' Dom dipped his head so it reached the top of mine. I stood on my tiptoes to give him a quick kiss on the lips without, I hoped, inflicting my alcoholic fumes on him.

'Madly,' I said. Dom's fingers found the zip at the back of the dress. He tried to lower it but was struggling. Perhaps I'd damaged the teeth with my efforts to seal the dress with me inside of it. Why wasn't I better for Dom? Why wasn't I the right fit for this wonderful life he'd given me? Why, even in this moment of gratitude, as Dom tried again to liberate me from the dress, did I still not particularly want to give my husband the one thing he asks of me, a body that, by some miracle, he sees without flaw?

'Oh no,' he said quietly as the zip resisted his force. 'Did I get the wrong size?'

'No. *No.* It's me. It's the right size. I'm the wrong shape.'

Dom gave the zip a yank so determined it almost knocked me off my feet. He pulled the dress down over my arms, before guiding it to the floor. He got to his knees, so his head was at level of my stomach, specifically, the fold of it above the line of my sensible underwear, which he kissed. He did so tenderly at

19

first, before it felt as though he was gathering my flesh together to create a handful of me to devour. 'You're the perfect shape,' he uttered between kisses. 'Never say you aren't.'

'*Dom,*' I said, letting some protest into my voice, hoping it sounded like I was objecting to the fact he thought me perfect, not, as I actually was, resisting my husband's somewhat extreme gestures of adoration for my body, as he practically buried his head in my flesh, his hands by now inside the back of my unsexy cotton underwear as if the whole package of me was the most arousing thing imaginable. How much more grateful I needed to be, for his care, for his endless support, for loving all the mess of me this much.

Dom edged my underwear down to my legs, then to my feet.

I think I might drink today.

Chapter Two

Day twenty-one, Saturday morning

Oh god. Oh god. Oh god. Gabriel.

Gabriel.

Is this real? I don't understand. I *do not* understand. Who would do this to him? I can't remember anything about being in this room last night, can I? I beg my brain to yield something. Something is trying to surface from the blurred depths of last night's memory: I remember being with Gabriel. Yes, I do remember his body, or rather the way his body moved mine. I think it was pretty physical; rough. Him, not me, I'm not into that, but I definitely remember having the kind of sex where he felt powerful. He was very strong, stronger than me. That must account for the aches and pains. Could I have drunkenly got confused and hurt him if he was a little forceful? Pushing him, slapping him away is one thing, but *this*? No, I wouldn't have done this. *I couldn't.* But Gabriel is dead and there is no one else here. No one but me.

What will they tell his family? Who will tell them? The police? What about the police? Shit, *the police.* And work? But forget all of that, how the hell am I going to explain any of this to Dom?

And the baby, she's going to find out this happened one day. How will I tell her how I ended up here? That's if they still let me see her; that's if they don't think I did this. I didn't. *I didn't. I didn't. I couldn't.*

OK, is there any way I can find out at least when this happened?

I reach for my phone on the bedside table. The time now is three thirty-two a.m. I check my messages. The last one I sent to Dom after nine yesterday evening.

My phone's nearly out of juice. Leaving it to charge in my room. Drinks will prob go on late, so I'll sign off now. Hope you have a settled night. Give the baby a kiss from me. Love you xxx

It doesn't read like a drunken message; there are no typos or random spaces. I clearly didn't come back here to charge my phone: the battery is currently at twenty per cent. Dom sent me quite a few more messages after I sent mine, none of which I read last night. The final one says:

I guess you must be busy enjoying yourself. Love you more than you'll ever know. Call me when you wake up XXX

He sent that around eleven thirty. Could I have somehow done this to Gabriel intentionally, or unintentionally, at some point in the four-hour window since then? I don't have that in me. Not to Gabriel, not to anyone.

So, someone else must have come into this room.

I need to make some kind of sense of this before I raise the alarm, before I call Dom, beg his forgiveness and plead with him to get over here and rescue me from this mess, just like he saved me from the train wreck my life was on the verge of becoming before him. What would he do if he were here? He'd check if there are any signs of forced entry. Yes. That's what I should do.

I unfreeze my limbs and get out of bed, not daring to turn on the light or look behind me as I hunt for some clothes. I can see what I was wearing yesterday is in a messy heap on the other bed in this room, together with Gabriel's clothes. I leave the pile untouched, assuming my clothes may now be *evidence* and head to my overnight bag in the corner of the room. I go to find my leggings and vest but notice the blood on my hands. I don't want to touch my things before I've rinsed it off, or risk putting my bloody fingerprints all over the room.

I get to the bathroom and flick on the light with my elbow, noticing more red staining across my arm. I want to wash all that off too, but I know I shouldn't and stick to washing my hands, watching the water turning a sickening pink as it swills down the sink. The police will need me to retain as much evidence as I can, so they can understand what happened to Gabriel and eliminate me from their enquiries. Because they will do that, won't they? And I *will* call the police, I only need to get a handle on things myself before I try to tell them what I think happened here. I take a breath and leave the bathroom, ignoring the quaking of my hands, my entire core.

I don't let myself look at Gabriel's body as I finally pull on my vest and leggings, as though if I can somehow ignore him, all of this might not be happening. Once dressed, I head to the door into the room from the corridor outside, scanning its edges for any kind of clue. I see nothing unusual: no signs of the lock being forced or the frame splintering. And the door is, indeed, locked from the inside. OK, what about the windows? I move to them, grazing the edge of the second bed in the room as I do, the one Sal was supposed to sleep in.

Sal. What happened to her last night? We were supposed to be sharing this room. An image emerges from the haze of my mind: Sal wincing. Was she upset? OK, it's coming back to me: I think one of the last things I remember is her heading home for the evening. Why did she leave me alone here when staying over together was her idea all along? She booked this room, begged us to stay here together. But on the other double bed, the one Gabriel and I did not sleep in, there's no trace of her, only our discarded clothes and underwear.

As I get closer to them, I notice a draught wafting from behind the curtains. I pull them back with my eyes closed. This is a ground-floor room and I'm terrified that the murderer may still be outside, waiting in the darkness for me, prolonging their diabolical sport. I make myself open my eyes, while being sure not to brush by or touch anything solid, thinking of the police dusting and recording each surface around me.

The floor-to-ceiling window is wide open. It's a large enough opening for someone to enter and drop onto the grass below once they'd committed their crime. The window isn't smashed or damaged in any way I can see. I don't remember much, but I really can't recall myself or Gabriel opening it.

My phone pings a notification, making my flesh leap from my bones. It must be Dom. My heart punches my chest. Oh god, what do I do? Call him right now if he's awake? Is that the most honest thing I could do? I want to tell him; I *need* to tell him what I've done and the mess I'm in now. But no, I can't do it yet; I don't know how I'd find the words to begin to tell my husband any of this. I gasp a breath into my lungs and prepare myself to read his message, like a missive from an alternative universe where I'm the person I was before last night:

I never should have let you go like I did yesterday. I want you next to me. If you don't come to me, I'm coming to find you . . .

Oh god.

I'm in room 213.

No. Please, no.

Yours, totally, still yours, Gabriel xxx

Chapter Three

Day zero to day one, Saturday to Sunday

The day could have gone far better from a drinking perspective. At the leisure centre, I took the baby to her swim class while Dom had his usual workout. Afterwards, I felt good: I'd had some decent what-you-might-call quality time with the baby, even if it wasn't much more than forty-five minutes. I also hoped, as I suppose I do most weekends, that Dom might be sufficiently physically spent he wouldn't want our standard Saturday sex on the sofa. Meanwhile, the scent of chlorine on my skin was making me feel faintly virtuous. I wanted to build on this and planned on having a glass of sparkling water with some fresh lime when we got back home, which was just after five, order some sashimi later on, cut the booze and the carbs and enjoy an all-round decent Saturday. But by the time I'd unpacked the swim bag in the utility room, I returned to the kitchen to see Dom pouring a large glass of white wine.

'Thought you looked like you could do with this,' he said, turning to return the rest of the bottle to the wine fridge. 'So many babies in that class!'

I didn't really feel like the wine, but I didn't want Dom to

26

think I wasn't grateful to him for thinking of me. I intended to drink it very slowly and to only have that glass all night; there was probably a third of the bottle in Dom's generous pour.

'Baby swim is always fun,' I said, taking the glass, then remembering the free–weights room overlooks the training pool. What might Dom have seen as I took the baby through her swimming exercises: me looking harassed having wrestled her into her swim nappy barely in time for the start of the class; probably because it's Dom who does the vast majority of nappy changes, another key area in which I lack both practice and skill. Perhaps he thought I looked bored at the twentieth tuneless rendition of 'Twinkle, Twinkle, Little Star' while encouraging the baby not to cry when I dunked her under the water as instructed?

'She loves it,' I said, gesturing to the baby who was at that moment pressing the same button on a musical fire engine over and over. *Nee-naw. Nee-naw. Nee-naw.* What I didn't tell Dom is that I kind of dread going to the class. I'd much rather sit and play with her somewhere, just me and her, but Dom says it's critical she starts to swim as soon as she can.

'Well, I think you deserve to relax tonight anyway. You were so great today, considering.' Dom knocked an open beer bottle gently against the side of my glass.

'Considering what?' I said quietly.

'Don't be like that, you were fine last night, honestly, like I already said, but I know you didn't sleep.'

'Sorry if my tossing and turning kept you awake.'

'You know me.' Dom came round to where I was, leaning against the kitchen island, and surrounded me. 'I don't need much to keep me up.' And I felt it: the faint pressure of his groin on me. He probably didn't even know he was doing it. So much for the workout calming him down; it seemed to have fired him up even more than usual.

'I was thinking about work. Anton,' I said.

Dom fell away and stepped back to view me.

'*Him* again. That guy's such an arsehole. I'd never treat anyone on my team the way he treats you. I mean I've faced some performance issues with some of my guys but—'

'I'm good at what I do.' I invited a laugh into my voice that didn't quite manifest. 'Or maybe I used to be.' For a moment, I saw myself in the office, in the time before they promoted Anton above me. I was heading into my mid-thirties and I finally felt like I knew what I was doing. As well as my standard duties of ghost-writing articles, interpreting research to develop messaging for fundraising and marketing campaigns and writing up case studies, some of the leadership team had begun to seek my expert eye if they had a presentation, speech or even an important email they wanted to hone. I'd become known as the Killer Queen of the Passive Voice, and I rather liked it.

'You can make your writing sound less remote and more alive if you ditch passive voice and choose active,' I told one director. 'The passive means the subjects of your sentences have the action done to them, so it's not *Upper-floor flats are preferred by service users.* With the active voice, your subject owns their action: *Service users prefer upper-floor flats.*'

I won a prestigious award for a campaign that went viral. My old manager, Reena, was never threatened by my successes.

I wanted to be that kind of leader too, when my time came, certain that it would. Reena became pregnant and recommended I should cover her maternity leave, confessing to me it was unlikely she would ever return, her male partner being the higher earner. I believed the timing of her departure was the cosmos lining things up for me at exactly the right time. Maybe what happened next was the universe telling me to never get too comfortable.

Anton.

Anton Bloch had been inherited from the previous comms lead, and, from what I understood soon after I was hired by Reena, had vastly overinflated his skills and experience gained in the private sector. He'd managed to cling on long enough to pass his probation and swerve being fully found out, or anyone caring enough to remove him. But, I grew to realise, he was actually the perfect candidate for promotion: Anton waved through bad ideas if they were from leadership; he proved himself quietly untalented so did not threaten anyone's authority; he was male. A rumour went round that leadership were reluctant to recruit another woman of child-bearing age. Being a parent wasn't something I felt particularly compelled to do, having seen the sorts of professional paralysis it brought women like my mother back in the day, and even in modern times with women like Reena. If I had a 'body clock' at all, I was deaf to its ticking. Besides, I wasn't even in a relationship (the housemate/friends-with-benefits situations I typically found myself in not counting). And I was, of course, still in a house share. Even if I wanted a baby, how could I? *Where* could I? In the interview, a forum where I should have been showcasing all my successes to date and everything I could offer in the future, I instead ended up oversharing the many emotional and material shortcomings of my adult existence that meant I was tactically unfit to breed. They recruited Anton.

Maybe if Anton had been good at what he did, better than me, I wouldn't have taken it so hard; perhaps if he didn't criticise my advocacy for accessible language over his preferred flowery sentences, over-formality and the deadening passive voice. Or maybe it was once I could see I was deemed a pregnancy flight risk above all my other professional characteristics, I no longer had the confidence to imagine a way forward at the charity I was working for, or any other.

I began to feel resolutely stuck in the mud of my life: no relationship and becoming something of the elder stateswoman of my house share, having watched the last in a long line of friends with benefits leave, and seen so many others come and go on to better places, pastures new, rendering me the only 'original' housemate left of the third line-up of co-residents. I think it was around this time that my alcohol intake began to climb, especially as I became subjected to Anton's 'management regime', which involved 'correcting' my copy and hogging all the interesting work. I began to feel like the poor writer he wanted me to be. I started to feel less than good about lots of things about myself. I turned to my mum for sympathy and understanding, but she seemed, as usual, preoccupied with my stepdad and supporting my half-brother in his post-university life. I had Sal, but she had Tim and her twin boys, and she'd managed to secure a senior role from the off at our charity, in part, I'm sure because the leadership team had judged her past any further baby-rearing as her boys headed into their teens. What people like Sal had, and I did not, started to matter. And then, along came Dom, who made everything possible for me all at once.

'I'm not talking about what you do,' Dom said, bringing me back to my life now – my impressive husband having my back; how far he has taken me since that fateful night we first met. 'Only how that arsehole seems to perceive how you're doing.' Dom wandered over to where the baby was sat on her playmat. 'If there's someone I don't think is pulling their weight . . .' He slid his frame down to the floor to play with the wooden building that came in the same handmade set as the musical fire engine, pressing down on a lever that caused a spray of wooden red-and-yellow flames to spring out from a slit in the roof, once, twice. The baby giggled, and crawled over to her dad, but only to traverse him so she could slap the flames down. Dom released the lever, so they disappeared before she was able. 'I work with my bottom quartiles positively. It's such an inefficient strategy your boss is using.'

'Anton's strategy is to manage me out,' I muttered, before taking a sip of wine. Apple, vanilla, alcohol. While I had genuinely not wanted to drink, the taste, the ice cold and background heat filling my mouth instantly told me I was making the right choice by letting myself have that one glass. *Now, you can relax*, the wine's cold-fire flavour said; the familiar, faint burn near the saliva glands under the recess of my tongue that always seems to warm me with a certain self-determination: *everything outside of this is for them; this is for you.*

'If he wants to manage you out, why not let him?' Dom said, wooden flames appearing once more before vanishing as quickly as they'd shot up, to the baby's growing frustration.

'What do you mean?'

'What I said. What I've always said. You don't need him or that place. You never needed to go back so soon after Agatha was born, or ever.'

'I know, and I'm so grateful to you for giving me the freedom to hit the eject button,' I told Dom with a prickle of guilt, knowing how much some women would love to have the choices he gives me. 'But I love what our charity does. On a good day, I know I do my bit for the women we help navigate the system, get away from bad housing; shady landlords. It matters to me,' I said, hoping not to have to rehash my reasons for going back to the office after just shy of three months of maternity leave and clinging onto a job that does seem to mostly make me miserable any further. When I returned so soon after the baby was born, it was because I wanted to prove that despite the odds being loaded against me, I wouldn't fold and give up my career, surrender all of my identity to motherhood. It was one of the easiest decisions I ever made, but one of the hardest to execute, both in terms of finding a nursery to take in such a young baby, and convincing Dom that a happy mum made for a happy baby. As much as I adored the baby, I needed to keep being Elle-at-work too. The reality was, the day-to-day drudgery, frequent boredom and loneliness of being on maternity leave, for which I wasn't at all mentally prepared, was sometimes utterly nullifying. I needed more.

'And I love that I get to work at the same place as Sal,' I added.

Sal is head of fundraising and a key reason I've managed to tolerate sticking around after Anton leapfrogged me. She's one of those people you meet very rarely in your life who come to you fully formed as a friend; as though you had a them-shaped hole you didn't even know about until that person slotted inside it perfectly. Sal keeps telling me to hang in there at work. She thinks karma will come for Anton soon and I should stick around to see it.

'All your job seems to do is make you unhappy. And the money's nothing,' Dom said.

'It's not much, but it's something to me,' I told my drink quietly, as though it was the only one that might hear me, before taking another sip.

Dom pushed himself up off the floor. 'I didn't mean it was *nothing* nothing, but obviously, we can survive without it. Realistically, you'll probably be going on maternity leave again soon enough anyway, right?'

I swallowed my mouthful quickly so I could rush out my answer. 'Definitely yes, pretty soon, with any luck.' I smiled over my shame. Of course Dom wants more children; he adores the baby, would die for her. He's amazing at being her father. When Dom has an aptitude for something, he goes for it. That's how it is for him and having more children. I swear, when I know I'm in a better condition for another pregnancy, birth and the aftermath, I honestly plan to let it happen and give Dom the family he wants. It's only because I'm not there yet that I've gone back on the pill temporarily. And I can't tell him any of this because it would rightly make him so deeply upset if he thought he and I weren't

33

quite on the same page. 'Do you think we should risk bringing a cheese plate or something to your mother's tomorrow?' I said, needing to change the subject fast.

Dom was at my side again, two hands on my shoulders, fingers working their way under my T-shirt, kneading my stiff flesh gently.

'Your value isn't related to your job, or about what *Mother* makes of you,' Dom said, 'it's about the future we're making together.'

I nodded, looking about our shining kitchen, in the embrace of my substantial husband and the small and beautiful child we created and to whom he is devoted. Such hefty anchors holding me to the path towards my future life. So, what explains why I still feel somehow adrift? How can I understand what compelled me to pour the rest of the bottle Dom had opened for me into two more large glasses and down my neck, even before he had put the baby to bed and before our somehow-inevitable Saturday sex on the sofa?

The morning after, and we were getting ready to depart for my mother-in-law's house. I washed down two ibuprofens for my booze headache with a Diet Coke for breakfast. I felt terrible. Stood in the dress Dom bought me the day before, I looked dreadful too, my disquiet deepening when I thought about the look I knew Patience would give me when she saw me in it.

Dom emerged from our dressing room with the baby decked out in her Sunday best. Dom too was looking as smart and put-together as always, in his well-cut jeans and a not-too-starchy pale blue shirt that set off the aquatic light in his eyes. The two of them

34

looked so gorgeous together, it made me even feel worse about myself. Was there any way I could wear something else to lunch at my mother-in-law's?

'Do you think,' I began to ask, as lightly as I could, 'it might be a little on the tight side? It feels ever-so-slightly clingy.'

'Nope.' Dom shook his head as if I was talking nonsense before appraising me. 'What I see is you in a great dress that shows all of you off.'

I smiled at him, my heart sinking, even at something as sweet as what he'd just said. Lots of women would be touched by their husband admiring their post-baby body so profoundly. Why couldn't I be one of them?

'Thank you,' I said to Dom out loud. *Sorry*, I said in my mind.

'Thank *you*,' he replied, coming to me to hold me.

'What for?'

'For being you.'

My arms rested on his chest as he held me. I held out a finger for the baby which she grabbed, before pawing at the dainty, pink-gold wristwatch Dom presented me with almost as soon as I'd given birth, as though something shiny might distract from the carnage of labour. The watch was tight on my wrist since that first day. Since late pregnancy, my wrists and fingers swelled, more pieces of me yet to return to my pre-baby dimensions. I've had to take my rings off and leave them hanging on a thin chain around my neck. I've never googled any of it, but from what Sal commented, I estimate I'm wearing three times my annual salary on my body; forever gifts from my forever man; further offerings I can never hope to equal.

At eleven fifty-one, as we walked over to my niece's birthday lunch at my mother-in-law's house, I mentally noted there were approximately twenty minutes until I could legitimately drink again, if that's what I really wanted and, in that moment, it seemed as though I did.

When we reached Patience's house, the gloomy Arts and Crafts villa surrounded by labyrinthine gardens where Dom grew up, it was Ol who opened the door.

'Hey, big brother,' Dom said, bringing his diminutive elder into a bear hug. If Dom is said bear, then Ol's physicality suggests cub, even though he's three years older. 'How's the birthday girl doing? She have a good day yesterday?'

'She's doing all right, I think. She's pretty tough,' said Ol.

'Tough like her mum, tough like her dad,' Dom said, gripping the side of Ol's shoulder, causing his brother to sway slightly on his feet. 'Flic would be so proud of you, mate. And, while we're at it, she'd want you to be happy. I've said it before, and I'll say it again—'

'Don't do that.' Ol shook his head.

'Cora's five now,' Dom continued unabated. 'It's been almost four years. You get one life, make the most of it; get out there again.'

'Yeah. OK. Maybe,' Ol told the floor.

'You know I only ever want what's best for you.'

'I do. Thanks, man; I know. When I'm ready, OK? I will *get myself out there*, but let's keep our focus on Cora today, eh?'

'You got it, buddy.' Dom looked about. 'What have you done with Mother?'

'Oh, she's upstairs, tending to some seedlings, getting them ready to share with *The Propagators* tomorrow, apparently.'

The Propagators are Patience's (I really don't want to say *coven* at this juncture, but if you knew her and imagined her spending time with women like her, you would struggle to say anything else) *collective* of older female gardening enthusiasts who meet regularly to share seeds, cuttings and, I should imagine, a great deal of bile about their daughters-in-law. Today was supposed to be about extending her motherless granddaughter's birthday, but The Widow Diva had already skewed focus onto her by not being there to greet us when she knew we'd arrive. I had no doubt she'd make a dramatic entrance before delivering whatever delicious food she'd planned to serve; another trick of hers, deploying her culinary skill in the manner of unspoken and attention-seeking martyrdom.

I watched Dom disappear deeper into the house, pulling the baby out of her buggy and putting her on his hip as he went to find Cora, leaving Ol with lingering thoughts of moving on from Flic, and me wondering why Dom was so invested in him doing so. Maybe, I thought, he wanted Ol to only look forward; accept Flic is no longer here and focus on the positives of today. It's very Dom to never took back. He probably thinks keeping Ol future-focused – which extends to diverting any attempts to steer the conversation back to Flic, her life, her death – is helping his big brother heal after losing his wife so young. Or maybe Dom can't bear to talk about Flic because it makes him think about the possibility of losing me. From very early on in our relationship, Dom made it clear that being without me would 'destroy' him.

My husband is someone who much prefers to swerve the things that hurt, and focus on the things that don't. It's this strength of mind that's helped me go low-contact with my mum, stepdad and younger brother.

Breaking away from them hasn't been easy, but neither was trying to overlook our issues, which is why it works better for me if I only contact them when absolutely necessary. I didn't have a terrible childhood, as such, even though my dad was completely absent, and me and Mum didn't have much money. She and I were a happy family of two, right up until I hit my teenage years and needed her more than ever. This was precisely when she met my stepdad, and he became her priority. He's not a bad guy, in fact he's perfectly solid, like my little brother, but his arrival pushed me to the outskirts of what was once my life, with the birth of my half-brother shunting me over an invisible fence around their new family unit.

Looking back, I suppose I can't blame my mum for moving on, particularly as she faced me growing up and building my own life away from her, but the whole thing left me feeling disposable. My mum has never taken on board how much being relegated to feeling like a spectator in our family hurt me. So, while my low contact with her is a sad and perpetual background ache, I remind myself this protects me from the bigger moments of anger, sadness and more subdued buzz of low self-worth growing louder whenever I'm with her, with them. It was Dom who enabled me to see a way of taking control of my family situation, helping me see how fighting for the familial justice I needed but would never arrive, was pointless. All I could do to help myself was focus on my own future, the family he and I might make, not that I knew at the time just how quickly I would become a mother myself. These days, my mum continues to question why I barely accept her calls or visit, but remains unable to acknowledge things about my childhood that still hurt, still matter.

All of this running through my head again made me wonder about Ol. As well as helping him focus on the next chapter of his life, I wondered if we needed to let him know it was OK to still be hurting; let him see we would always bear witness to his grief and it was OK if this would always need to co-exist with the energy it takes to keep going forward.

'Hey, Ol,' I said, banishing a burgeoning rush of something like grief for my family, a feeling I've become used to dampening down whenever it flared up. 'How you bearing up?' We came together in a hug. Over Ol's shoulder, I found my eyes level with a photograph I didn't remember seeing before: a portrait of a handsome young woman, cornflower-blue eyes, shining hair in thick, dark waves falling to her shoulders. She looked lovely, so vivacious. A cousin? A family friend perhaps? I wondered why I'd never noticed the image before in amongst the otherwise deathly energy of Patience's hallway but refocused my attention back on Ol.

'You know . . .' Ol's damp eyes fell to the dark floorboards. 'It's always bittersweet, Cora's birthday, isn't it?'

'I'm so sorry, Ol.'

'It was fine . . . we're fine.' Ol swallowed down tears, his kind features flushing.

'Well, if you ever want to talk . . .'

'You're here.' A voice came from the top of the stairs.

There was the ever-gothic silhouette of Patience.

If Ol took after their father Hugo, who died from heart issues not long before Flic got ill, in his distinctly less intimidating physical presence, then Dom was all Patience. Sufficiently elusive about her age and weathering so exceptionally well without anything as common as *tweakments* or surgical intervention, so not even her sons could date her accurately; Patience is somewhere between sixty-four and over seventy. But then she has, apparently, benefitted from great genes and never having to worry about anything so ugly as money. She came from a wealthy family and continues to reap the financial rewards from the rise and rise of Graham Nurseries, the family business of nationwide garden centres established by Dom's father, and, under Ol's direction, a thriving online enterprise too. Although the system of foreboding pathways, head-high plants, dark dead ends and hidden corners comprising her outside space demonstrates Patience's gardening expertise, imagining her physically getting her hands dirty was almost impossible.

'Patience,' I said, addressing the dusky figure moving demurely down the staircase. 'How are your seedlings?' I took a step away from Ol, who muttered something about checking on Cora, leaving Patience and I alone.

'Finding the light, Elle, I'm happy to say.'

There she was in all her glory at the foot of the stairs, all five feet eleven inches of her; ashen hair curled back on top of itself and pushed towards her crown, giving her even more height and a timeless sort of presence; the Princess Anne of Suburbia. She wore wide-legged, stiff grey trousers, a white shirt of impeccable quality tucked in at the waist. She's the type of woman who's as narrow approaching her dotage as she was on her wedding day, though being openly proud about that, as one might, would be deemed by the likes of Patience as profoundly vulgar.

'I kept them in the shadows, you see, to encourage them to grow towards illumination,' she told the middle distance, before turning to me. 'New dress, is it?' Her eyes, the same aquatic tone as Dom's, ran over every bulge and stretch of me as she leant in to give me the briefest and most perfunctory of embraces and a single kiss near the air by my cheek.

'Oh, yes,' I said, trying not to let my hands cross my body defensively, all the while knowing it was useless because every piece of me screamed my limitations to Patience. Me wearing a dress Dom had bought and that was far too good for me was, for Patience, only the latest manifestation of the greater problem of me being partnered with her son, a man miles beyond what someone like me should ever expect or deserve.

'Dominic chose it; did he buy it for you?'

'He did, yes.'

Patience simply nodded, a smile tightening her cold-cream complexion for a flicker, no further words needed to confirm her abundantly clear sentiments on me in the dress. I followed her into the dining room, pulling it pointlessly down over my hips.

'Aunty Elle!'

Little Cora greeted me by gripping me as high as she could reach, which was around my constricted waist. I gazed down at her, resting my hands on her head of soft, sandy hair. Becoming her aunt was so easy, one of the joys amongst the greater relief

41

when Dom found me. How was it that becoming a mother was so much harder, my connection with the baby, when I let myself think about it, so much more difficult to come by than my bond with my niece?

'Happy birthday, lovely girl,' I said, prising Cora off my middle, but only so I could kneel down and take her into my arms, my whole body momentarily relaxing at her emphatic embrace. 'How was yesterday? Did you have lots of fun on your bouncy castle?'

'It was brilliant but Maisie got a nosebleed, and she wanted to get out and tell her mummy, but the boys were being really silly, and they wouldn't stop bouncing and let her off.'

'Oh no! Poor Maisie. Was she OK in the end? Did the boys says sorry?'

'We all know boys don't apologise.' Patience had retrieved a handful of silver cutlery from the long sideboard behind me and was laying heavy dessert spoons across the top line of each place setting.

'Do we?' I said, directing my words at Cora, not my mother-in-law. 'Well, I think they should.'

Patience's features shifted inscrutably as she smoothed an invisible crease in the white tablecloth at the head of the table, a position Patience had only recently taken to sitting at, even though Hugo had been gone for years.

'There's thinking about something and wishing it was so,' Patience said, sighing. 'And then —' she looked at me, dead on '— well, then there's the reality one sometimes feels nothing can be done to affect, no matter what your hopes may be.'

'Hello, Mother,' Dom said briskly, having returned from the kitchen, specifically Hugo's cellar, accessible through a dark door at the back of the room. He had two bottles between his sturdy fingers. 'Who's ready for a drink, then?'

'Me, yes.' I shot up to my feet and I heard the urgency in my voice; I'm confident Patience did too. 'Yes, please.'

We sat, Patience at one end of the table, Ol and Cora to one side, Dom and I on the other, the baby in an ancient plastic highchair from God knows when that must have once been Ol's, then Dom's. I was, as has been usual, sat opposite Ol. He and I have an undiscussed habit of catching each other's gaze whenever Patience says anything extra-Patience. Today, it was a sly reference to some of the parents of the children at Cora's party.

'The school's catchment area must include the estate on the main road. They're to be admired for doing the best with what they have,' said Patience, just as she placed on the table one of her *centrepiece pies*, her comment causing Ol and I to find each other's reaction for half a beat.

'Game pie,' Dom said, focusing on what he'd correctly identified as the filling of Patience's offering, leaving the glance between Ol and I unwitnessed. 'You've really excelled yourself on child-friendly pickings today, Mother.' While Dom's comment was sarcastic and quite unpleasant, given all the effort Patience would have undoubtedly put into the food, it was an issue only because she insists Cora must eat whatever the grown-ups do without dispensation. Dom, in turn, had today insisted *he* give the baby batons of al dente vegetables and strips of organic chicken.

43

Before long, Cora had eaten her pastry and left all the meat, and the baby was ready for a nap in her buggy. Dom pushed her gently back and forth with one hand, alternating his fork and his glass in his free hand until she finally stopped grizzling.

Over lunch, there was, at first, champagne, which, I reasoned, it might seem rude not to drink, the day being a celebration after all. That first drink slipped down so easily, seamlessly becoming a second and, before I could stop him, Dom tipped the end of the bottle into my flute. By the time he uncorked a very full-bodied Italian red, an Amarone della Valpolicella, apparently, I was in the zone. I had a booze buzz and didn't want to let it go. I did try to make myself slow down, but it was no good; the conversational tone set by Patience was as tense as the fabric of my dress. It was a miserable meal. Poor Cora was as bored as a child could be and when Ol good-humouredly offered her his phone to play with, he was prevented from doing so by his mother, which left Cora quietly upset. Taking another draw on my Amarone, I imagined what might happen if I got to my feet and screamed out on Cora's behalf: *Her mum is dead and if she wants to play with her dad's phone and he says it's OK, then it's fucking well OK, Patience!* But I didn't. I only drank the contents of the glass in front of me more quickly, to swill away the voice in my mind, the rage sat in my throat that, if released, risked ruining what little good has come of me being brought into Dom's family.

Eventually, the conversation loosened, turning to the subject of work. Ol asked Dom about the latest deal he's about to do with a big supermarket, one that will help 'protect revenue' (that is, use AI-enabled facial recognition technology to identify shoplifters

44

before they even know they're going to steal) and make Dom even richer.

'How are things with the online business, Ol?' I asked, because Dom had just completed something of a monologue about the intricacies of his supermarket deal. By this stage, when I spoke, I was aware I had to concentrate on getting my words into the air while not betraying even the slightest hint of a slur, or revealing the fact I was working so hard to achieve this.

'It's good; busy. I've got a big new corporate customer, which is great,' Ol told me, unconvincingly.

'Great but . . .?'

'Well, it wouldn't be an understatement to say there are some days when it feels like his sole purpose in life is to make *my* life hell,' Ol said with a rueful smile.

'Sounds rough.' And also, familiar. Ol could have been describing my working life with Anton. 'What's this customer doing?'

'Whatever we deliver it's not right, not enough, not what he expected. Take your pick. He's just one of those people.'

'I know the type. Sorry you're going through it.'

'Something I can step in on?' asked Dom.

'Not this time,' Ol said, which, for some reason, prompted Patience to draw in an audible breath. Ol glanced at her, then diverted his attention to me. 'So, your boss still not behaving himself either?' The question was directed at me, but Ol's eyes were back on his mother who was, at that moment, staring melodramatically into the middle distance for no other reason I could think of than to seek attention.

'Hardly,' Dom answered for me, tipping the last of the Amarone into my glass, placing the bottle on the table and using the hand nearest me to rub my back. 'He's trying to manage Elle out.'

'We don't know that,' I told Ol.

'And I suppose you've told Elle she doesn't need to fight that eventuality, Dominic?' Patience asked.

'I have, as a matter of fact,' Dom said, which seemed to visibly irk her.

She recalibrated almost instantly, her hands still before her on the pale tablecloth; she watched them as she spoke to me next: 'And how would *you* feel about that, Elle?'

I felt every cell of Patience's attention on me, even though she did not deign to look my way. *Don't slur. Do not slur,* I told myself while considering what I might say. In the hiatus, Dom spoke up instead.

'Imagine it –' Dom turned to me '– how do you normally feel on a Sunday night? How are you feeling right now? Your usual downer-panic-neg mood, or whatever, creeping up on you already?'

And there was me thinking I was doing an OK job of not showing my Sunday-for-Monday dread.

'All that could go away,' Dom continued. 'Let your boss make your working life untenable, see if you care. Or better still, go now, hand in your notice, get out on your own terms, enjoy more time with me and Agatha, before we add a little brother or sister to the mix.'

'Her own terms?' Patience said, a dark-grey eyebrow rising on her high forehead as she looped back to Dom's earlier phrasing.

Dom hesitated for half a second, sent a cautionary glance at his mother before returning to me. 'Resign tomorrow. With the new deal, we definitely don't need the income.'

'Don't *we* now.' Patience sighed, as she sunk a silver cake slicer into a ceremonial-looking pavlova.

'I want to keep working,' I told Dom. 'I want to stay in my job, Patience,' I told my mother-in-law. 'Don't worry about that. Donchoo worry 'bout me.'

It happened; I had stumbled. I had slurred. She heard it; Dom heard it. Even Cora looked up from the tremulous tower of napkin rings she was stacking to look at me as though something had happened to her aunty. I think something has happened to me: functional alcoholism. I held Patience's gaze, and she mine. Meanwhile, the baby began to wake, a whiny cry emerging from her buggy. I was almost relieved.

'I'm not worried about you, Elle,' Patience said, with a hint of entirely mirthless laughter in her tone. She handed Dom a portion of dessert and left her seat to head to the buggy before he could get to her first. Patience freed the baby from her buggy and moved a strand of sleep-damp hair from where it was plastered against her cheek. 'Should I be?'

Chapter Four

Day twenty-one, Saturday morning

Is this what a heart attack feels like? If the man dead in my bed isn't Gabriel, then who the hell is it? Gabriel is the only man I've wanted in a long time. He was certainly the only man there last night I had any interest in. Wait, maybe he sent that text before he came here? Perhaps it's only just come through now. Maybe this message was how our night together started. I don't know what's worse, right now: the chance Gabriel is still dead or the risk that the man dead in my bed is a total stranger.

My phone's just pinged again. Gabriel? No. This time, it is Dom:

You're online – how come you're up? Everything OK? Miss you. You missing me? Video call? XXX

Oh god. No. No, no, no. I need to put him off:

Hey, you up with the baby? Don't you worry about me. Woke up needing some water, going back to sleep now for a bit. Hope she lets you get back to bed soon. I love you.

I really love you, Dom. I'm so, so sorry.

Please give our baby a big hug and a kiss from her mum.

Fuck. Oh fuck.

Can't wait to see you both. All my love Exxxx

Finally, I feel my tears surfacing. I take back everything I felt before: I want to go back to the fork in the road and choose a completely different course than I did last night. I'll obey the Marriage Rule 'til my dying day, or as long as Dom wants me to. I'm about to sob, but a knock at the door stops me.

Oh Jesus.

'Elle, it's me. Open the door.'

No.

'*Please.* Let's talk.'

Please, please go away.

'Elle? I can hear you're in there. Listen, whatever happened last night, I think we can get past it.'

I take a breath and move closer to the door. Gabriel is alive; thank god he's not dead, but who the hell is that in the bed? I peer over my shoulder at the shadowed smudge of the body's outline. 'What about last night, Gabriel? Tell me.'

'Elle! You *are* there. Good. Listen, let me in and we can process everything together.'

'Please, Gabriel,' I whisper to the wood. 'Can you keep your voice down? Also, *everything*? What do you mean, *everything*?'

'I really don't want to have this conversation through a door.'

'Neither do I, but now isn't a great time.'

'So, when is? When else are we going to get a chance like this? You never let me see you outside of work. We need to talk properly; why not now?'

I look at the stranger's body behind me again, try to blink some sense into my mind, something that could help me now, send Gabriel away but not before he's given me some crumb of information on how that man may have got here.

'Because . . . because I don't trust myself to just talk to you. You know how things are with us. We can't keep doing what we've been doing, OK? That part of us is over. But I want to hear what you have to say about last night . . . Gabriel?'

'I don't understand you, Elle.' Gabriel sounds crushed. '*It's over.* If that's really true, then why did you make like you were serious about us going to the next level, what, six, seven hours ago?' *Six or seven hours.* OK. So, I haven't seen Gabriel since around the same time I texted Dom last night. 'Are those the actions of someone who's serious about stopping where we've been heading? Elle?'

'I know we've been getting close, but things are different now. If you could just tell me what you think was happening last night we can leave it there for now. Please, Gabriel.'

'Jesus, Elle, if you're so convinced you and me don't have a serious connection, what was all that about last night? I . . . I don't know what's going on with you. I never have.'

'I'm so sorry, Gabriel. Life's got pretty crazy since you came into it. I'm really confused myself right now.'

'Can't I—'

'No! That's not going to happen.'

'God, Elle . . . You know, when I said I needed some time to think about everything, can you please tell me this one thing: why did you almost immediately go and do whatever *that* was? I mean, were you trying to make me jealous? You know you'd never need to do that.'

Jealous? Who on earth with?

'Gabriel, why would I—'

'You didn't have to make me watch you disappear like that. With *him*.'

'I don't know what or who you're talking about.'

'Wait . . . Are you not alone?'

'No, I—'

'That's why you won't open the door, because he's still there with you now?'

'Who, Gabriel?'

'Come on, Elle. I saw how you were with him; *everyone* did.'

'Please, Gabriel, *who*?'

'Anton, of course. Who else?'

Chapter Five

Day two, Monday

'Elle, I really didn't want us to go through this all over again, but you've given me no choice. I think you already know where this is going isn't good enough.'

It was late on Monday morning and I'd been summoned over to Anton's desk to be told why the draft campaign messages he'd taken it upon himself to review on Friday were not up to scratch. They were never going to be. Anton had been up to his usual tricks, skimming the shared drive for my projects, copy I wasn't ready to share, so he could strangle my words at birth. There were typos, half-formed thoughts, placeholders. I would never share anything in the kind of state this was in, and especially not with Anton. But my document was nevertheless open on his screen, veined with extensive red Tracked Changes.

'As I explained, Anton, it wasn't ready for review.'

I tried to stand close enough so he'd know I was willing to take whatever feedback he had for me on board – even though I absolutely was not – but far away enough so there was less danger of Anton smelling the booze my body was still metabolising and the pungency of my breath, which I worried was punching through the last Smint I'd popped. Then, a terrible hangxiety thought: was Anton's assessment of where my copy was heading fair? Did my draft campaign messages represent the foundations of my very best, most original work? Possibly not. OK, *probably* not.

I had, I suppose, dialled in some of my draft content recently, and possibly my work for the last campaign too. If I was being completely honest, ever since they promoted Anton above me, bringing the best of myself to my job, pushing myself to be as sharp and inventive as I once believed I was, had felt broadly pointless, especially after my maternity leave, when I'd confirmed to leadership they were right about me all along: I'd gone off to have a baby when I might have otherwise been heading towards the height of my career. Still, I had to stand my ground with Anton. If I didn't, he might take even more of it from me.

'Could you break down where you think we could do better?' I said with as much evenness as I could, though inside I was raging at myself, but also at Anton because even on my worst day, I knew my copy was better than his.

Anton sighed, and in a display of overplayed exasperation, pushed himself away from his desk so he could rest his elbows on his knees and contemplate the myriad of ways my work was subpar.

'Look at my revisions. Take it from there,' he practically sneered, his top incisors, which stuck out at the best of times, seeming to jut out even more acutely on his top lip, as though his indignation at my copy had forced them even further out of alignment. Then it struck me: Anton wasn't going to give me direction because he simply did not know how. And even if he did know better than me, there would be no chance he'd share that insight with me anyway. Anton's small, pewter eyes remained on the screen. 'I think if you go away, read it again, I don't know, leave the office, walk round the block while you think about it, you'd realise why and how you need to . . .' he thought about it a moment '. . . I don't know, reframe this whole thing.' He sat up to gesture vaguely at my document on his screen as though it was defiled. He would have liked it very much if I'd dealt with his unconstructive criticism by leaving the office, going AWOL before lunchtime; another plank with which to build his case for getting rid of me. In fact, this whole little display was probably all part of his masterplan. I wasn't about to make it easier for him to execute.

'I don't think I need the walk, but I'll definitely take another swing at the copy.'

Anton waved me away. I began the trudge back to my desk. 'Oh,' he called out after me, 'I've shared this draft with leadership, by the way.'

'But it's not ready,' I said, and you could almost, *almost* hear the panicked tears that immediately wanted to burst free. 'I hadn't even got it in shape for your review.'

Anton shrugged. 'I thought it would be helpful to sense-check what step you were on re the strategic staircase.'

Steps you were on re the strategic staircase, a childish little voice crowed in my head. He loved to use whatever corporate claptrap he could to justify sending out my copy when it wasn't in final form. I'd started to save my work only on my desktop when I first realised he was accessing my kick-off drafts. But Anton had insisted it was new *IT policy* we had to save our work on the shared drive. I vowed to create a new file within a file within a file on my desktop to house my work-in-progress. I'd call it something wholly innocuous and boring, like *Archived messages* because I'm increasingly convinced the only *strategic staircase* Anton is interested in is the one that takes me down and out of there so he can promote his mediocre mini-me Caleb to my position and therefore be fully confident he's safe from anyone genuinely capable. I wanted to show him that wasn't about to happen without a fight.

'OK, Anton. Do you imagine any of the leadership team have any specific feedback I should bear in mind, now they've seen the work to date? I should probably book some time with them, one-to-one, engage them so we can climb the strategic staircase together.'

Anton looked instantly panicked at the idea of me having an excuse to work again with our senior colleagues, particularly the ones who've recently indicated they'd rather work with me directly on the bigger-ticket comms. Anton shook his head. 'Leadership aren't here to solutionise for you, Elle. You need to figure it out for yourself. Oh, and don't rush the next iteration. Camp out on it a while.'

Solutionise. Camp out. It's Anton spouting this sort of bullshit I hear in my head on my cycle home, in my nightmares, when I'm in the bath rehearsing how another rubbish day might play out. I wonder if he knows how much I hate him. Probably not. All I ever give him, as I suppose I do everyone else in my life but Sal, is sweetness and light. I duly left Anton's space with a smile on my face and a 'Thanks for the feedback!'

I texted Sal as I walked back to my desk:

Early lunch? Wondering if we could camp out on a few issues re LW. Perhaps you can solutionise over ways I can get LW killed and get away with it? Look forward to hearing your feedback Exx

By the time I'd sat down, I'd received Sal's response to my breezy sarcasm:

Roger this. See you in Pret, 12? Can only stay for 20. PS Regards your earlier query, what if you were to weaponise a jacket potato? One could throw said weapon with some force at LW's head and, at the very least, dispolalise of murder weapon by internalising it with tuna and cheese? Happy to discuss. Sxxx

'It could be he's cracking under the pressure. I don't think he's totally bad,' Sal said half an hour later on the opposite side of our usual table in Pret a Manger, her soft Australian accent elongating the 'a' sound on *bad*. 'I mean, it would definitely piss me off, being sent scuttling back to my seat like a naughty schoolgirl, but I reckon he might just be *cascading down* some of the shit he's been getting from on high.' She took an enormous bite of her ham and cheese baguette. Unlike me, Sal has the metabolism of a teenage boy. She's never had to worry about the pounds piling onto her skinny frame, even after she had her twins.

'Oooh, what kind of shit?' I asked. Knowing Anton was struggling would be some salve to the constant bruising of my ego.

Sal chewed quickly, swallowing her mouthful down with an emphatic glug of her Coke and checking the time on her phone, her next meeting imminent. 'Elle, you know I'll be in major doo-doo if I get caught out telling you things I shouldn't.'

I waited patiently. Sal is great at many things, but keeping secrets has never been one of them.

'*Mate!* I *can't!*'

'Oh please, Sal, throw me a bone. I'm dying here.' I was joking of course, but when I see these words written down now, I shudder. *I'm dying here.* I wonder if I am. Sometimes it feels as though my life is slowly killing me: work stress, my career going backwards, the drinking, broken nights, keeping Dom happy, showing how grateful I am for all he's given me. Am I sweetness and light on the outside, a slow, bleak death happening on the inside? Have I let myself become passive? Because it's started to seem like my life keeps doing things to me, I am not doing things to my life.

'*Please?*' I begged Sal.

She sighed, checked about her to make sure that no one else from work was in Pret, and spoke conspiratorially. 'He's getting ridden pretty hard by leadership. The last major campaign: it tanked. Revenues were on the floor that quarter compared to the same period last year. The messages Anton's leading on to get donors to keep giving, for whatever reason, they're just not landing. Reckon he might be on pretty thin ice.'

57

'Right,' I said. 'I see.'

'Happy now? . . . Elle?'

'Sure. Anyway, how are Zak and Lewis doing?'

Sal went on to tell me about the latest sporting exploits of her teenaged boys, plans for her parents to come visit later on in the summer, if she and Tim could afford to pay for their flights, which I think was doubtful for reasons I'm ashamed to say I can't recall because while I was nodding and making the right noises at Sal, my mind was somewhere else. That last campaign, the one that failed to connect with potential donors, which raised no money, was mine. And the spike in donations that happened last year? That was when I was on maternity leave. There was the truth, in data, in black and white: my contribution to the charity I love was worthless.

'Hey, you in there?' Sal asked me. 'You alright?'

'Yep, fine, sorry, I zoned out for a second. What were you saying?'

Sal tilted her head. 'How's Agatha?' She took another sip of her Coke, her eyes still on me. 'How's Dom doing?'

'Yeah, she's great, he's great. That deal I mentioned last week, with the supermarket, Dom seems pretty confident it's going ahead.'

Sal nodded. 'Tealeafs beware! Dom the cam man's comin' for ya!'

'Something like that.' I gave a quiet, unconvincing laugh, thinking about all of Dom's success compared to my career, which once looked promising but was then thwarted by patriarchal forces, and now seemed to be heading towards complete malfunction because I lacked the competence I had once taken as read. The very least I could become, given my professional life, was a woman able to make a decent fist of her family life, to be a good mother and a better wife. But I had no particular aptitude in this space either. Perhaps, then, the very least I could do was not to want to run away whenever Dom touched me.

'And how are things between you guys?' Sal asked, perhaps sensing my sadness.

'What do you mean?' I asked, worried again I might have said something horrible about Dom when I was at her place on Friday, something that maybe Tim might have overheard, something at risk of getting back to Dom. My pulse kicked up a gear.

Sal shrugged. 'I mean what I mean. Things with you and Dom alright?'

'Yes.' I shook my head defensively. 'Why shouldn't they be?'

'No reason.' Sal watched me for a second, waiting for more.

'Dom's *Dom*. Still incredibly hands-on with the baby, very hands-on with me.'

'Hands-on with you?' Sal asked, and now it was my turn to look about the place to ensure no one could hear us.

'After you had the boys, after you'd been together a while, did Tim, you know, *calm down* at all?'

'As in, stop pestering me for sex the whole damn time? Yeah. What about Dom?'

'Sal. If he could have sex every day, twice a day, he would.'

'And you?'

'Quite honestly, if you told me I never had to have sex again for the rest of my life, right now, I wouldn't be in the slightest bit bothered.'

'I see.' Sal nodded. 'That's a tough one.'

59

'The truth is, sometimes I'd actually really like it if we could have significantly less sex.'

Sal nodded some more, seemed to think about something for a moment, before looking at me straight on.

'You *do* know the Marriage Rule, right?'

'The Marriage Rule? You sound serious.'

Sal leant in close. 'Elle, there's just one rule you need to follow for a happy marriage.'

'O-K,' I said uncertainly, 'tell me more.'

'It's super simple: you have to keep on having sex with your spouse whenever they want it, even if you don't.'

I laughed. Sal did not. I forked the tuna salad in front of me, waiting for her to crack into a smile. 'You mean it? You genuinely believe that's the one *Marriage Rule?*'

'That's what I'm telling you.'

'Have sex whenever they want it? And if you don't want to?'

'Then you don't want to.'

'But that's breaking the Marriage Rule, according to your nineteen fifties housewife *Rule of Subjugation*.'

'That would be true. So, I suppose, the question is, are you prepared to keep doing something you don't want to do for the sake of keeping Dom happy; for the sake of staying married?'

My mouth dropped in outrage. This type of talk was the last thing I'd have expected from devoted feminist Sal. She was the person you would least anticipate coming at my problem with advice that seemed tantamount to *Lie back and think of England*.

'I can't believe you actually—'

'That's the rule of staying married, Elle. Think about it.'

'I mean, it would definitely keep Dom happy, but . . .' I was bewildered as to why my fearsome, women-defending, thoroughly modern friend was suggesting I needed to accept a life of sexual servitude to maintain my marriage, but worse than this, I wondered whether what Sal had told me was actually true.

While I'd been speaking, Sal had screwed her baguette wrapper into a tight ball. She stood up and took a final swig of her Coke can. 'And if you're not happy following the Marriage Rule, you probably need to ask yourself why. Gotta go.'

And it was at this point I thought about what alcohol we had in the house that I might give myself permission to fall on when I got home if I really felt like I needed to when the day was through.

'But—'

'I think that's your man calling,' Sal sung as she left, after nodding at Dom's face popping up for his usual lunchtime call.

'Hey, babe,' I said to him, still distracted by the sight of Sal coolly leaving Pret, as though she had not just lit a fire under everything I thought about her and everything I thought marriage should be about: honesty, compromise, support – and absolutely not delivering yourself up whenever your husband decided he wanted sex.

'Are you too busy to talk?' Dom said, instantly picking up on my tone.

'No. No. I'm all yours. Did you go into the office today?'

'I felt like working at Mum's. She's just taken Agatha out for a stroll, so I'm all alone in the attic.'

'That sounds nice,' I said without really thinking.

'Does it?' Dom said a little confused, hurt even.

'I mean to have some peace and quiet for once, that must be nice; no one in your team asking you for something, interrupting your flow,' I stumbled.

'You OK?'

'I'm about the same as I was when I saw you a few hours ago.'

'Oh. You don't feel like talking today. OK.'

'No. No, that's not it. Everything's fine, work is . . . it's the usual.'

'Well, you know what I say to that.'

'I do,' I said, sneaking a bite of salad.

'What are you eating?'

This may sound mad, but I suppose I've taken to lying about what I eat when I'm at work and Dom calls me at lunchtime. My husband loves my body as it is. He doesn't like the idea of me being hungry at work, which I often am, the thin soups and light salads I accept as my penance for all the calories I throw away on booze.

'I couldn't resist, but I had a huge ham and cheese baguette, with a full-fat Coke,' I told him, doing what I usually did, which was tell him whatever I'd seen Sal eat.

'Did you have crisps too?'

'Salt and vinegar,' I improvised.

'Did you put them in the baguette and crunch them all together?'

'I may have. Is that gross?'

'No. Not gross at all. What you did sounds . . . delicious.'

Something in Dom's voice had changed. I knew this tone. Dom wasn't appalled at my messy-sounding sandwich. If I wasn't very much mistaken, he was a twinge turned on by it. My husband's thresholds when it came to me, I have come to realise, in part by writing my log these last few days, were extremely low.

'What are you eating now?' Dom asked, letting out a breath. He sounded as though he was stretching, or possibly something else. I felt incredibly weird, but it seemed a little unfair to spoil his mood. I suppose Sal's Marriage Rule was freshly lodged in my mind. Besides, I reasoned, if there was some way I could help Dom deal with his own needs now over the phone, he might leave me alone in bed later. 'I can hear you're still eating,' Dom said, his cadence low. 'Tell me. What are you putting in your mouth right now?'

'*Dom*,' I said, scooping up the almost full plastic salad bowl and dropping it and my fork in the bin on my way out. 'I'm in the middle of Pret.'

'You don't want to tell me what cake, what chocolate you're eating now?'

I headed out into the street, speaking quietly and slowly into the phone, feeling weird, feeling ridiculous, feeling the tiniest bit icky over what I think I was being asked to do by my husband, but doing it anyway.

'Well, I actually wanted some cake *and* some chocolate.'

'You wanted them both?'

'I did.'

'You wanted to eat it all.'

I took a deep breath and squeezed my eyes shut for a second, readying myself to give Dom what it sounded like he wanted. I bit my top lip, scrunched up my eyes and started to speak.

'The cake looked so moist, and the chocolate so rich and . . .' I avoided catching the eye of Anton's protégé Caleb who was at that moment walking past me in the street, turning my face and cupping my hand over my mouth and the phone. 'And it looked so sticky . . .'

'Yes?'

'Yes, so I ate them both.'

I could hear Dom's breath quickening on the end of the line. 'With your fingers?' he asked, the tone of his voice rising on the last word of his question.

'I got cake all over them.'

'And your face?'

'Yes,' I said, rushing out the next words, 'my lips and my chin and my cheeks were all smeared with chocolate and my face was stuffed full and . . . do you want to know something?' I added, stalling for time, trying to think of how to elongate whatever we were doing for Dom to finish what I knew for sure he was now doing.

'Yes,' Dom whispered, air catching in his throat. 'Yes, please.'

'I absolutely loved it. And I wanted more and more even though I was so full.'

'You were so full? Was your skirt tight on your belly?'

I blinked, surprised, maybe even a bit shocked at this turn of our interaction but feeling obliged to go along with it anyway. 'So tight. My clothes were so tight . . .' I was stalling now, unable to imagine what the right thing to say next might be. 'My skirt was so tight, my belly was so big, I couldn't breathe.'

A quick and decisive huff on the line.

Thank god. It seemed to be over quickly. I was almost at the reception of our building. I didn't know what to say next, wasn't entirely sure I wanted to say anything more anyway. This wasn't something we'd ever done before. Had I done OK? I wondered. I also felt, I don't know, maybe a little strange; I had just had phone sex with my husband, fuelled, of all things, by the idea of me overeating. Did I know my husband at all?

Silence for a beat, some faint rustling, some movement, before Dom came back on the line, his voice now slack with satisfaction. 'My god. Look what you made me do. Jesus!' He laughed at himself, at us, I suppose.

'It wasn't me,' I said, joking along with him, but when I caught my reflection in the glass doors to the lift, I saw I was frowning. 'I didn't make you do anything.' I corrected my expression into the smile I wanted him to hear in my voice.

'Yes, you did. You can't help it. *I* can't. I'm so turned on by you. I'm turned on by everything you do. I can't wait to see you later.'

'Me too.'

'I love being married to you, Elle Graham. Gotta go. See you at home for round two.'

Although I had barely eaten anything at lunch, I found I had no hunger at all except for the cold, vanilla-sour Sauvignon Blanc I knew was waiting for me in the wine fridge.

Chapter Six

Day twenty-one, Saturday

I can barely breathe: the sex I could barely recall was not with Gabriel, the man some part of me believed was worth throwing my marriage away for, but with Anton, my physically and spiritually repulsive boss, someone I openly despised.

Could it be my aches and pains this morning are not the lasting impression of pent-up desire being finally released by Gabriel and me into each other, but something fuelled, surely, by hate? And the fact I feel like I'm hurting from my head to my thighs and everything in between: was it even sex? Because I simply can't ever imagine consenting to sex with Anton. Rape, then? Did intimate violence, not the passion of multiple, overlapping episodes of intercourse, account for my soreness? Wouldn't I know for sure if I had, indeed, been assaulted?

But isn't that what so many women say when a man has harmed them without her identifying it as pain, as assault? Because perhaps men have executed their crimes somewhere in the margins of acceptability, places where it's possible to frame their violence as expressions of desire or admiration, not power and subjugation. *She liked it rough; it was a crime of passion; a sex game gone wrong.* I deal with the stories of women worn down by these concepts all the time at work, women laid low by men and their *just-abouts,* abhorrent things placed in the sphere of kink and confusion over what a woman was consenting to, what she might feasibly enjoy and what will certainly leave her in unacceptable pain. And the humiliations I've seen women suffer nevertheless leave too many of them not howling in rage at the overpowering of her will, of her debasement, but instead, wrestling with morning-after questions posed only to herself: *I don't feel right, but am I overreacting? Maybe I'm a prude if I don't want to do that again? I hurt but maybe I'm just not as adventurous as other women?* Don't some women, so worn down by man's systems of abuse and of the erosion of her boundaries, walk away from something a man has done to them, that's if they get to walk away at all, thinking: *I'm sure he didn't mean to hurt me. He didn't know I wasn't into choking. He got carried away in the heat of the moment. It didn't feel right, and I did not want it to happen, but it wasn't* **rape**?

But when I think of the word 'rape' I can't attach it to myself; because I don't want to believe it, or because I don't feel I'm anything like the kind of women we help. I don't live like them. I am rich. I live in a large house in a desirable neighbourhood. I have a middle-class job. And I am alive; Anton, dead. So, can I really be the victim not the aggressor? And even if I am, would a court, a judge, a jury ever believe me?

I force myself to look at the outline of his head in the semi-darkness. I can see from here it is him, Anton. Because I know it is him, I recognise I am very much the suspect. Oh god, what have I done? What ever should I do now?

Gabriel has gone quiet, but I know he's still there on the other side of the door.

'Go, please, Gabriel. We're done here.'

'This conversation or you and me?'

'I'm sorry, Gabriel, all of it. It's all done now. You should go.'

A pause, a deep breath, then I hear footsteps retreating down the corridor outside. I am alone again. I cannot stall going to Anton's body any longer. I approach it from the side nearest the window. There is so much blood, on the sheets and the walls, I wonder how it could have all come from him. I bend down to the height of the body, bracing myself as I use the very tips of my fingernails to pinch the sheet near the head. It is damp with blood, red spots spurting out in a diabolical spread across the crumpled pillow to the side of the head. I follow the spurt pattern, turning around to see the spray on the wall beside the window. Some of the blood has also reached the edge of the curtains nearest him. I pull the wet, reddened sheet away again, just enough to reveal the face. It is horrific. Anton's eyes are glassy and grey, slightly open. I do not want to look at them, at him, do not want to make myself see any further detail from this scene, but I need information. Maybe I can begin where it ended: the fatal injury.

I pull the sheet back further, holding my breath. There it is.

A neck wound.

The cut itself is almost indecipherable in the darkness but I can still make out congealed blood in and about a sickening trench across his throat. Bile rises from my stomach as I imagine the diabolic projection of blood from Anton's veins. So, a fatal neck wound; inflicted with what? A knife? I think it through and

68

feel something like relief; I didn't have a knife in my possession. That suggests some degree of premeditation. This can't be me. The only thing I think I had on my mind last night by the sounds of it was getting Gabriel into bed, that's until I unfathomably turned my attention onto Anton. I don't have any clue how that would have happened, but I do know for sure I had no plans to hurt anyone last night.

'Not even you, Anton,' I say to his face and it's then I notice his hair. Its untidy tufts of characterless brown with some kind of greasy wax in it don't appear simply post-sleep mussed or even post-coital dishevelled: there's something unmistakably violent about the mess of it. A chunk of hair shoots away from Anton's scalp at an acute angle, as though someone had gathered it in their fist. There's something about it that I can't imagine it being left that way from the throes of even warped power-play hate sex, or in a scenario where I might be fighting desperately to deter Anton, to make him stop. No, it very much seems to me that whoever had Anton's hair in their grasp was using it to escort his throat closer to the blade. I recover his face with the sheet and take a step back.

I look at my hands. Could they have killed? I look for any evidence I've been holding a knife, an accidental score or abrasion perhaps, and instead notice my fingernails. On one of my hands, the index fingernail has broken; on the other, the nail of the middle digit and the thumbnail have faint, ghostly white bars across them that broadly align with my fingertips. Only now do I register the angry heat under what seem to be fracture lines. I shouldn't have washed my hands. What was I thinking? I couldn't

69

have been thinking at all because if someone didn't know better, it could easily look as if I was trying to destroy evidence of the violence between Anton and me. And, on the other hand, if I have been assaulted and needed to plead self-defence, perhaps now I won't have the flecks of Anton's skin under my nails to prove it.

This thought, and perhaps also the disorientation that's only growing with every new discovery, sends me stumbling to the bathroom where I finally vomit. Another mystery. I remember drinking red. Yes, I remember now, there was sparkling white wine, but the last, maybe the only thing I can just about recall drinking was some red wine. But my vomit isn't particularly red-wine-coloured so I couldn't have drunk that much. Maybe there's a bit less flesh on me to absorb the units than there was a few weeks ago. How else but being out of my mind on alcohol could account for how I apparently ended up 'going off with Anton' as Gabriel described and the fact everything about last night happened in the shadows of my memory?

I feel another surge of nausea and instinctively splash my face with cold water. Drips fall to my neck and down to the white vest I threw on soon after I woke up in this living nightmare. I grab the hand towel by the sink, stand up straight before the mirror. I'm about to dab myself dry when I notice faint smears of blood on my cheek, smeared dots on my neck, blurs of pinkish red near the top of the vest.

No.

I've almost rid my face and upper body of the remaining evidence of the blood splatters that would likely locate me right in the vicinity when Anton's neck was fatally slashed, perhaps even facing him; evidence I have now unthinkingly all but destroyed; evidence that could suggest I did this to Anton. If anyone could have imagined I was innocent now, every small decision of mine seems to make this possibility vanishingly tiny. And all of it makes me think I've never needed Dom more than I do right now.

Dom is the one person who will know for sure I could never hurt Anton. He's made it his life's purpose to watch over me, hasn't he? I'm sure he'll do whatever he can to keep me close to him now and forever, shield me from my poor decisions, from cleaning myself up to the point it could look as though I'm covering my tracks, from hanging onto a job I realise now would have been far better to let go, and, of course, from whatever I've done that's put me in the position I'm in now. I desperately want to call him, but I can't do that yet. I need to get some kind of story straight, and I can't do that if I have no idea what that story is.

The only thing that's currently clear is that a man I openly hated is dead, a man there are multiple and undeniable WhatsApps and emails about, professing my repulsion for him, a man who in my darkest Sunday-night moments, I actively wished would die, suffering horribly, alone and in pain. There would be no need for anyone to spring the evidence on me. I know already how it could look all look: my Sunday-dread wishes coming true. Only, he wasn't alone at the moment of his death, as I had speculated and wished for many times; my vile boss died with his bare skin next to mine. I need to throw up again but my stomach is empty.

I'm frozen now, sat on the floor in front of Anton, my back to his body, my mind desperately clawing around for what else my

71

memory might possibly yield. My body begins to give way to self-soothing rocking. It makes me think of Dom shushing the baby to sleep, cradling her in his arms, a sight I feel I may never see again. Because while the window was open and someone else could have got in here, I know this: I had motive to kill Anton Bloch, and this motive is heavily evidenced.

Who will the police tell first about Anton being dead? Who are his next of kin, the person or people who miss Anton the most? I don't want to google Anton now. Instead, I recall my unhealthy levels of internet sleuthing when I'd tried to work out what made the man who'd taken my job from me so remarkable the leadership team couldn't see past my child-bearing age.

Anton was probably five or more years older than me. The job he took from me was his first senior role, as far as LinkedIn could tell me, in the charity sector. He was, to me then, another self-aggrandising blow-in from the private sector. Since eschewing some city broking firm where he was in some kind of PR, he had, apparently, thrown himself into a series of charitable and fundraising endeavours, in particular, lone-running escapades he enjoyed detailing on social media. I disliked him so deeply, the posts seemed like little more than an orchestrated campaign to look like a 'good bloke' with a sincere commitment to the not-for-profit sector. Later, when I snooped while I was on maternity leave, his volunteering and fundraising efforts seemed to intensify. I remember also never seeing any evidence of a serious relationship, or even friends beyond those other Lycra-bound middle-aged men he might grip under the finish-line banners of his charity events. Anton's park runs and half marathons also seemed to me about filling time. It's one of the reasons so many of the messages the police will surely read between me and Sal are peppered with the letters *LW*, the initials of my codename for him: *Lonely Wanker*.

I'm sorry. I am so, so sorry; to Anton, to anyone who cared for him. He didn't deserve this. I don't know what I may have done, but if I am to blame for this in any way, if there is something I could have done to have prevented his death, I am desperately sorry my issues at work may have somehow come to this. I'm not a violent person, or I didn't think I was. But then, I didn't think I was a lot of things it turned out I was.

There's nothing else for it, I'm going to call Dom and then the police, just as soon as I can steady my breath. But when I imagine myself dialling nine-nine-nine, then speaking the words of a woman turning herself in for what, being out of it while her hated boss was murdered – *being* a suspected murderer – it all sounds so insane, so enormous, so final, I feel I can't breathe at all. I pull myself off the floor and stumble towards the open window to try to get some air inside me.

I see something moving quickly in the middle distance outside.

A person walking fast, almost breaking into a run.

They're familiar, no, unmistakable, even in this dark hour. Her steel crown of Princess Anne hair catching the hazed moonlight, my mother-in-law rushes towards the exit of the hotel car park.

Chapter Seven

After lunch, I tried to not let myself think too much about the weird phone sex with Dom and instead messaged Sal, wanting to know what she really meant with her Marriage Rule chat, whether it applied to her and did this therefore mean she was having sex endlessly with Tim, even after more than fifteen years together, whether she wanted to or not. But Sal didn't seem ready to explain herself any further. Instinctively, I was appalled at the idea of this so-called rule being at the heart of her enduring marriage, of any that go the course, and any universe where Sal's Marriage Rule was the one thing that might allow me to succeed at mine.

When I got home, Patience was there, as was usual on the days she took care of the baby. She and Dom must have migrated with the baby back to the house post-lunch, having spent the morning at Patience's. Dom insists it's vital to the baby's development she forms a close bond with her grandmother, rather than with her key worker at nursery, though I get the idea his mother could take or leave her caring responsibilities, not least because of the many charged 'discussions' she and Dom have had on their opposing approaches to childcare and parenting. 'You're the professional wordsmith, Elle, *to parent* wasn't even a verb when the boys were small. Make of that what you will,' she had once said, loftily bringing to an end yet another 'conversation' about the relative detriments (Dom's stance) and benefits (Patience's position) of giving babies dummies.

'Good day?' I asked Patience, quickly rinsing my hands before retrieving the baby from her play pen, or 'baby jail' as I have privately termed it, an instrument of containment bought by Patience so that she might carry on about her day, reading her *Daily Telegraph*, perhaps sending the odd email to the team managing Graham Nurseries if something occurred to her, some description of some bulb, shrub or other that wasn't quite to her liking on the website. To Patience, the baby jail meant there was no way the baby would be denied the chance to learn how to 'entertain herself' or risk 'over-stimulation'. I was secretly glad she was in her jail when I got home; that way I knew she'd at least prefer me to it, with Dom not being an option in that moment. It very quietly broke my heart that she seemed to prefer her father to me, but perhaps that's the tax I must pay for Dom being so present.

'Oh,' Patience said when I liberated the baby. She was watching me from the dining room table where she was reading her paper. 'Agatha was perfectly happy there.'

'Hello, you,' I said to the baby, ignoring my mother-in-law for a moment so I could nuzzle my nose into her cheek, hating how strongly she smelt of Patience's old-fashioned perfume, the soapy, bergamot scent of *Je Reviens* after her day with her grandmother. 'I haven't seen her since this morning,' I said to Patience, smiling, using every ounce of my energy to keep irritation from creeping into my voice. I held the baby a little more tightly to me and kissed her cheek.

'And somehow she survived,' Patience breathed to the page of her newspaper as she turned it.

'Oh, did her dress get dirty?' I said, ignoring Patience's last snide remark, to instead ask what had happened to the outfit Dom had put on her that day, something he had bought for her after a recent growth spurt.

'I'm afraid she hated it. She was getting very cross indeed with the buttons and so on.'

'Right.'

Patience left her seat. 'When the boys were Agatha's age, they lived in romper suits, so much better for movement. Dominic was walking by the age Agatha is now.'

'No, I wasn't, Mother.' Dom had come downstairs from his office. He wandered over and gave me, then the baby a quick kiss, his hand squeezing my shoulder in a way that told me he was on my side, though he didn't need to; Dom was always Team Elle when it came to me versus his mother. Dom took the baby off me.

'I think I know my own child, Dominic. I think I know my own mind.'

'Of course you do, Mum. No one's saying you don't.' Dom passed his mother on the way to the kitchen where I guessed he'd gone to retrieve Agatha's meal from the fridge, the baby on his hip. He turned to me and rolled his eyes from behind his mother's back before winking at me. I can admit, I had to stifle a guilty laugh.

'That is precisely what you are saying.' Patience looked up from her paper to glance not at Dom but over at me.

'It's fine, Mum, honestly,' Dom said as he peered up and down the fridge shelves. Meanwhile, Patience held my gaze, as though expecting, wanting me to say something to counter Dom's somewhat patronising words. I had nothing to say to her. It was all I could do to send a meaningless smile in her direction, one that was not returned.

'Mother, did you happen to come across some sweet potato wedges I roasted for Agatha?'

'Yes, I pureed them and fed them to her about twenty minutes ago.'

'*Puree*? Mum, Agatha is doing baby-led weaning. There's no need to mush up her food and spoon feed her; we want her to learn and enjoy different food textures.'

At this, Patience let the page in her fingers drop, raised an eyebrow and reached for her camel-coloured mac. She spoke to me as she belted it at her narrow waist. 'I turned him from a six-pound mite to what he is today. And it all began with puree.' She walked over to me and spoke quietly into my ear. 'Formula too.'

We caught each other's eye. While it perhaps deservedly wiped the underlying smirk off my face, this felt to me like an incredibly low blow. I had not been able to disguise from Patience, from Dom, Sal or anyone, how challenging and painful I had found breastfeeding, in fact almost everything about those earliest months with my newborn. I'd been such a mess, Dom recruited a night nanny 'maternal nurse' and had her on speed dial for those nights when it seemed to clear to him I simply couldn't cope.

And when he did call her, while the guilt killed me, having that safety net saved my life because sometimes the whole newborn experience was like jumping off a cliff and never quite reaching the ground. Not only could I barely cope with the physical and the spiritual demands of having something so precious but so desperately dependant on me, I could barely imagine how anyone managed it, even if, unlike mine, their pregnancy and baby had been planned and longed for.

My body was ill-prepared, despite Dom's best efforts. He took such great care of me throughout my pregnancy, cooking the most nutritious meals, setting the conditions in our bedroom to the right temperature and humidity, optimising pillow formations so I might sleep as my body swelled. He even searched for and recruited a one-to-one pregnancy yoga and hypno-birthing expert to support me in the final stretch. But the labour still proved long and ultimately featured every kind of intervention Dom had so hoped we might avoid. I had to be induced, I begged for an epidural once the contractions kicked in and the final removal of the baby required both ventouse and episiotomy. And when the baby finally left me, I tore. When it was my turn to take over, my body failed: it did not relinquish her efficiently and independently and it would not allow me to supply her with milk without putting me through excruciating pain. I felt as though I'd failed; myself, Dom but mostly that innocent baby, so pure and perfect she deserved only the best I could give her. But giving her the very best of me seemed only to bring out the worst of myself, something on which Patience was only too happy to capitalise.

'Give up,' she had said to me one awful afternoon in the first couple of weeks, making sure Dom was out of the room when she did. 'Let me give her a bottle of formula. Let me take her.'

'No! Get away from us!' I screamed, which made the baby squeal and cry, and Dom rush in.

'What did you say to her?' he demanded from his mother.

Patience remained silent, keeping her eyes on me, apparently unafraid of Dom's anger and untroubled by my outburst. 'Nothing.'

Dom did not believe her. 'I think it's important you remember when to keep your thoughts to yourself, Mother, no matter how *helpful* I'm sure you think you're being.'

Patience and Dom shared a charged mutual glare. Waiting to see who would blink first as the baby continued to cry with escalating volume was excruciating. In the end, Patience shifted her view to me, then the baby. Her expression changed. She removed herself from our room without another word. Dom took the baby, and me, into his arms and I sobbed into his chest, so thankful that in a world I understood to be full of mummy's boys unable to stand up to their matriarchs on behalf of their wives, here was my defender. Back in our kitchen, ten months later, Dom was once again standing up for me to his mother.

'I assume you'd still like me to come on Thursday.' Patience folded her paper and lodged it under her arm.

'Of course, Mother,' said Dom.

'As you prefer.' Patience moved to leave the room.

'Bye, Patience,' I called out after her. 'Thank you!'

She had reached the doorway to the hall. Dom, who was by now chopping an alternate range of whole vegetables for

79

the baby, could not see his mother. On hearing me thank her, Patience stopped. She turned around. One. Two. Three seconds she watched me, waiting until the strained smile left my face. Her look said, pure and simple: *I see you.* After another agonising moment, Patience finally turned and left.

Dom was all over me the minute he'd got the baby down, finding me in the kitchen. Given how he'd had my back with his mother, I felt I owed it to him not to resist and besides, I had not been able to deny myself one, OK, two large glasses of wine that I'd sunk as he settled the baby. Though I felt at first guilty about pouring myself a drink when I shouldn't really feel the need on a Monday night, the fact was, I *did* feel the need after my day with Anton, the weird conversation with Sal, the strange phone sex with Dom. The booze soon left me feeling more relaxed, though I still can't say I was massively in the mood when Dom came to find me.

'Oh my god, I've been thinking about you since I put the phone down after lunch.' He had me in his arms and was mouthing my neck, just as I was about to drain the pasta, my small contribution to the dinner he had planned and prepared.

'Care*ful*!' I said, hot salted water splashing on my wrist, a blast of boiling steam in my face.

I just about managed to rest the pan on the draining board before Dom spun me around, telling me between kisses, 'You have no idea what you do to me.'

'Oh, you give me a pretty good idea.'

Dom froze, let me go and came up to his full height. 'Shall I stop? I just thought, I mean I managed to get Agatha out like a light, eventually, and—'

'And of course, I don't want you to stop,' I said, because Dom looked so wounded, and he had just spent the last hour bathing and getting our baby to bed.

I pulled him towards me, inviting him to kiss me, asking him to press his body hard into mine again, my back against the Belfast sink. He sent one hand up under my dress. I expected to feel his fingers travelling to the place between my legs, but instead, they found the roll of my stomach under the waist of my dress, his thumb and finger holding the fold in a firm pinch, the other fingers soon joining on the opposite side. The whole gesture felt extremely odd. I know I should be grateful he desired me despite, or even because, of the pieces of me I liked the least, but Dom's recent fixation on my stomach, probably the most out of control part of me, left me wanting sex even less than I already did.

We did it, there in the kitchen, the whole time my mind somewhere else; planning a new cycle route I might try in the morning, thinking about how I was going to get through another day with Anton, considering, many times, how I might be able to justify not only finishing the white with the pasta, but also opening something red for the rest of the evening ahead. The first two glasses of wine, or perhaps how I felt about myself after our at-sink clinch, seemed to have overcome what was left of my best intentions to limit my intake.

Chapter Eight

Day twenty-one, Saturday morning

From the window of my ground-floor hotel room, I watch Patience almost running through the car park exit. She slows only to take out her phone from the pocket of her camel mac, making a call just before she reaches the street and moves out of my sight.

What was my mother-in-law doing here? Has Patience been spying on me because she suspected I was having an affair? Did she come here to get final proof for Dom of me being no good and that he should leave me and take my baby with him? Maybe she'd tried to get a picture with her phone through the open window, saw me with Anton and lost her mind; gone at him with one of her propagation instruments, or slashed Anton's neck with her pruning knife? It all seems so utterly insane, but what else is my mother-in-law doing all but running away from the scene of the crime at quarter to four in the morning?

She has never approved of me and never wanted me to marry her son. I have plenty of evidence of this; countless messages my husband has forwarded to me from his mother over the last three years, whenever she sought to sabotage our relationship, which was at every critical stage. By sharing her messages, I think Dom was showing me from the very start he would be on my team over his mother's every time she asked him to choose. I don't know what I've been thinking lately; how I've ever lost sight of the fact he deserves a better wife than the one I've turned out to be. I have, in fact, proved Patience's every instinct about me correct. Still, I don't deserve this, if it is Patience who has done this to Anton, to me.

But this is madness, surely. Patience is capable of a lot of things, but a violent murder? No, I really don't think so. Besides anything else, something as direct as murder simply isn't Patience's style; her preferred methods of sabotage are far more underhand. I retreat back into the room, dropping myself onto the floor, leaning against the corner of Anton's death bed where I pull out my phone, scrolling way back to rediscover all the forwarded messages from Dom by Patience, right back to the first one he shared with me:

I don't think Elle is the type of girl you should be forming any kind of meaningful relationship with.

My mother-in-law sent this to my husband after my agonising first meeting with her, when she spent two hours investigating how and by whom I'd been brought up, barely able to conceal her disdain at my unextraordinary past. Difficult, but no abject poverty, neglect, abuse or jail time, but also not much in the way of a relationship with my family since I'd decided to go low contact.

Dom introduced me to the notion of going low-contact. It was a tactic he'd used in business relationships that didn't benefit him enough to justify a proactive approach to making it better, while the big bang of cutting ties would have generated too much kickback. I'd minimised my family's ability to make me feel terrible as part of the transformation of my life. I wasn't living old Elle's life anymore. Not letting myself feel like I was being forced to be her by my family made total sense.

As far as how Patience felt about me then, I know for a fact she's only ever believed my reasons for being with Dom were financial. While I do enjoy not having to worry about running out of money to pay my phone bill, being able to buy new shoes if I need to – and I definitely relished being able to leave the house share – I don't have expensive tastes and I don't like spending what has always felt like Dom's money. I don't drive a luxury car; I barely drive at all; I don't care for the designer dresses, watches and jewellery my husband lavishes on me. There really is no evidence to suggest to Patience I was, or am, some kind of gold digger, but when I read some further messages she sent to my husband at key moments in our relationship, it's clear this would be one of the more pleasant names she would attach to me.

I read again the missive she sent after Dom had proposed:

This is horribly rushed. I don't know what you think you're going to achieve but I advise you strongly against it.

And the message she sent to him after we'd told her the wedding date was confirmed:

I cannot say this strongly enough: I am warning you now, do not to marry this girl.

I found another message from Patience to Dom, one Dom forwarded me soon after he'd announced my pregnancy to her:

There is no way on earth Elle is ready to be a mother.

And the following spout of hate my mother-in-law sent soon after she'd threatened to wean the baby off my breastmilk, to take my baby away from me:

I told you she wouldn't cope. This will not end well.

Is there a case to say Patience may have been capable of killing Anton less in a fit of rage over my betrayal of her son, and more because she wants me out of the way? Framing me for murder would certainly be one way of finally achieving what I've known from the very start: Patience wants me gone. She has even said as much to my face.

I'd taken the decision, supported by Dom, not to invite my family to my wedding day. I was ready to embrace my husband's family as my own; Ol and Cora, and, yes, I was even ready to give Patience another chance, despite the poison she'd attempted to drip in my husband's ear about my character and motivations. Two days before we were due to get married, Patience had arranged a 'pre-wedding dinner' at her house, where Dom was staying in his old attic room in the nights before the big day, perhaps trying to make the wedding feel a little more traditional than it might. So many of the other rituals and signifiers were missing; I had no father to give me away, no mother of the bride I wanted there to dab her eyes as I said my vows. And because of Patience's watchful eye on whether I might be a spendthrift of Dom's money, and perhaps because I didn't want a big wedding anyway, I was happy to go along with Dom's idea of inviting only a handful of guests. On my side, there were a couple of girls from the house share I'd stayed in touch with, even though I hadn't seen them much at all since finding Dom, and I had no bridesmaids as such, only Sal as my maid of honour.

For the pre-wedding dinner, Patience had lit candles in the gloomy dining room, but it only made the place feel even more oppressive. I was nervous about the wedding, or perhaps – I can admit it now – the marriage. Patience did, I suppose, have a point about the timing. Dom and I hadn't been together as long as many other couples, but that shouldn't have given her any reason to assume we weren't real or that my motivation to 'sprint up the aisle', as I know she'd termed it, was anything other than her son becoming everything to me and me being ready to commit to that.

Like many brides, I'd lost weight in the run-up to my day. Unlike working to get rid of my paunch recently, my weight loss then was not at all intentional. For weeks I was too nervous, too churned up to eat. That night at the pre-wedding dinner, I recall Patience had cooked a spring lamb pie. I could not stomach it. I pushed my food about my plate, fixated on the sight of pieces of the young animal spilling from its egg-washed tomb at the centre of the table. Ol and Dom insisted on clearing up after dinner, leaving Patience and I alone. I remember now, my relief that Dom had topped up my wine glass before he and Ol left the room with the dirty dishes. His mother peered at me from her side of the table, having not yet taken her husband's seat at its head.

'I don't know if it's something about the candlelight, but you look quite ghastly, Elle,' Patience said, surely the last thing any bride wants to hear before her wedding.

'Ghastly?' I repeated dumbly, before quickly recalibrating. It was often something like this between Patience and me, especially when we found ourselves alone. She'd say something sharp, something to test me, to see if she was able to drive a wedge between me and Dom, to explore any way possible to scare me off committing my life to her son. I had to always stay alert, ready to absorb her latest blow, show she couldn't knock me off course. 'Hopefully it's nothing make-up can't fix.' I smiled. Dom's mother merely watched me, calculating her next line of attack.

After a moment of silence she asked, 'Was there something wrong with my food tonight?'

'No. God, no, it was delicious, as always. I suppose I'm—'

'You've hardly had a bite. Something troubling you?'

'No, I think I'm just—'

'I'm going to say this to you now and say this once.' Patience leant over the table, checking the door to be sure Dom and Ol were not about to return. 'You could take it all away now, if you wanted to.'

'Take what away?' I asked, working to keep the smile on my face, so she and I could imagine that she was joking. But Patience Graham never jokes. Patience has no discernible sense of humour whatsoever.

'You don't love my son.'

I gasped. My jaw fell.

'I know. You know.' Patience's Baltic eyes flicked between my face and the door. Being overheard was the only way she would be incriminated, and she knew it. She was entirely confident I wouldn't say anything to Dom about this conversation. Because looking back, she was probably right.

From her perspective, Patience imagined she could see I wasn't entirely sure I loved Dom the way he loved me, the way a wife should ideally love a husband, but I was going through with it anyway. Who else, what else did I have? If I were to give in to pre-wedding nerves, the chill I could feel on my feet, what were my alternatives to married life with Dom: contacting my old landlord and seeing if one of my former housemates had vacated so I could retake my place amongst them; trying to get a better-paying job with some miracle employer in the charity sector who could see past my child-bearing age; applying for a mortgage no lender in their right mind would ever give me, in light of my not-at-all-high salary and patchy credit history? No, I couldn't do that to myself. And I did care about Dom, I did like being with him; I did hope, one day, to develop the depth and quality of feeling that I could see Sal had for Tim, that perhaps Patience could see Flic had held for Ol and that I did not yet wholly experience for Dom but honestly believed I would as we grew together. Because that strong, handsome, romantic man loved me in a way no one else ever had, loved me not for all I could possibly be, but complete with all my shortcomings. That was more than enough for me to be ready to build a life with Dom and, despite what Patience believed, it was nothing to do with money.

'I don't know where this is coming from, Patience.'

'You can still walk away. Go, Elle. Leave this relationship while you still have the chance. If it's money you need, I'll give it to you. Take yourself out of my son's life.'

'Patience,' I said quietly, also keen not to be heard, not to have Patience's outburst sour my upcoming wedding, or give Dom any cause for concern, 'I don't need or want your money. And I'm not going anywhere,' I told her firmly. Then, I softened, working to suggest it was reasonable to interpret the appalling, brutal things she was saying to me as coming from a good place, or at least an origin of ambiguity, not from a state of unequivocal hate. 'I know seeing your son get married must be a potentially challenging time. It would be understandable if you were feeling conflicting emotions.'

Her eyes were touched by the faintest injection of tears, glistening in the unsure flicker of the candles.

'Maybe,' I continued, 'it's making you think of when Dom was a baby, and you can't believe your youngest boy's getting married?'

Patience blinked away her tears. 'That is not what this is about.'

'Perhaps it's making you remember your own wedding day; bringing out thoughts of your husband?' I asked as softly as I could. Patience's features remained still, except for her eyes, which she had shut tightly. I had struck a chord. I continued, 'I can understand if this is difficult for you with Hugo, with the man you promised your life to, not being here, for you, for your son on his wedding day. I can imagine that perhaps there are times when you feel lonely. But Patience, that is not down to me. That won't change just because you manage to scare me off your son, keep your baby boy single forever.'

Patience gave a faint shake of her head and opened her eyes.

'I mean you and your family no harm,' I went on, 'I only want to make a life with your son, who loves me. Please, be happy for him, for us. Please, don't say mean things like that again. It's incredibly hurtful. And, you should know, I do love your son, very much,' I said, my stomach falling when I made my last statement. I suppose I did know this wasn't entirely true, no matter how much I wanted it to be.

'You hardly know him,' she muttered to her hands, still and flat on the tablecloth.

'I believe I've known Dom longer than you knew your husband before you were married?'

Both Patience and I heard Ol and Dom's chatter getting louder as they moved to leave the kitchen. We would not be alone for much longer.

'That's correct,' Patience said. 'But that still doesn't make it right.'

I gave a sigh, smiled and shook my head, still trying to pretend what Patience had said was misguided, not hateful, even though by that stage I fully suspected she had arranged the dinner not to celebrate my impending nuptials, but to prevent them.

'What are you two chatting about so conspiratorially?' Dom's two hands were on my shoulders. 'You about to bust out the baby photos, Mum? Tell my wife-to-be what a naughty boy I was?'

'You weren't naughty, bud,' Ol said, walking back to the side of the table where Patience sat. 'You were . . .' He smiled at his 'little'

90

much larger brother. 'You were just what we needed.' Ol tipped his glass in Dom's direction.

'I've only ever done what any good brother would,' Dom said. For some reason, this made Ol look as though he might cry. Patience too. Dom picked up on it and in his very Dom way, moved to pivot the conversation to a significantly less emotional place. 'So, go on; what were you two talking about?' He had clearly also picked up on the residual tension between his mother and his bride.

Patience eyed me. I laid my hand on one of Dom's. 'Your mother was just giving me some pre-marital advice.' I caught her eye, hopeful Patience might, if not go along with this, then at least not show me up as a complete liar.

'Anything you can use?' Dom asked me, his attention darting between me and his mother.

'That's for your wife to know and you to find out,' Patience said, rising from her seat. 'I have some cuttings that need my attention.'

'You go do that, Mum,' said Dom, rolling his eyes at me, unseen by his mother who was already drifting past us. Dom retook his seat next to me, topped up my glass, then Ol's and finally his. Patience, meanwhile, had stopped at the doorway. I sensed her still watching me and turned around. She stepped deliberately back towards me. I froze. She dipped down to give me two careful kisses on each of my cheeks. They felt like kisses of death.

'Good luck for your wedding day,' she said quietly. She did not say these words, but I heard them as she brought herself to her full height: *You're going to need it.*

91

Despite all the evidence of her mistrust, of her hate for me, the idea that Patience attacked Anton with her pruning knife or similar, either in a moment of rage or in a more elaborate plan to get me out of her son's life remains utterly ridiculous. Nothing makes sense. It is pure insanity to imagine Patience as Anton's murderer. Maybe that wasn't even her I saw. If my mind was ever going to play tricks on me, tonight would be the night to do so.

Then, I smell something; odd, but familiar. I turn my head this way and that in search of the source. Eventually, I leave the floor, tracing the scent up Anton's death shroud like a blood hound until I reach the epicentre of the fragrance.

The sheet that covers the face of my murdered boss smells distinctly of *Je Reviens*.

Chapter Nine

Day three, Tuesday

The morning after Sal had apparently revealed the secret of enduring relationships, I realised I had effectively gone along with the Marriage Rule in the kitchen, just a few hours after I'd been appalled by it. I wondered, what would have happened if I'd told Dom the truth about how I was feeling, that I really didn't want to have sex? What if I were to consistently break the Marriage Rule, and only have sex, even phone sex, when I wanted to? And what if that's not many times a week, twice a day, but a few times a year; what would happen to my marriage then?

Then, I reasoned, as I mindlessly broke up pieces of banana for the baby to feed herself for breakfast – as Dom had asked me to do while he prepared some optimal assembly of superfoods for her later that day – aren't the real rules of marriage the vows you make? And aren't these all about sticking with your spouse no matter what, which would include, surely, whatever troughs your libido may be pulled into by having children, by the way that child or children have made you feel about your body, yourself, the kind of person you are and hoped you would, or would not, be? But didn't I also make a further vow to promise my physical life to him too: *with this ring I thee wed, with my body I thee worship*? And if I were to break this pledge, wouldn't Dom be in his rights to seek sex with someone else? How would I feel if he had an affair, maybe one purely based on sex? Would that be devastating, or the perfect arrangement, so long as we could stay together with the baby? I played out explaining such a scenario to Sal, immediately hearing her threaten to *tear Dom a new one*, if he ever betrayed me in this way.

I introduced Sal to Dom a few months after I met him, soon after I'd moved into his house, the one I live in now. Sal wanted to know who the guy was who had 'kidnapped me', the man who was 'eating up my evenings' and sending huge, heavy bouquets of flowers to work, their thumping arrival on my desk making me flush with warmth for Dom but also embarrassment. Was everyone else thinking what I was: what did I possibly have about me to justify such extravagant, public gestures? When I told Dom, in the gentlest terms I could find, he should realise there was no need to declare his love for me so publicly, I think he thought I was joking, *protesting too much*. He ended up sending even more for a time. While like Dom, Sal believed me to be worth every petal of those bouquets, she became increasingly intrigued about 'this Dom' and asked to meet him as soon as she could. But I didn't want to introduce Dom to Sal's robust sense of humour until I was sure he and I were strong enough to withstand it.

I also knew Sal was worried when I moved in with Dom so fast, a development partly driven by my tenancy agreement on the house share coming up for renewal. I'd shared with Dom I

94

wasn't over the moon at renewing for a further twelve months, but not because I was expecting, or encouraging Dom to invite me to live with him, though when he did, I agreed. Why not? I wanted what I had with him to be solidified; or maybe it was that I wanted my life to feel more grounded. I loved the fact I didn't need to sign on again for another year. Instead, I could join the ranks of former housemates who'd given their notice and got their deposits back; *I* was finally the one who got to say goodbye to the people remaining in the house share. I loved that Dom had made that possible for me.

House or no house, Sal would never have put me with someone like Dom, a fiscally secure, entrepreneurial alpha male. The kind of guys I'd been with before were a lot more like me: not notably successful or financially secure, somewhat adrift, in our old house share or someone else's, with the notion of property ownership a distant fantasy. I imagine Sal probably thought I'd end up with someone more like her husband, Tim, the kind of guy who doesn't take life or work desperately seriously and has a gentler approach, perhaps, to what constitutes an existence lived well.

Tim is a would-be surfer bum trapped in the body and life of a forty-five-year-old insurance executive. Sal met him when he was on a year out in Australia. They clicked. Sal fancied 'a couple of years' in the UK and Tim and Sal found there was no way they could unclick. Two years morphed into two babies and the promise of the rest of their lives. I had hoped Sal might see Dom and me progressing at the rate we did because she knew sometimes a man can take you by surprise and take your life to places you weren't expecting. And yet, I suppose when Dom has asked me over the years whether Sal 'has a problem' with him, when I reassure him that Sal 'thinks you're great', I know I'm not being one hundred per cent truthful. Maybe that's because Sal is something of a wilful contrarian and, fair enough, sometimes this winds Dom up. Sal is the kind of person who likes to take an oppositional view, sometimes for the sheer sport of the spar. Maybe that's where her stark argument for the Marriage Rule was coming from and maybe that's why she continues to kick Dom's tyres so robustly, something which began from the very first time they met.

'Jesus,' she said, appraising all of Dom when he walked into the bar where she and I were waiting for him. 'Why does a great big specimen like you still feel they need to send hundred-buck bouquets to a girl's place of work? You not reckon you had her on *Hello*?'

'*Sal*,' I cautioned, so desperate for my best friend to feel as good about this life raft of a man as I did, and for him to love Sal as much as I did.

Dom laughed, though his eyes narrowed, as he paused to examine his adversary, the person he knew he might need on-side to truly keep me.

'I'm not a complacent man. I'll use whatever I have at my disposal to seal the deal,' Dom said to Sal over my head as he hugged me hello.

'Will you now?' Sal said. 'Well, let's see what you've got going for you.'

'I should warn you, Sal,' Dom said, taking a seat and swiping up the drinks menu from the table, 'I enjoy being tested.'

I eyed him, then Sal, my stomach clenching at the tension between them, even if it was good-humoured.

'And you should know,' said Sal, 'I'm a details woman.'

Dom held out the wide span of his arms, suggesting he was, to Sal, an open book whose pages she was free to read. I felt I loved him very much for that gesture in that moment, that on top of how he'd blown my life to pieces in what felt like the best way, dismantling everything that felt wrong about my existence bit by bit: the way I'd stopped over-compromising in relationships with my family, the way being with him almost neutralised the pain of my abortive promotion, of my once-depressing housing situation. I gave all of myself over to Dom, back then. Now, I could barely give him the one thing I could really offer him, my body, sex.

I was still chewing all of this over when I got to my desk that morning. I logged on and stared at the screen, then spent the first two hours of the day throwing some more ideas at my proposed campaign messaging. At some point, Anton's mini-me Caleb asked me how it was going and if I needed any help. I told him no thanks as politely as I could, then decided it was best to send a holding email and a work-in-progress document to Anton, who'd been away from his desk for much of the morning, before he thought about chasing me. I wanted to demonstrate I was focused on delivering what was expected, and that my new draft proved I didn't need Caleb's help to get something workable over the line. In composing the email, I employed some of Anton's bullshit vocabulary, hoping it might put him in a better mood to receive my work:

Hi Anton,

Sorry if you're a bit busy today, but I thought I'd run my new messaging direction of travel up the flagpole before working these through the updated plan. Look forward to hearing your feedback on the attached.

Many thanks,
Elle

I sent the message, feeling not too brilliant about the stage my work was at, but hoping I'd pacified Anton for the time being. I went to get a coffee on my own, with Sal working from home that day, something I preferred to avoid if possible myself. I was far more productive away from the house and, in truth, away from Dom, who tended to take my working from home as an almost cast-iron guarantee for lunch-hour sex if he was home too and the baby was at nursery.

There was no corporate guff to cushion the intent of Anton's feedback. When I returned to my desk, there was a print-out of my revised document waiting for me on my keyboard. Through my words, not even in red Tracked Changes, was a thick black diagonal line the length of the page and one word in capitals scrawled in the bottom right-hand corner of the page:

NO.

Before I could stop them, I felt the tears in my eyes. No. *No.* I would not be a woman who cries in the office. I took a deep breath in, swallowed and pushed my fingertips hard into my tear ducts.

'And this here's our current copywriter, Elle.'

I turned around to see Anton stood behind me, and twisted my faintly horrified, flushed, tearful face towards him. There was another figure to his left, the sunshine reflecting off the river outside my window illuminating one side of his face.

'Elle,' Anton said, 'meet Gabriel.'

Chapter Ten

Day twenty-one, Saturday morning

I think my mother-in-law must have been in this room, right near Anton's body. Or perhaps, it's only that indelible scent of hers has been transferred to my outer clothes via the baby? It's all feeling like too much of a coincidence, surely?

It's almost four now. Anton's body is cooling next to me. Maybe by now it's beginning to decompose. Thank god the window is already open. I don't want to inhale his cells, breaking down and away from him, incorporating back into the air, back to the earth's soil and water, when only a few hours ago he was whole, with an entire existence ahead of him. Even though I hated him, I feel genuinely and deeply sorry this is Anton's fate. I know I need to make things if not right, then at least just.

I also know I can't stay like this much longer, but I don't understand how to do whatever I need to do next if I want to see my baby again, because I realise how this looks, how unlikely it is that my mother-in-law killed Anton, but I want my chance to live freely, to get back to my baby and make everything right.

Oh god.

The hotel phone by the bed rings.

A single ring.

Internal call.

Reception? Housekeeping? Security? Can they smell Anton already? Has Patience or someone else reported me? If I don't answer it, surely someone will come to the room and then I will lose whatever control I have of this situation.

'Hello?'

'Ms Cotton?'

'Yes?'

'This is the night manager with your four a.m. wake-up call.'

'Wake-up call?'

'Yes. We spoke late last night.'

'We did?'

'That's right. You said you specifically wanted to give yourself a message that it was time to wake up now.'

'Wake up at four? Really?'

'You were . . . a little worse for wear, shall we say. You mentioned to yourself you thought four o'clock was the earliest you might hear a call . . . Are you still there, Ms Cotton?'

'Yes. Did I say anything else?'

'No, not to my memory . . . Ms Cotton?'

'Yes?'

'Is everything OK? Is there anything you need or I can do for you?'

'No. No. I'm fine. I'm . . . I don't suppose you happen to know if I was alone when I called you?'

101

'I know the other name on the room booking checked out last night. Mrs Sally Porter?'

'Oh, right, yes.' Yes, that confirms it, Sal went home.

'Is there anything else I can help you with?'

'No. No, thank you.'

'OK, well, breakfast is from six thirty, so you have a bit of time to kill.'

'Yes. Thank you.'

Sal.

I need to call Sal.

She'll go crazy if I call at this time, won't she? Though she did accept all those three a.m. desperate calls when the baby chewed on me until I bled in those first weeks after she arrived. That was a crisis, so is this, an even worse one. Who else have I got to help me; who else besides Dom?

I call her number, doubting she'll hear her phone.

'Sal? Hi. You OK? I didn't think you'd be up. Sorry.'

'No, um, yeah, I . . . Did you already try to call me? I've just got a voicemail. I think that's what woke me.'

'That wasn't me.'

'Whatever, anyway, was there something you wanted to tell me?'

'No. I don't know . . . I think I was bit more pissed than I wanted to be last night.'

'Oh yeah? You calling me 'cos you've done something you shouldn't have, or something so good you couldn't wait to tell me about it?'

'Sal. I don't think I remember too much about last night.'

'Do you remember having what looked like a deep and meaningful with Gabriel? That was the last thing I saw when I was getting my things.'

'When was that?'

'I dunno exactly, after nine, I guess?'

'You guess or you know?'

'I can check my phone. I called Tim about two minutes after I saw you guys getting into it from where I was standing. Do you remember I wasn't feeling too clever? What's the matter with you?'

'Getting into what?'

'I don't know, but it's you and Gabriel, so I could take a guess. Did anything happen, then?'

'Did you see me talk to Anton?'

'Anton? No, you may have done after I left. What, are you worried you got pissed and gave him what-for?'

'Yeah, I don't know. I feel . . . it's only everything feels a bit mixed up right now.' I can't cry, but that's all I want to do right now.

'You alright there?'

'I don't know that I am, Sal.' I want to tell her everything. Hearing the warmth of her voice is like the sound of the distant past. I want to fall apart.

'Hey, don't cry over it, mate. You've only done what billions of women have done before you. Trust me, you don't need to feel guilty.'

'What do you think I've done, Sal?' I ask through my tears.

'All you've done is get something you wanted. You're probably thinking that's selfish, maybe even wrong, and maybe, technically, to some people it is, but I think things like this happen for a reason because they need to.'

'There was nothing I *needed* to do, Sal! I don't know what I did last night, anyway. I only know that everything is wrong now, whatever happened was totally wrong.'

'Alright, Elle, it's OK. I hear you, I do, but try not to panic. You want me to jump in the car and come and get you? Or maybe I can kidnap you later, save you from baby swim?'

'That doesn't sound like my life.' I feel quite numb now.

'Mate, calm down. Whatever you did or didn't do last night, only two people know, and you can't even remember. If what you want is to draw a line under it and forget it ever happened, you can. That's possible. You can do that, OK? If that's what you really want.'

'That isn't something I can do.' My temples are fizzing; I can't stay on the phone with Sal much longer. 'Sal, I left a message to myself last night via reception. I can't remember making it. I wanted to tell myself it was time to wake up.'

'Who knows what the pissed mind convinces itself is a good idea and what really isn't . . . Elle?'

I've stopped listening to Sal; it's all I can do to sweep across the scene before me again, searching for anything like sense.

'*Elle?* You still there?'

'I have to go. Sorry if I woke you up. Thanks for taking my call.'

'You have nothing to thank me for. And no reason to apologise.'

I end the call but remain staring blankly at my phone.

Was there an outside chance I'd taken some photos that would give me any new ideas on how I got here? I swipe through my image library. The last picture I took was one Dom asked me to take of him and the baby at home, one he'd been so happy with, he'd gone ahead and set it as my phone's wallpaper. I can't bear to see it: an image of them both, so innocent, unimpeded by app icons. I retreat to my home screen where their bright faces are obscured by fitness and calorie-counting apps, and my email tile. I register I have mail. I noticed it before but assumed because it had arrived overnight it must be spam, but in my desperation for insight, and perhaps to give me another reason to stall before making my move to tell Dom, or the police, or both, I check the message.

At around midnight, just before I made the call to the night manager, I sent myself an email. There is no message, only the following letters in the subject line:

don'tt rust SLAk   DnT trsuy Sal   DponT TRUST SAL

Chapter Eleven

Day three, Tuesday

It transpired Anton had recruited someone to develop messages for a standalone campaign. It was another slap in the face. A big ad agency has offered to do some work for us pro bono. Some months ago, I'd suggested to the leadership team an idea for a campaign to challenge local objections to new housing developments, something that would reframe the 'not in my backyard'-type attitude. We had research suggesting the kind of messages related to our service users that might start turning the tide if we were able to land them. Working with the agency creatives to help deliver the project would have been a step up, or at least a step in the right direction, for both our service users and me. But now whoever this Gabriel was had arrived on the scene, it looked as though there wasn't anywhere for me to move at all.

'Elle, Gabriel has a lot of experience creating messages that stick; copy that resonates,' Anton told me, clearly implying this wasn't something I was capable of doing anymore, if I ever was, even if the central concept for the entire campaign was mine.

'That's so great,' I said, grinning at Anton and shooting a look at Gabriel, my eyes dead with disappointment. Gabriel, meanwhile, scanned my desk, noticing the shard of crystal, the award I won for my work, what felt like a lifetime ago.

'Wait, is it Elle *Cotton*?' Gabriel asked me.

'I'm her,' I said, and his features relaxed into a soft, dimpled smile, his fingers reaching into a crest of thick mahogany waves.

'You came up with that massive viral campaign last year.'

'If it's the one you're thinking of and the one I worked on, that was more like three, three-and-a-half years ago,' I said and I think I may have blushed. No one's said anything good about my output at work for so long.

'I use that example all the time when I'm onboarding people. I show them your work and tell them that's what I need. I mean, that and my own finest outputs too, obviously,' he said, blinking in mock modesty. 'You know, the kind of stuff I showed Anton to let me get my hands on the agency gig.'

'Naturally,' I said, going along with his performance and suddenly not appearing to mind at all that he'd effectively taken an exciting new workstream from me. 'And you've onboarded exactly *how* many people to your team? For all I know, that could be one person.'

'Well—'

'I think I'll leave you two to get better acquainted,' Anton interrupted, feeling perhaps a little uncomfortable that we'd started to talk as if he wasn't there. 'Elle, you'll be working for Gabriel on the agency project if that's what he wants.'

I nodded eagerly while inside bristling at how Anton had talked about me *working for Gabriel* and *if that's what he wants*. Simple phrases deployed in a way that reduces me, my time and skill to a commodity to be called on or dismissed at will, without much thought or consideration, and a commodity with a low market value in Anton's eyes at that.

'*With*,' Gabriel said to Anton, though he was still looking at me. 'Elle Cotton will be working *with* me if she's happy to.'

'I am. I definitely am.'

The award Gabriel had noticed was for one of the last projects I'd completed before I failed to get my promotion and Anton leapfrogged me. I'd had to clear my desk during my maternity leave. Reintroducing the award to the office felt a bit like jumping up and down on the spot and reminding Anton and mini-me Caleb: *Look! I used to be somebody!* I almost left the award collecting dust along with the rest of the items I cleared before my mat leave to wait in a box under my desk. This included the silver-framed photo of me and Dom, him standing behind me in one of the shadiest nooks of Patience's garden, his arms wrapped protectively around me. Dom had given me the framed image to display at work soon after I'd moved in with him. Unlike my award, it still lay in the box at my feet, gathering dust along with the unread instructions IT gave me on how to change my email address to my married name the year before I had the baby.

After our first, very pleasant, meeting, Gabriel was set up to work at a desk diagonally opposite mine. Perhaps it's him knowing of my past successes, my former incarnation as someone with a bright career ahead of them, that made me somewhat self-conscious, the gaping divide between who I was then, and who I became. When I next went to the loo, I found myself looking in the mirror much longer than I usually would.

I despaired of what I saw, in particular, my hair. It used to be thick and wavy, with a natural kink that formed a reliable blondish arch around my face, flowing out to my shoulders. Since the baby, the texture has changed. Nowadays it defaults to flat and greasy, the colour a darker, far less luminous shade, the arch around my skull collapsed. In the toilets, I shook my fingertips through my roots to encourage some volume that might frame my face more sympathetically, then prodded my stomach pouch below the waistband of my linen trousers. I tightened my belt another notch to remind me to hold my core with more determination.

I returned to my desk feeling unattractive and dull, the dissonance between the Elle Cotton whom Gabriel knows of and Elle Graham insurmountable. Dom bought me yet another present, which should be arriving today. When he saw how much I enjoyed the expensive Amarone from his late father's cellar at lunch on Sunday, he ordered a case to come to the house. It was twelve forty-five when I began to think about opening it.

Then, an email arrived:

Subject: Lunch?

Hi Elle,

Could I please take you out for something to eat if you're not too busy. I really need your brain if we're going to make the most of the agency time. No worries if you're busy.

Gabriel

I replied:

Love to.
Elle

Then deleted that draft and wrote something cooler and more professional. I deleted that draft because it sounded too haughty, before becoming aware I'd spent too long agonising over my response, meaning Gabriel would know the disproportionate effort I was expending trying to create the perfect email to his simple request for a working lunch. In the end, I dashed off something and pressed send before I could think about it any further. I must have been in texting-Sal-at-work mode because this is what I wrote:

Yes. Exx

I had a lovely lunch with Gabriel, which is great because from now on, I'll be working alongside him a lot more. Spending that time talking with him about the origins of the campaign and my initial thoughts on the messages had started to awaken something of the old me. It made me think how much I want to be her again and maybe I have for a while. The difference after talking to Gabriel was that I started to have the tiniest bit of confidence that getting back to who I was might be genuinely possible.

As I made my way home, my belt bit further into my stomach as I bent towards my handlebars. I cycled past the leisure centre on the new route I'd planned, a little longer but more scenic with less traffic than my standard route, giving me a little more time to think, get my head in the baby-and-Dom-zone after my unexpectedly refreshing day in the office. On the street outside the centre, I spotted an A-board. It was advertising personal training sessions. I stopped. Without waiting to hear in my head all the reasons I should not call it, I dialled the number listed. A young-sounding man called Jordan answered. Within minutes I had my first session booked for early the next morning before work, telling myself that Dom would be fine with it. I hardly do anything for the baby in the morning anyway, he's pretty much got it covered. Besides, if I get my pre-baby fitness back, I'll have more energy in the long term. I'll get a bit closer to be the best I can be, for the baby, and for my husband.

On the final leg of my cycle, I imagined I felt fitter already, the gesture of taking more control of my body already convincing me I was somehow stronger than before. Despite Dom's offer to crack open the case of the finest Amarone waiting for me when I reached the house, I did not drink a drop.

Chapter Twelve

Day twenty-one, Saturday morning

Don't trust Sal? Why not? We got past what happened between her and Dom at Patience's house last week didn't we, even if Dom hasn't? She wanted to spend time with me, which is why she booked us a room to share for after the away day. And Sal sounded genuinely worried at the state of me when I just called her, not to mention thrilled at the idea of me getting together with Gabriel. None of this is the behaviour of someone who had any notion of what happened in this room last night. Evidence of my mother-in-law being implicated I could just about take, but: *Don't trust Sal?* My best friend being somehow part of this mess is completely beyond my comprehension.

Come on, what else can I find out from this room?

I check the outline of Anton once more. The folds of the bloodied sheet covering him are catching shafts of the dawn now seeping in above the curtains. This could be my last morning of freedom and I'm spending it with him. Anton, I also realise, is the only person I can turn to for any answers; the only person who can tell me more about last night before I lose complete control over my existence. What further secrets might his body hold if I'm brave enough to search it more closely?

I approach him once more, intending to examine what I can of him while disturbing the scene as little as possible. I pinch back the covers once again and this time, the paling gloom means I can take in his horrific unblinking eyes and still face in more detail. Now I can see there's blood on his lip, leaking from a split below the biting surface of his protruding incisors, which are exposed; yellowish and dry. I remember something. A background pain, on my shoulder, the skin joining my neck to my collarbone.

I rush to the mirror.

I can see them now, one, two impressions, uneven but unmistakable: teeth marks. Anton bit me.

I go back to his body, bile rising again. Because I know now what the bite marks, my broken nails, and all the pain inside and about me are telling me: I did not consent to sex with Anton. I had once thought him only interested in degrading me professionally. When that failed, it seems he resorted to disempowering me in the most emphatic and sickening way a man knows how.

Maybe the blood on his lips could even be mine, not his, from when he sunk his teeth into me. And if this is the case, then the blood that shot from Anton's veins into the world, onto the sheets and the wall, is surely nothing to do with my spying mother-in-law, Sal, or anyone else. It's all down to me. It's all starting to make horrific sense.

Because I'm being taken by rage that's surging from deep within; a blast of startling power and righteousness. And if I'm feeling like this in the cold, growing light of day, then how did I feel when it was happening, when he finally stopped? Was I so furious I found a knife from somewhere and slashed his jugular? For the first time, I do genuinely think it could have been me. I look at my palms. They could be hands that murdered.

I refocus on Anton's body, desperate to find something that will tell me I'm innocent. I follow the line of the arm that's reaching out of the bed, hanging down into the air above the carpet. I can see strands of hair, dark blonde, unmistakably mine, caught between his knuckles. A memory: my head, pushed to his crotch, hair raising from my scalp. Heat where the follicles have been emptied of their strands. My mouth opened to take him in, despite the pain, despite the servile humiliation of it all. Oh god. That happened. I could not have consented to it and there is a terrifyingly strong chance I took instant, inebriated revenge for the crime.

I can see something else in the shadows, near a crease of over-sheet that's reached the carpet near where Anton's hand hangs. A short pencil. A hotel pad too. Anton has scrawled something on it.

I shine my phone's torch on the pad, my breath like flames in my chest. The writing is frustratingly faint. Anton must have written it as he lay there, dying. After he had raped me, and I did whatever I did to kill him.

This is what I can see:

EG
Mum

Chapter Thirteen

Day four, Wednesday

'If this is what you want then, you should go for it. So long as you're doing it for the right reasons,' Dom said when I asked if it was OK if I left early to go to my first personal training session.

'And what would be the right reasons?'

'I don't know, staying fit without having to inhale all that pollution when you cycle.'

'I definitely wouldn't mind getting fitter,' I told him, feeling guilty and not knowing why I didn't ask Dom the night before. Maybe I was nervous about admitting I wanted something for myself, when I had so much already. Or maybe a part of the Elle Cotton jangling inside me was struck by the oddness of asking another person what I might do with my morning. It's a big adjustment being a parent, being a wife, especially when both happened to me so quickly.

Though I'm obviously so grateful for the life I have, it's only now I'm able to catch my breath, take stock of how I ended up asking another person for permission to do something as uncontroversial as exercise, that I realised how it's taken only three years to go from an entirely independent, if frustrated, young woman with a life unknown ahead of her, to someone who felt so much older sometimes, and with all her remaining years and all the moments that will make up those years largely accounted for.

'And what would be the wrong reasons?' I asked Dom, smiling through my disquiet, not wanting to show him how much starting training was beginning to mean to me.

'The right reasons would be the right reasons for you. The wrong reasons would be if you think doing this would make me happy. You know I don't want you to change.'

'Change? I mean I suppose I would like to have more energy. Is that a right reason?' I said, widening my smile.

'What did you say you trainer's name was?' Dom asked.

'I didn't, but it's Jordan.'

Dom nodded. 'And she's supposed to be good, is she?'

'Yes,' I said, realising that, of course, I wasn't correcting Dom on wrongly assuming my trainer is female. But I really didn't want to derail his approval as, I supposed, Jordan's true identity might.

'Well, go for it.' Dom picked up the baby from her cot. 'We can cope without you here, can't we, Agatha?' He kissed the baby's cheek. 'How often will you go?'

'Twice, maybe three times a week, if that's OK?'

'Of course. Why wouldn't it be?'

'No reason,' I said. 'Thank you.'

I stood in the centre of a heavy chrome rectangle I was reliably informed was called a 'trap bar' designed for deadlifting. Jordan – twenties, a semi-professional footballer as well as a personal trainer with a stomach like iron and a completely unintimidating disposition – stood behind me, both of us watching me in the full-length mirror ahead. Attached to chrome poles sticking out at the end of the frame were two circular weights resting on the floor.

'This looks pretty heavy, Jordan.' I spoke to my reflection.

'You've got this, let's go. Bend those knees, push up through your heels, chin up, chest up, like I showed you in the warm-up.'

'I'm not sure I can do this,' I said, nevertheless squatting down in preparation to lift.

'Looking at you, I'd say you're much stronger than you think.' I watched Jordan as he viewed my legs, and perhaps my bum too, but not in a creepy way, in the kind of manner you might use while undertaking a risk assessment. I nodded, then turned once more to the mirror; the spill of flab below the waistband of my leggings as I bent, the extra inch of side-arse fudging into the top of my legs, pushing my silhouette to places it had never been before the baby. I had my hair in an unforgiving ponytail and I was already red-faced from the vigorous warm-up. Nevertheless, I grabbed each side of the frame, puffed out a breath and heaved its weights free of the floor, locking my knees when I straightened as I'd been instructed. It was heavy, but not backbreakingly so. I did the lift. I didn't even look too bad doing it.

'Very nice. Let's go again,' said Jordan.

I completed my set, quads buzzing. I imagined ley lines of energy from my hips through to the floor coming alive while the skin on my palms heated with the friction from the texturised metal of the trap bar's handles. The next set, we added more weight and while those lifts were more challenging, I completed them. And when the time came for me to do weighted squats, using a bar with two weights slid onto each end that sat across the back my neck and shoulders, I was unafraid. The same when Jordan instructed me in the ways of the faintly ridiculous-looking but explosively aerobic kettle bell swings, where I threaded the weight through my legs before shooting it out in front of me. At the end of the session, I was incredibly sweaty, a little shaky but more than anything, I felt proud of myself and hungry for the next time.

'You want a warm-down? Let's stretch it out. Lie down,' said Jordan.

I did as I was told without really knowing what I was agreeing to. I lowered myself down onto the nearest gym mat. Jordan knelt and took my leg, bent it at the knee, opened my hip to the side and used the edge of his body to push all his weight on it. I could feel an exquisite tension in the muscles connecting my hips to my groin. He stopped for a second before asking me to breathe deeply as he pushed a little more before repeating the sequence again. God, it felt good.

'Deep breath in.' Jordan released one leg, then folded the other and applied the same pressure. 'And breathe out.' I looked away as Jordan released the pressure and pushed again, trying to not to gasp, doing my best to hide just how much I was enjoying what he was doing. I felt guilty and a little appalled at myself as I tried to process why this contact was so pleasurable. Was it because it had been so satisfying to activate muscles I'd not used before? It was certainly thrilling to know there were parts of me holding strength untapped. But the truth was, there was something else that had been dormant within me being reactivated: the ability to be aroused. I was as exhilarated as I was disturbed. I realised, I couldn't remember the last time I'd been genuinely turned on by Dom. A maelstrom of guilt swept through me: I was getting aroused by the actions of an innocent man I wasn't employing for any kind of sexual service, but my body wanted to commodify him in that way anyway. But worse than this, I hadn't come close to feeling that way with Dom for months, perhaps years since we first got together. And then, when I really thought about it, had I ever connected with Dom in that breathless, burning, addictive way as I had some men?

As I headed to work after a shower at the gym, I shed these darker feelings and tried to focus on sweeter sensations, the blood pumping through my muscles, the early summer sun wanting to freckle my knees after I'd knotted the dress I was wearing at my thighs to cycle safely. I felt every breath of wind on my skin, tingling with my own pulse, right up until I turned into the entrance sloping down to the basement of my office building where I park my bike. I'd dismounted, leaning the frame of my bicycle against me as I unclipped my helmet, when I heard a voice.

'Morning. Good ride in?'

It was Gabriel, dismounting his own bike behind me.

'Oh hi. Great, thanks,' I said, self-conscious of the amount of leg I was showing and knowing how bad my helmet hair would doubtless be. 'You?' I asked as I slid my front wheel into the tight metal frame ahead, him slipping his wheel into the one next to mine. I hurried to unknot my dress.

'Glorious. Such a beautiful day,' Gabriel said. The weather

certainly appeared to suit him, a faint flush about his face, dark eyes glistening and his easy-going smile bright. 'Hey, I was thinking about a cycle up the Thames Path at lunch, take advantage of the sun. Wanna come?'

I thought about, then dismissed the vague plan I had with Sal to take our Pret offerings to the riverside together.

'Sounds great.'

A sunny day would typically send my mind to the evening, where I could justify taking a glass of wine into the garden. Instead, I realised I was happy to embrace the sun as an opportunity for the pleasures to be had inside my own skin, instead of finding alcohol-fuelled ways to get out of it. *I am not going to drink today*, I thought as I headed to the lift with Gabriel.

My phone rang.

Dom seemed to be calling and texting a lot more of late. I wondered if it was the stress of the supermarket deal. Maybe Dom was using me to distract himself from whatever challenges he may have been facing, or maybe he was trying to buoy me up because he knew what a bad time I was having with Anton. Either way, he'd sent fifteen or so WhatsApp messages yesterday, on top of our usual lunchtime call. This call from Dom, then, was a bit unusual, but not entirely unexpected.

'I'm going to have to take this,' I said to Gabriel. 'See you up there.'

He gave me the thumbs-up as the lift doors closed.

'Hey, you alright?' I said to Dom.

'Thank god you're OK.'

'Why, what's the matter?'

'There was a cyclist seriously injured on your route in. A female in her thirties.'

'Oh no, that's awful. I'm fine, obviously.'

'Obviously? How was I to know?' Dom sounded hurt, as though I was laughing at him.

'Not like that. Only, you can tell I'm fine because I'm talking to you.'

'There but for the grace of God.'

'Yes,' I said, unsure of what else I sensed my husband wanted me to say.

'How was your session with Jordan?'

'It was great, thank you.'

'She put you through your paces?'

I took a breath before I spoke again. 'Jordan's actually a male trainer.'

'Oh. You said you were being trained by a woman.'

'I'm not sure – I don't think I did. Anyway, he's a very young, very sweet meathead,' I said, feeling a bit obliged to talk down about Jordan for some reason, but also needled with guilt for doing so. 'I'll introduce you if he's around on Saturday when you go for your workout.'

'Do that. Jesus, I'm so relieved you're OK. I really thought we could have lost you. I hate you riding that thing; the accidents, never mind the fumes. Honestly, I thought you'd give up cycling once you had Agatha.'

'I love my bike,' I said, my words losing volume with each one I uttered, the rest of the sentence dying silently before it had a chance to be spoken: *it makes me feel so free.*

'Yeah, but it's so dangerous. We don't want to lose you. Besides, you'll be skin and bone with your training *and* your cycling. You'll disappear. Seriously, you should think about giving up your bike. I can drop you into work.'

'No,' I rushed out. 'I mean, don't worry, I can get the bus.'

'So, no more cycling?' Dom sighed. 'Amazing. Thank god for that. That's one thing I can rest easy about today.'

'Yes.'

'Gotta go. Love you, gorgeous. Can't wait to see you later. What do you fancy eating tonight?'

'Something light, maybe? I think the sun's lasting all day. Be nice to sit outside with a drink.'

'Sounds perfect.'

At first, I thought I felt excitable during my lunchtime ride with Gabriel because I knew it would be one of my last for a time. I understood what Dom was saying about cycling; it is taking a risk with my life every day, though I'm a pretty conservative sort of cyclist. I rarely jump a red or slip in between a bus and the pavement. But the idea of denying the baby a life with her mother because of my own selfish needs was enough for me to retire my bike for now. In the meantime, as I cycled in Gabriel's slipstream up the Thames Path, past London Bridge and onto Bankside, I savoured the power my muscles released into the pedals, the warm breeze on my face and arms. And at the sight of Gabriel's back, in a T-shirt with the sleeves rolled up, dazzling white in the sunlight, I felt, perhaps, the bittersweet flavour of saying goodbye. He seemed so carefree as he slipped with dexterity through the crowds on a bike I would soon be impressed to learn he built with his own hands. I wondered whether the nub of anxiety in my stomach was down to a kind of anticipatory grief over the fact I wouldn't be able to enjoy that familiar sense of liberty my bike gave me for a while.

The river looked beautiful, glassy, and unusually green in the midday sun. Gabriel had the idea we could grab a loaf and some tomatoes from Borough Market as we passed. We glided through the narrow walkways before cycling towards an open patch of grass in the cool shadows of the Tate Modern. We threw down our bikes and our respective jumpers, tore hunks out of the loaf and popped the ripe tomatoes, sweet and fragrant, into our mouths, the sweat from my fingertips salting each morsel deliciously. When we'd finished eating, Gabriel lay back on the grass with his eyes closed. I did the same. My anxiety from earlier shot through my stomach afresh, reaching into my lungs and troubling my throat. I wondered if, to other people, Gabriel and I might look like a couple.

Lying down next to each other, we talked about work, yes, but also about hopes and dreams, and our childhoods. 'My family is Portuguese,' Gabriel told me as the minutes raced by. 'I had a great childhood, full of strong and passionate women, my mum and my avó, my grandma.' I heard Gabriel move, opening my eyes to see his face turned to mine. 'Would it be completely weird if I said that's probably why I'm always so attracted to women with a bit of toughness about them?' I shook my head through a smile before sighing deeply. My mum, she wasn't perfect, but she must have needed to be pretty strong all those years when it was just us.

I knew if, for some reason, I didn't have Dom, I'd never cope on my own with my baby as she had with hers. A thump of missing her dreadfully, wanting to know how she'd managed, hit me hard. I swallowed the sudden wash of emotion threatening to burst out of me.

'I'm so sorry,' said Gabriel. 'Did I say something to upset you?'

'It's not you.' I gulped down the tears now fighting their way to my surface. 'You're only making me think about some things I haven't wanted to for a while.'

'Go on.' Gabriel's soft, almost-black eyes looked right into me. He dropped his arms from where they had been resting on his stomach to the grass either side of his body, and propped himself up to give me all of his attention. I too sat up before speaking again.

'I haven't spoken to my mum for a while. We don't really speak. I mean, there are reasons why, but it makes me . . . I mean, it's so sad it has to be that way, right?'

'Would you like to keep talking about it?' Gabriel asked me carefully. 'It's OK if you do; OK if you don't.'

I sighed once more but my chest remained taut and my stomach churned. I could not dispense of the tension growing inside me. 'I don't know what I'd say to my mum anymore. There's a lot of hurt. I've tried to move past it in my own way, but maybe . . . I don't know.' I let my hair flop down over my face. I didn't want anyone, and especially not a colleague I'd known for barely one day, seeing me as emotional as I was.

'Ignoring something doesn't make it not real. Is it the sort of thing you could ever think about dealing with head-on?' Gabriel said gently, and when he did, he moved a strand of hair away from my face, his fingertips feathering a line across my cheek. The gentleness, the sudden intimacy made me shiver. And then, I began to cry for real. I had no choice. Gabriel immediately came right to my side, sitting his body close to mine as he brought me into an embrace. The musk of the skin on his neck, the faint fragrance of whatever product he'd used on his curls, enveloped me. I could feel the warmth of his back through his T-shirt where my hand had found itself. I imagined allowing my fingers to reach below the fabric resting on his lower spine, thinking how I'd flick the material aside to reach the skin there, how it might feel as I inched up to his shoulder blades with the tips of my fingers. Meanwhile, I was letting Gabriel stroke my hair. I didn't move when his fingers travelled to the nape of my neck, where he rhythmically circled his fingers in a soothing motion that seemed to alter me. Blood rushed from my core to pulse between my legs. His lifted the chain around my neck lightly with his fingers.

'The rings on this. Your mum's? Grandma's?'

That was the point in the day when I should have told him the truth. Those rings, those commitments, were mine. But that didn't happen. In fact, that's when I knew I would not turn the conversation with Gabriel around to the fact I have a husband, a baby; that's when I knew I would go home later and rename my boozer's log *Miscellaneous* and locate it in a folder within a folder I would rename as *Archived messages*.

Gabriel moved so his cheek was next to mine. An incremental turn of his head or mine and our lips would meet. How profoundly I wanted this to happen, how deeply I knew I could and should not allow it. I forced myself to break away, disorientated with the desire thudding through every bit of me.

'I'm so sorry,' Gabriel said. 'I didn't mean to make you uncomfortable.'

'I think I'd better head back now.'

Gabriel nodded. 'I really am so sorry. I find you extremely attractive, but I shouldn't have acted on it. Should I?'

And this was the point where I should have told Gabriel that he should not, that I wasn't single. But to my shame, I didn't want to.

I knotted my dress, perhaps a little higher than it needed to be on my thigh. 'Please, don't worry.' I pulled my bike up off the grass. 'I'll see you at the office.'

'OK, Elle.'

I cycled away, fast, finally understanding what that turmoil in my stomach and chest was from before; it was the nervousness of someone who wanted to be touched, who maybe knew this would be easy to invite. Gabriel had signalled he'd have liked to get closer to me from the second he saw me and realised he was meeting 'Elle Cotton'.

He returned to the office five minutes after I'd got back. As Gabriel retook his seat diagonally across from mine, he gave me the kind of small, sideways smile that spoke of something shared, secret and dangerous. My head felt light; adrenaline, deep desire, and utter guilt combining. I jumped in my chair when my phone rang. Dom. I rushed out of my seat to take the call in the nearest empty meeting room, a glassed-off space behind my desk, struggling to breathe as I readied myself to act and sound normal.

Though my back was to him, I felt watched by Gabriel the entire time.

'Hey, how are you?' I said, trying to sound simply happy to hear from him, but not so cheery Dom would suspect I was masking something.

'Sorry I couldn't call you till now, my twelve thirty went on. And on,' Dom said.

I forced myself to concentrate on the sound of my husband's voice, to have it ground me, pull me back from the heavenly fantasies I'd escaped to in the minutes since Gabriel had touched me. I needed to reset myself as Dom's wife, not give my husband a reason to think I was anything else but the woman he thinks he knows.

'I thought as much when I was waiting for you to call,' I lied. 'How was your morning?'

'Pretty damned good. We're almost good to go on the deal. It's happening, Elle. This is going to set us up for life.'

'Oh Dom, that's fantastic. You must be over the moon.'

'Aren't you?' he said, perhaps a fraction confused, hurt even, which made his voice sound sharper than usual.

'Of course. It's just you've been working so hard to get it over the line. I'm happy for you that it's finally almost there.'

'This is almost there for us, darling. *Us*. Things don't happen to you and me as individuals anymore. What impacts me, impacts you. What happens in your life, happens in mine, happens to Agatha.'

'Yes,' I said, rubbing my eyes as though coming round from the trance Gabriel had put me in. What on earth had I been thinking? I had *not* been thinking about the baby. I'd crossed a line that made me unfaithful to her, as well as to my husband. What was wrong with me?

'Are you OK? You sound peaky. Did Jordan take it all out of you? I hope not. I had an idea we could make love under the stars tonight.'

'God, I'm not sure how next door would like that,' I said, attempting to laugh over my stomach churning as an image fused itself behind my eyelids: Dom with his trousers round his ankles, having me up against the side return.

'That doesn't sound like fun?' Dom could not hide the offence, the upset he'd taken from my tone.

'Of course. I was joking. I can't wait,' I said.

'So, it's a date then?'

'You don't need to book that sort of thing in with me,' I said, trying to laugh once more while wondering, for an instant, whether it was better to know what was coming for me and when, rather than living under the constant threat of sex with my husband.

'No. I don't.' Dom sounded quite satisfied with himself. I left my seat and turned ready to leave the meeting room. Gabriel caught my eye from his desk. My heart pounded, in residual want for him and in desolation at the idea of having to go home to my husband's house, to have dry, desireless sex with him in a suburban garden. I lost my next breath, imagining Elle Cotton heading instead to Soho with Gabriel for drinks and dinner, but cycling back to his after barely one drink so we might fuck all night in one wet blur like it was our last day on earth.

'Well, I'd better get back to it before Anton—'

'Elle,' Dom said, 'you sure you're feeling OK?'

'Me? Yes.'

'You don't sound like yourself. Wait, you don't think you could be . . . ?'

'No,' I said quietly. 'I don't think so. I'd really better—'

'That's right. You can't be pregnant. It's impossible.'

I lost another breath, this one in panic. How could Dom have found my pills? I keep them in the toe of some boxed boots in our dressing room. Had he finally worked out why he hasn't got me pregnant these past months and gone looking for the evidence?

'Why is it impossible?' I asked quietly.

'Because you're not due on now for three weeks.'

'You've been tracking my cycle?' I asked, not quick enough in my reactions to keep the horror from my voice. I corrected myself, lightening my tone. 'How are you managing that?'

'I want to be the husband you need me to be every day. I want to optimise your life. If I know where your hormones are, I can do that better. It's a simple app. It only needed a few metrics.'

'Metrics,' I repeated dumbly.

'It's one of the reasons I'm not one hundred per cent crazy about you lifting weights with your guy at the gym. Maybe we can find you a pre-partum specialist who can support your body with the next pregnancy. That's probably the priority right now, not trying to conform with some beauty expectation that, to me, is frankly a little generic.'

'Probably,' I parroted.

'Leave it with me,' Dom said. 'I know a guy who knows a girl.'

129

'OK. Thanks,' I whispered, the sourdough rising from my stomach into my gullet.

I fell back into my chair and gripped the arm to will the nausea away, knowing my sickness was nothing to do with pregnancy.

'Off you go now,' commanded Dom. 'I'll see *you* when you get home.'

I ended the call, feeling desperate and desperately alone. I wanted to confide in Sal but was worried she might throw the whole Marriage Rule in my face or present my life's options with more clarity than I was ready to see them. And there was no way I could call my mum, contacting her out of the blue to tell her the life I'd made out of her sight was apparently beginning to fall apart.

I thought I couldn't feel any worse. Then, I heard Anton's voice, muffled but audible in the adjoining meeting room. It's where he takes his regular one-on-one catch-up with his boss, the director of comms, the man who rated my work but ultimately promoted Anton over me.

'Yeah, for sure,' Anton said. 'Let's hope she steps up to work with my contractor on the agency project ...Yeah, I think we've spoken before about the *challenges*. I've tried to open doors for her, but you know what I've been telling you: I do everything I can to support her, but it's probably best we don't hold our breath for her turning it around. Sometimes doing the right thing for your people is to accept their authentic selves, and honestly, what I think Elle Graham is, first and foremost to herself is *Mum,* and maybe *Mum* is all she really wants to be.'

He said the word *Mum* like a slur. But then, didn't I, sometimes? Being one was never a priority for me, not really. And didn't I try to secure the senior role Anton got by asserting that *Mum* was not a status I valued highly and therefore planned to pursue?

The day had started so well, banked left to somewhere beautiful and rare, but ultimately became another day in the office where *Mum* ended up crying in the toilet and wishing she'd been quick enough to set her phone to record what Anton had just said about her.

Chapter Fourteen

Day twenty-one, Saturday

EG

Mum

Was Anton using his dying moments to taunt me? A final dig before death took him after what I'd done? Or was this Anton apologising deliriously as the blood drained from him? Another memory pokes through my consciousness: me, jabbing my finger in the air front of Anton's chest. He grabbed it, aggressively, or in self-defence maybe. I remember now; I *did* want to have it out with him. I'd had enough of his behaviour, and when he came to talk to me last night, I wanted to tell him it was time he stopped what he'd been doing to me. It wasn't me 'going off' with him, like Gabriel accused me of, it was me telling Anton I wasn't about to let him get rid of me once and for all. So, did Anton move to pacify me with booze, then take his revenge on me when I couldn't fight him anymore? Only I did fight back, hard, way too hard.

My phone is ringing again. Dom? No, it's Gabriel. What does he want now? Maybe I can get something more from him on what he thought he saw going on with me and Anton.

'Gabriel?'

'If you're wondering why I'm still up, it's because I can't sleep. I'm too upset.'

'I'm so sorry. I never meant for any of this to happen. Listen, what did I say to you when I went to speak with Anton? I honestly can't remember a great deal.'

'That right, is it? Did you also forget you had a husband? Forget you had a baby? Forget to mention any of this at any point in the last three weeks?'

'I—'

'Was Sal in on your little game the whole time? You played me, Elle. You used me.'

'How did you—?'

'Find out I'd been lied to by a married woman with a *kid*? After you'd got rid of me just now, I wanted to understand what was going on with you, since you wouldn't tell me. So, I did something I promised myself never to do to someone I'm dating, or whatever it is we've been doing: I gave in and googled you.'

'Right,' I say, somewhat amazed, impressed he hadn't done that yet. He's much the better person than I am, for so many reasons.

'You're not Elle Cotton anymore, not really, you just hadn't bothered to change your maiden name on your work email yet, didn't bother telling me those rings on your neck are yours after all? I knew, I *knew* Sal was up to something with you. You know,

133

when we caught up after Fundraising Committee and she told me you were staying at the hotel; she may as well have winked and told me to pack my toothbrush. She booked you a room so you could do what you wanted with me without your husband getting wind.'

'No, of course not. I don't know why Sal would—'

'Dominic. Good-looking guy. And rich. But one man not enough for you? Two not enough? You had to have Anton too?'

'I don't know what it looked like, but it wasn't what you think it was. What *did* it look like? What exactly did Sal say to you?'

'Tell me Anton's not in your room with you right now. Go on. Tell me and lie to me again.'

I pause. 'Anton isn't here.'

'I can tell you're lying, Elle. You're a great liar, but not this time.'

'Gabriel, please, I—'

'I found your husband's mobile number online.'

Oh god, no.

'I have it right here in my phone. Either you tell him, or I will.'

'Please, Gabriel, no.'

'Why not? You need to face up to your lies and start telling the truth, Elle. That's the last thing I'm going to say to you.'

'Gabriel. If you can just let me—'

Gabriel hangs up.

I can't breathe.

I can't do this.

But I have to. I *have* to do this now, before I lose what little control I have left of managing whatever happened in this room.

134

Oh god. Fuck. My fingers are quivering so much it's a struggle to even dial his number.

'Dom?'

'Elle?' he says foggily and in a half-whisper that suggests he's only just resettled the baby, my poor, sweet baby; my blameless husband.

'Dom, I am so sorry.'

'Why are you sorry? . . . Elle?'

'Dom, I need to tell you something. I've done something terrible. Can you please come to the hotel? Come now and please, don't answer your phone if you get a call from a number you don't recognise.'

Chapter Fifteen

Day six, Friday

Dom and I had just got back from an early dinner at Sal and Tim's, having left the baby with Patience. My husband presented me with a large pour of the Amarone from the case he chose for me. It tasted delicious and at more than fifteen per cent alcohol, it was delectably nullifying too. I could drink Amarone forever, I thought. After what happened earlier that night, I felt I might do just that.

'So, what's my wife done to upset you? I've been getting it in the ear about you not having lunch with her all week,' Tim asked me, soon after we'd sat down for dinner. Sal issued an uneven smile to the jam jar of salad dressing she was about to shake. At this stage, Dom was on his standard setting when he was at Tim and Sal's; an unexcitable fondness for Tim, a lovely man but one my husband recognised as having neither the physical nor fiscal prowess he did. With Sal, Dom maintained his usual spiced sort of civility.

'We had lunch on Monday,' I said as nonchalantly as I could to Tim, my heart galloping in anticipation. Where might this conversation veer? What might get revealed in front of Dom?

Not by what I said, necessarily, but what I didn't; my pauses, the tiniest tightness in my voice, the micro-movements of my mouth, the way I stroked the neck of my fork as I spoke, recalling Monday, feeling like it was another lifetime, the one before Gabriel.

Since whatever he and I did in the shadows of the Tate, I have enjoyed no fewer than five out-of-office encounters with Gabriel, two lunches and three coffees. These interactions were chaste but somehow extremely intimate. In the office, our collaboration has been natural and productive; away from it, our conversations have spanned far and wide. He has made me laugh. Quite honestly, quite appallingly, it hadn't taken much at all for me to want everything and all of him.

My desire for Gabriel was like a black hole at the centre of my existence, an awe-inspiring but deathly power sucking in my every waking thought, my vision of what the future might be, and a dark lens through which I was now viewing my past choices. I was sure Dom had noticed a change in me: I'd told him I was enjoying my training with Jordan and didn't want to switch. It was a wholly uncharacteristic display of single-mindedness that stunned him into a wounded silence which then prompted me to promise I'd swap to his 'pre-birth' trainer if it looked like I was getting too thin.

So, when Tim asked what appeared to be an innocent question about my non-availability that week, I felt as though I was in danger of being laid entirely bare before my husband. Dom would be able to understand why even when I was in the room with him, I was somewhere else, replaying the last conversation with Gabriel, imagining being undressed by him, conjuring how startling the tip of his tongue would feel on me. He would know, surely, it was Gabriel's body I imagined in mine when he made love to me. Dom would know it all. Somewhere, I knew I was doomed. I knew how rapid, how dangerous this unstoppable force of mine was, but it was proving impossible to resist, even as everything I knew and ought to be working with every fibre of my being to protect, was being disrupted, distorted and pulled to its destructive centre.

'Ah, I know my place,' Sal said, sloshing salad dressing into a large wooden salad bowl, then sinking two prongs into it and folding the leaves onto each other. I hoped that was the end of the conversation. I was preparing to ask Tim some vague, open question about his work to change the subject when Sal spoke up again as she doled out the first portion of salad onto waiting side plates on the dining table. 'Elle's working on a hot-shot ad agency project.' She handed me the first plate as I clenched internally at Sal saying *hot* in the context of my work with Gabriel. I instinctively knew we were in the danger zone. 'I might be missing my old mucker at Pret,' Sal continued, 'but it's good to see you with some lead in your pencil at work again.'

Lead in my pencil. Oh god.

Sal returned her attention to the salad bowl, but had picked up, as I had, on how focused Dom was on our exchange, even though he was not looking at either of us. As Sal handed him his plate, I sensed a waiting escalation in her usual mischief around him, but this time, I didn't like it one bit. 'This one —' Sal ticked her head towards me '— she's probably not mentioned it because she's too modest, but she's been drafted in to work her magic on a seriously visible project.'

'That's great,' Dom said, turning to me. 'Why didn't you tell me?' He was smiling but I could see he was upset at the idea of Sal knowing something significant about me he did not. I immediately imagined the heightened volume of calls and WhatsApp messages I might expect in the week ahead. Dom had begun to play with the saltshaker in front of him, tapping its punctured steel top rhythmically with the fingernail of his index finger; a surface distraction from far deeper feelings.

'It's really early days,' I told Dom. 'I've barely started working on it.'

'Well, I'm looking forward to a stunning victory soon; put you back where you should be at work,' Sal told me, handing Tim his plate.

'And where is that, exactly?' Dom asked Sal.

'Showing the Steves up for their bang-average mediocrity,' said Sal, finally serving herself and taking her seat, before gesturing to me to help myself to the heap of scallops and mussels from the steaming serving dish in the centre of the table.

'The Steves?' Dom asked Sal, in a tone of bafflement laced with what sounded to my ears like anticipatory resentment.

Tim placed a bread board with a sliced baguette and a square of butter on the table and took his seat opposite Dom. 'You don't know about the Steves? *The Steves* is our wives' endearing term for the legions of middle management and senior men who think they run the show and, well, technically do but probably shouldn't.'

139

'*Steve's leading on that. Let's see if Steve'll sign it off. Let's take Steve's temperature on this,*' Sal gruffy impersonated our generic man clubbing up with another to prop up their fiefdoms.

'Has there ever been a genuine overrepresentation of actual men called Steve?' Tim asked.

Sal thought about it. 'I mean, there's one now on the leadership team, and there was definitely about two at one point, but it just works, doesn't it? A catch-all term for the distinctly unexceptional white guys who rise to the surface nevertheless, mostly because their work histories aren't broken by babies and by virtue of sticking around and appearing to the Steve above them as the right Steve for the job.'

'Wow, Sal. So cynical!' Dom said. 'Is this a view you share?' He turned to me. 'I assume Anton is a Steve?' He blinked. 'Am *I* a Steve?'

'Of course not,' I said, topping up Sal's glass of white wine, before moving to Tim's, then Dom's. I hadn't really wanted to drink for days, and had barely done so most of that week, but I willed there would be a decent slug left for me in that bottle.

'Don't you worry your pretty little head about that, mate,' Sal said to Dom, that strange energy she's always had around him searing the air; a little goading, a tone that says: *Go on, try it.* I have always at once loved and hated hearing it; that night, I was firmly in the latter zone.

'Now, now, let's keep it friendly,' said Tim, also used to the arch way his spouse talked to mine. 'For what it's worth, I'm pretty sure *I'm* a Steve,' Tim told Dom. 'It's not a bad life, but you, my friend, are in no way a Steve and definitely have it much better. Elle mentioned your deal to Sal, congrats.' Tim moved his glass to Dom's, who smiled modestly at the table, while I silently thanked Tim for the prompt before praying the conversation had moved away from dangerous territory permanently.

'Thank you, Tim. It is kind of a big deal,' Dom said.

'A big deal, or a *big deal*?' Sal asked, also bringing her glass to make a dull connection with Dom's. I joined the toast and took a large sip of the white. It didn't taste great in the adrenaline-bitterness of my mouth, but I gulped it anyway.

'Both. Pretty soon, I think it's fair to say, the Steves of this world won't be troubling Elle for too much longer.' Dom's hand reached for my thigh under the table, his blue eyes feeling like too-bright beams shining into my every recess.

'Are you fucking leaving us?' Sal asked.

'It's up to Elle, obviously.' Dom took a sip of wine. 'But I know what a toll working with your man Anton is taking on her.'

'He's not my man. We're on the same level, but he's not on my team,' Sal corrected Dom.

'Sure,' Dom said, placing his glass back on the table so he could acquiesce to Sal with his hands in the air.

'And besides, Elle's job isn't wall-to-wall Anton.' *Oh god, please don't go there, Sal.* 'In fact, she's just started working with someone pretty cool.' The tender scallop I'd just put in my mouth became an unassailable lump.

'Oh?' said Dom with a tight smile, inviting my response. I knew my face would be flushed with guilt. It was vital I didn't betray myself in introducing Gabriel into my husband's sphere of knowledge.

141

I forced the rubber boulder of the scallop down my throat, then took a long, sour sip of my wine, my throat recoiling, the rest of my body welcoming its impact. I started to cough, adding extra drama, pause and potential meaning to my response to Dom's enquiry. My attempts to brush the existence of Gabriel away were an abject, and likely deserved, failure. 'Why would you say he's *cool?*' I spluttered in Sal's direction. I did not want Gabriel's name in my mouth this close to my husband; I did not want Dom to have even the tiniest idea of how sweet his name felt on my lips, a word I had taken to uttering in my mind, and breathing to myself when I took a bath and locked the door, sending my fingers onto and into myself, thinking only of him. I swallowed and decided on my best defensive stance.

'I'm just as experienced as him. He's obviously some kind of crony of Anton's he's drafted in to take a potentially interesting workstream away from me.'

Sal looked perplexed. 'I thought he seemed all right. You've not said anything about him being an arse.'

'He's not an arse,' I said, feeling the full force of my husband's scrutiny, or perhaps it was my paranoia, my guilt making me hypersensitive. 'I mean, he seems fine, but he is a bit of a Steve who Anton thought he needed to bring in for the ad agency project over me.' I turned to Dom. 'That's what I've just started working on, but Anton's brought on this guy over my head.'

'Fine is right,' Sal said definitively, referring to my earlier comment. 'When he introduced himself to my team,' she told Tim, 'he damn-near reversed my perimenopause.'

'Fuck's sake, Sal. Calm down.' Tim said it in mock outrage,

though his eyeroll lacked a certain comedy and struck me as a little loaded. Tim caught himself and said in a far more Tim-like way, 'If I talked about a woman at work like that I'd be dead meat. You can't be getting all hot and bothered about some young buck at work; one false move and you'll be dragged to HR.'

'Don't worry, darling,' Sal said to Tim, catching my eye and scuffing Dom's attention as she left her seat to fetch a jug of water on the sideboard behind her. 'I don't think *I'm* his type.'

'Ah-ha! *That's* why this is the first I've heard about him!' Dom slapped the table hard enough it made the saltshaker jump. My stomach dropped. I felt as though I needed the bathroom desperately. 'What's this young buck's name?' Dom asked all of us, as though we were all in on a secret he was not.

'It's Gabriel,' I rushed, shaking my head at Sal, all the while sensing Dom's laser focus on me. Whatever I said next I needed to sound as disinterested and untroubled by Gabriel as I possibly could. And I couldn't go off to the bathroom as I urgently needed to because this would only confirm to Dom Gabriel's significance. 'And I've got better things to do than be part of inappropriate conversations about colleagues. My credit record is poor enough at work as it is without having to worry about frankly juvenile rumours.'

'Rumours?' Dom shot a look between Sal and me. 'Is there *chatter* about you and this Gabriel? Should I be worried, darling?' Dom asked with an expression that an observer might take as jovial, but that I knew spoke of a genuine and deep-seated insecurity I would have to attend to later.

'*Petrified*,' said Sal, which forced him to look at her. Dom waited; she waited, apparently relishing the deadlock while she gave Dom the deadeye. 'Tim cooked the main course.'

After this, there were weak jokes about dry meat and wet vegetables. Dom laughed along. Eventually, I was able to take myself to the bathroom where I emptied my bowels. My hands shook as I washed them. I breathed my heart into something like a regular beat and returned to the table. The tension appeared to have dissipated. Dom was walking Tim through the last phase of getting his deal through, something about 'background checks' and 'due diligence', a conversation that continued as they headed to the kitchen where Dom went to help Tim finish preparing the fêted main course. As they left the room, Sal's boys arrived home from their friend's house. Any chance I'd had to reprimand her for her comments on Gabriel were gone. In a way, I was grateful not to have to speak of him again so soon, because rather than douse the embers, it could easily add fire to the flame. The less I said about Gabriel the better, the smaller my black hole felt. If no one else witnessed it but me, perhaps I could pretend it did not exist at all.

But Gabriel was now all too real to my husband. I knew Dom would bank what was said about Gabriel, my small gestures of discomfort, as well as my telltale coughing, and he would have noted, too, my prolonged stay in the bathroom. I also knew he would not bring it up immediately once we'd left Sal and Tim's; this would suggest the insecurity Dom did his best to hide but that seeped everywhere all the time nevertheless. For all his stature and presence, all his success, Dom's self-esteem had always needed me to tend to it for as long as I'd known him. He didn't deserve to feel insecure, not before me, and especially not since he'd given me everything and wanted to give me even more. Yet still, as I watched Dom bidding Sal, Tim and the boys goodbye for the evening, my mind was once again drifting somewhere else, to an imagined future where it was Gabriel saying goodbye to my friends for the night, and instead of dreading the possibility of dealing with Dom's inevitable grilling and then having to have sex with him, or thinking of some excuse that would only propel his scrutiny to new heights, I fantasised about living in a world where I could not wait to get my partner to myself again. That's how it would be with Gabriel. Why wasn't it him who caught me that night a few years ago? Why was it not a soul mate the cosmos presented to me, but a saviour?

I wondered if my husband had always known he was more life raft than true love to me, and that's why he had always gone over and above for me, including tolerating Sal's endless ribbing, submitting to spending time with her and Tim. Yes, my husband deserved so much more and who would I really be without him anyway? Who else would love me like Dom had? As we headed to the car, my mind scurried up an unlit path into the future: what would a Friday night really look like if Dom and I were to split? Firstly, would I only get the baby every other weekend? And what of those weekends without her? Realistically, would whatever I had with Gabriel wither to nothing in the destructive force of real-life step-parenting and divorce? That's if there was anything there at all; I'd only known him for less than a week, for Christ's sake. Then, a sickening thought: what if Dom, so wounded by my rejection and angered by my infidelity, applied for sole custody? He could easily prove he was the main carer. I'd be a failed mother, so much worse than a failed wife. What if no one else could ever love me? How could anyone else love when I'd hate myself so much if I couldn't be there for my baby?

My bowels turned again.

My imagination had raced to the darkest version of my future. Dom had a surely unbeatable case to be the baby's only real parent. He wouldn't ever forgive me for giving up on our marriage. He would have the evidence, the motivation and the money to support his plea for sole custody. I'd never get to live with my daughter again. He could argue the baby might come to harm if she was with me alone; he'd bring it all to court, my post-natal state, the fact I went back to work the minute I could, the everyday audit of all the things he did, and I did not do, for my daughter. All the times I've nearly hurt her because I was drunk. I've seen how Dom was when someone didn't do his bidding at work, when a supplier had let him down, the way he has exploded, then crumbled when members of his team he'd believed were loyal ultimately resigned. With Dom, I'd seen first-hand how it's all or nothing.

I knew I had to abandon my all-consuming thoughts of Gabriel, pull myself away from the black chasm of my desire into which everything good about my existence might be drawn into and destroyed. I couldn't risk living without my baby. I could never leave my husband. I was completely stupid to think I ever could or should.

After dinner at Sal and Tim's, we picked up the baby from Patience's house, neither of us talking very much. For me, this confirmed how much Dom had been upset by the conversation about *the hot young buck putting lead in his wife's pencil*; I could almost hear the words scraping at Dom's ego. I was primed to show Dom whatever he needed to be assured Gabriel was no threat and that I was all his.

'Sal was a bit much this evening, don't you think?' I said as we drove home, hoping to invite him to question me there and then, with the baby beginning to doze in the back seat, him focused on driving, not on me. There were a number of reasons it was best for the interrogation to happen at that moment, including how much I wanted the freedom to sink into the deep red of my Amarone obliteration unimpeded.

'No more than usual,' Dom said. He thought on it a moment longer. 'Though I have to say, it isn't the first time she's treated you like her kid sister. I do wonder whether you've outgrown her sometimes.'

I nodded, wanting to show him how much I was in his territory, convincing myself that I too could really step away from the abyss of my obsession with Gabriel and back into the gravity of my real life with Dom. 'I hear you. I mean, she's not *that* much older than me, but sometimes . . . I don't know . . .' I let my sentence drift, inviting Dom to fill in the gaps, readying myself to agree with whatever he said next, further progress away from my event horizon.

'Maybe it's time you recalibrated,' Dom said. 'You know, if you wanted to take a break, tell her you needed to spend more time with Agatha, I would support you. I'd completely understand.'

I had been hoping Dom might make some pointed comments

147

about Sal I might back up. I never expected he would practically suggest cutting ties with her. But given how on the back foot I felt after the revelations about Gabriel at the dinner table, I struggled to find the words to argue against what Dom seemed to be proposing, though I wasn't about to commit to it.

'Maybe.' I said it casually and looked out of my window, as if I lived in a world where I could take or leave Sal's friendship. I hoped we might be able to leave it there, but Dom was seeking certainty.

'We only get one life, Elle.' He reached over and laid a hand on my leg. 'Let's not waste any more of it on people who don't make us more than we are.'

I rested my hand on his and gave it a squeeze, my smile a tacit agreement but not an out-and-out commitment to abandon Sal.

'I do wonder if Sal talking stupid shit about you with some guy at work is just a distraction from what's going on with her and Tim,' said Dom.

'What's going on with them?' I asked, shocked. I hadn't a clue about whatever it was Dom was referring to – why hadn't Sal told me? Then I instantly remembered I'd cancelled our lunches that week, all because of my ridiculous obsession. I realised I was not only a fool, a terrible wife and mother, I was an appalling friend.

'All is not well in the house of Sal,' said Dom.

'Why?'

'Tim told me, in the kitchen. They're in deep shit, financially. They're probably not going to make Zak and Lewis's fees next term, barely made them last term.'

'God. That's awful. I had no idea.' I was sickened at my own self-absorption, my temporary insanity over Gabriel, knowing how upset Sal must have been about the prospect of pulling her boys out of their private school, and how dreadful it was she hadn't felt either willing, but most likely, able to confide in me. The twins started at the local school, but they never settled in. Then, the bullying started. Sal never saw herself as someone who'd send her kids to private school but would do anything to make sure her children were happy. Could I really say the same about me and the baby? After all, I'd been entertaining a fantasy of life without her father, without me. I glanced back at her, by now fast asleep in her car seat. By remaining committed to her father, to doing whatever I could in my power to make sure he felt happy and secure, certain that I was on his side, I knew I could say to myself I did all I could to stay by her side too.

'Oh yes. It's pretty bleak,' said Dom, perhaps betraying a little too much satisfaction he knew more than I did about the shortfalls of my best friend's life, or maybe even *because* of the crisis Sal was facing. Given how Dom felt he'd put up with Sal's spikiness over the last three years, it would not have surprised me if he was enjoying a shade of Schadenfreude. 'Tim was practically weeping. It's driving a real wedge between him and Sal.'

'I'm stunned.' I stared straight ahead.

'I'm sure Tim knows you and I share everything,' Dom said as we hit a red and he took the moment to look right at me. 'But probably best not to say anything to Sal. And maybe give it a couple of weeks before cooling things off with her.' *Oh my god, he's serious.* 'Give me a chance to help them first.'

'Help them how?' I asked, my insides freezing. Dom was

149

determined I decouple myself from Sal. How could I ever do that? And how could I do that now I knew she would need my support?

The lights turned green. Dom sped away from the car in the next lane. 'What's the point in me having all this money if I can't help people when they need it.' My husband smiled to himself.

'What do you mean?'

'On Monday, I'm going to pay the boys' school fees for the term and all of next year. I'll tell the school I wish to be anonymous. I don't want to humiliate Tim.'

'Oh Dom, that would be amazing.' It was my turn to lay a hand on his leg. 'You're such a good man,' I said, telling myself it was true, leaning into the idea of it being so. I needed it to be true. How else was I going to do this, the rest of my life? How was I going to get through the night, the next week, next month, all the nights and months of the years ahead until my dying day? I needed to persuade Dom he was loved by me, that there was no reason I shouldn't be allowed to remain in the front row of my baby's life. I set myself a target: it would be me who initiated sex later that night, no matter how much I did not want to. I would go above and beyond Sal's Marriage Rule to convince Dom there was no danger, that we were secure, that there never was and never would be anyone else; I loved him and planned to do so forever.

'And you're a great woman who deserves better than a friend who talks to you like Sal. Hopefully, with the school-fees monkey off her back, she won't take it so hard when you stop seeing her.' Dom glanced over at me, to check that what he said had pleased me further.

'Hopefully.'

The car felt hot and small. The baby began to grizzle in the back seat. I rolled down my window and hoped the wind would blast my tears back into their ducts.

As well as the three-quarters of a bottle of wine I'd managed to drink at dinner, I drank a whole bottle of Amarone almost to myself; Dom drank only a small glass and a couple of beers. I just about remember having sex. I don't remember going to bed.

Chapter Sixteen

Day twenty-one, Saturday

'What have you done that's terrible, Elle?'

'Oh Dom, it's worse than you could possibly imagine. I am so, so sorry.'

Dom remains silent for a moment, goes to speak, stops himself. More silence for an agonising pause before he speaks with a determination that's instinctively comforting in its familiarity. 'Elle, whatever it is, whatever you've done, we can get through it together, OK? What's happened? Just get it out. I'm already thinking the worst.'

'What do you think I've done, Dom?'

Another pause. 'I don't know; maybe you've done something that you shouldn't have with that Gabriel guy Sal was going on about? Something you regret, now you've sobered up and realised he wasn't worth it?'

'No. Nothing to do with him.'

'*No?*'

'No.'

I can hear Dom's breath, deep and urgent. 'Who, then? What? . . . Elle. Just tell me, please. I'm so confused right now.'

'Oh Dom . . . I think I've killed Anton.'

'*You* . . . you've *what?*'

'Anton. He's here in the room I was supposed to be sharing with Sal but she went home. He's—'

'You've *killed* Anton? I don't—You *think*, or you know? Shit.'

'I know. He's dead. I don't remember how it happened. I don't remember much at all.'

'Right. Shit. Jesus. Jesus Christ.' Dom lets out a deep sigh. 'Right. OK. What exactly do you remember? Tell me everything you can recall.'

'I just about remember talking to Anton at the drinks reception. Then I woke up and . . . He's in my hotel bed. I was lying next to him. And he's dead.'

'Fuck. *Fuck!*'

'I know. I know. I'm so sorry. It's beyond anything—'

'Wait, how do you know Anton didn't die in his sleep? Maybe he had a heart issue, or he's had too much to drink and choked or something.'

'No, Dom. He's clearly been murdered. There's a great big cut across his neck. He's bled to death, at a guess, and I am just guessing. I have no idea what happened.'

'He's . . . he's had his neck slashed? And you did that to him?'

'I don't know who else could or would because, Dom . . . I think Anton raped me.'

'Oh god. Oh god, no. Right, I'm coming, I'm coming to you right now.'

'Don't bring Agatha here. But don't take her to your mum's. She might not— I mean, please, don't involve her.'

153

'OK, you're right. I'll call the night nanny agency. Just don't leave that room and don't touch anything, OK?'

'I won't. Please, get here quickly. I need you, Dom.'

I didn't want Dom arriving through the hotel reception to raise any suspicions, so asked him to park the car down the street and come into my room via the window. I know this risks tampering with the scene or whatever, but what's the alternative: Dom negotiating with the night manager at reception to enter the hotel at this hour? That's way too dangerous. No one else can be involved until I know more, until, with Dom's help, I exhaust the options of what I could possibly do or say to make any of this any better for me so I can see my baby again.

Dom messages me. He's walking towards the car park now. I'm so relieved, but utterly terrified in a miasma of my own shame and filth. When he comes through those curtains, I expect I will want to bury myself in him, have him hold me, tell me everything is going to be alright, but I won't. I feel sullied, below contempt. I don't honestly know why he'd do anything for me now, let alone hold me in his arms.

I open the curtains like a warped Juliet to Dom's dark Romeo. Thankfully, Dom is already walking in the right direction towards my room, I only need to summon him to me with a quick wave. I note how my husband has dressed for the occasion, wearing a dark baseball cap with a black sweater and jogging pants.

Dom pauses before he enters my room. He produces and pulls on a pair of latex gloves, the type he uses when he's cutting chillies, and then a pair of blue, elasticated plastic overshoes, I assume left

154

over from when he painted the nursery the baby is due to move into. When he is sure both the gloves and overshoes are secure, Dom hoists himself through the window in a workmanlike fashion that, again, offers me some comfort; here is my practical and proactive husband doing what he always does for me. Once inside the room, Dom stands still for a moment and begins to take in all he can see before him. He can't hide his shock, his sickness. He looks at me for the briefest of moments, registering the horror I must look – the smears of blood, the bite marks. But then, I too am shocked at the sight of my husband. In his cap, gloves, and overshoes, he looks like some kind of prowler or more likely a forensic investigator in this scene from the horror movie that is my life now. Dom mouths some inaudible words; his eyes narrow as he looks about the room, the bed, the blood-spattered walls, before turning back to me. He takes a deep breath and says in a familiar, assured tone: 'Under there, right?' gesturing to the elongated lump in the bed closest to the window.

'Yes.'

Dom goes to Anton's body and does exactly as I had earlier, pinching the sodden over-sheet near his face between the ends of his gloved fingers, peeling the fabric back enough to reveal the mess of Anton's face and neck. But unlike me, my husband does not wince or sicken.

'Do you know—' Dom begins before pausing. 'Any idea if what was used to inflict the wound is still in here?' I note his unwillingness to ascribe ownership of the act of murder to his wife by using the active voice.

'Oh god, I don't know. I hadn't even . . .'

Why didn't I hunt for the murder weapon, see if it fit into my hand, check if holding it might chip any more memories free from the concrete of my mind? And I feel it: for the first time since I can't remember when, I am so glad to see my husband.

Dom drops to the floor, as though performing some kind of press-up, his head near where I had found the notepad with the mystifying *EG Mum* scrawl.

'Come,' Dom commands, and I do as I am told. He pulls out a small torch from the back pocket of his jogging pants, more evidence of a preparedness that makes me so glad he is here. 'Look, there.' Dom shines his light towards the floor under the bed. I crouch down to join him. 'See that?'

A wine bottle. It's been smashed; a cruel, clean curled spike across what was once the cylinder of the vessel. I can see it was a bottle of Amarone.

'Do you remember— I mean, did anyone smash the bottle when you were here?'

'No,' I say, dumbly, while Dom gets to his feet and looks about the room once more.

'Have you trodden on any shards?'

'No. No, I haven't.'

Dom stalks about the room, peering at the floor, looking at the hard edges of the table, a section of open shelves attached to the wardrobe, any site where a wine bottle may have been converted into a murder weapon. He hovers near a vase of dried flowers, as though he's about to pick it up for some reason, but instead, moves past it to dart into the bathroom. I follow, waiting by the door as he scans the small en suite from left to right for what he's looking for, finally peering behind the frosted screen of the bath/shower.

'OK,' Dom says, exhaling deeply, nodding, not in approval, but in the way people do when they're trying to force a reluctant thought to process.

'Let me see, please.'

Dom steps aside. 'OK, but make sure you don't touch the shower screen or anything. We don't want your fingerprints anywhere near here.'

'If they aren't already.'

'We don't know that. We don't know anything yet, OK?' Dom touches my shoulder reassuringly, before remembering the latex gloves he's wearing and withdrawing his hand, or perhaps it's that my husband no longer really wants to touch me, and who could blame him for that.

I angle myself so I can see inside the bath/shower enclosure. There's a drying pool of red wine lingering around the plughole, drips down the back edge near the taps, glass shards and a single curled section including the base of the bottle on its side. I look to Dom, frowning deeply; something about the bottle being here is perturbing him.

'What is it?' I ask.

Dom swallows. 'The fact whoever did that to Anton effectively created the murder weapon in one room, then took it to another . . . I don't know.'

'What? What do you mean?'

'I'm not an expert, but it could mean the police, lawyers, whoever, they may have reason to believe it wasn't self-defence, or manslaughter. This may make it seem like there was some degree of premeditation to cause significant injury.'

'Like someone almost planned it?'

Dom nods. 'Is there any evidence whatsoever anyone could find suggesting you wanted Anton to come to harm? That you held enmity towards him? Anything that could suggest a motive?'

'Yes,' I whimper.

The bathroom tiles below my feet feel cold and fluid. The next thing I remember, I'm on the floor, Dom is cradling my head in his lap, his ungloved hand stroking my hair. When I realise where I am, I turn to cling to him, as though we are both at sea. I'm so very grateful for his touch, for having him here. Then, a hideous realisation: if Dom becomes implicated in this mess, in potentially perverting the course of justice or whatever, who will look after the baby. Patience? I know Dom is far from perfect, but at least I know he's a competent carer, and with me out the picture, he'll be less angry, surely. The thought of Patience bringing up my baby is too appalling to contemplate. Rather than summoning him, I should have made sure Dom was as far away from here as possible.

'I'm so sorry, Dom. You need to go home to our baby now, please. I never should have called you. You don't deserve any of this and neither does she. Go. Leave me.'

I can sense Dom's head shaking, the warmth of his fingers, now stroking the top of my spine below my neck. He remains silent.

'Will . . . will you please look after the baby?' I continue. 'Now, when she's growing up, especially when she's a teenager, even after she leaves home, always? Will you take care of her?' My voice is croaking, full of tears. 'What am I talking about?' I berate myself. 'I know you will, it's all you do.' I wipe a tear from my eye. I see my girl, aged fifteen or so, tall and lean, like Dom, him at her side, but not me. 'And Dom, will you please tell her I'm sorry, one day? Will you tell her how much I love her and that I'm not bad, just stupid, just so, so stupid?'

'No.'

I pull myself free, sit up and peer into his eyes.

'Please, Dom. *Please.*' The ice in Dom's determined eyes freezes the veins in my face and neck, right through to my heart. 'Please, she needs to know that I never meant to not be in her life.'

'No.' Dom's eyes don't shift.

'I know I've done you so wrong, I know I've fucked up in the worst imaginable way, but, Dom, I'm still her mum. Please, make sure she knows I love her and that I'm sorry.'

'I'm not going to do that.'

'Why not?' I am very afraid now, at this turn in him, something I have seen hints of; something that has left me chilled many times before, the switch flipped from charming man to something else, from life raft to millstone, the pillow he places below my head to one he might hold in front of my face.

'Because *I* am going to get you out of this.'

Chapter Seventeen

Day seven, Saturday

I'd arranged our movements so I could introduce Dom to Jordan in the gym, feeling that if I presented my charming, buff trainer on my own terms it might neutralise any potential threat Dom might feel since I told him I didn't want to switch trainers. It's probably the placebo effect after only a couple of sessions this week, or maybe wishful thinking in light of my red wine hangover and the need to harden my resolve against my Gabriel-shaped abyss, but I really imagined I could feel previously soft pieces of me coalescing into fibres of muscle: strands of something harder than before in my shoulders, deep within my stomach. I have to believe I can be stronger than I actually feel.

I'd managed to negotiate Dom taking the baby for lunch in the café after baby swim and his own Saturday free weights routine (in the moments immediately after I let him have me, too hungover to protest otherwise, forming a plan in my head while it was happening), encouraging him to walk me up to the floor where I do my sessions. As we walked to Jordan's training zone, I braced myself for my husband's reaction to the sight of my fit, young and very personable personal trainer.

'Hi, Jordan,' I said, feeling deeply self-conscious, but trying to be as casual as I could. 'This is my husband, Dom.'

'And this is Agatha,' said Dom, who was holding the baby on his hip, one arm around her.

'Alright, mate,' Jordan said to Dom. 'Hello, little one.' Jordan gave the baby's fingers a little shake between his own fingers and thumb before reaching for Dom's free hand. 'You looking for a trainer too?' he asked Dom as they shook hands. My husband did that slightly Donald Trump thing, where men take another man's hand and bring the other man's whole body into their own space in an attempt to dominate. 'Whoa, maybe not!' Jordan said good-naturedly. 'That's some grip you've got there, mate.' Jordan pulled away, smiling as he rubbed his hand.

'Sorry,' Dom said with a showy kind of wince at himself. 'I sometimes don't know my own strength. Neither does she.' Dom gestured over towards me. 'Am I right, Jordan?' There was a pointedness in the way Dom deployed Jordan's name.

'Yeah, she's strong, but we're gonna get you even stronger, aren't we, Elle? You ready for today?'

'As I'll ever be. I'm afraid I don't even have five per cent of my husband's upper body strength,' I said, trying to catch Dom's eye, bringing to mind all the times I've had to ask him to take a lid off a jar, unscrew a tap for me. But Dom's vision was fixed on Jordan, who was clearly keen to crack on with our session and get The Husband out of the way. Dom, meanwhile, was focused on showing he would not be shooed quite so easily. I suppose it made sense; Dom probably understands how physically close trainer and trainee can get.

161

I'd be uncomfortable if Dom had a hot young female trainer. Wouldn't I?

'Well, I'll leave you two to it,' Dom said, finally. 'Say goodbye to Mummy.' Dom tilted the baby towards me. She seemed wholly uninterested in me, but then I think that most of the time about the baby; she's almost totally fixated on Dom. For his part, Dom obviously picked up more affection than I did in the baby's demeanour. 'Ah, don't be upset, Mummy will be back with us soon.' I was immediately flooded me with the guilt I'd been trying to ignore. It was bad enough I'd left her for five days a week since she was tiny, now maybe it seemed like I couldn't even handle a whole Saturday with her.

'Why don't I have her after lunch? I'll take her to the park. You can get some work done before we go to your mum's,' I rushed.

Dom considered my idea for a moment. 'Actually, that could work. I need to get the bounce on some emails before Monday. Final bits and pieces before we sign on the dotted line. You . . .' Dom said, leaning towards me once more, 'are . . .' he kissed me on the mouth, his lips open, his free hand firm around my chin '. . . my angel.' He kissed me again, lingering for a couple of seconds. Behind me, I sensed Jordan turning away, and saw from the corner of my eye he had suddenly found reason to move a kettle bell a couple of inches to the left of where it sat. And it happened: despite my dry mouth, the ache behind my eyes left over from the previous night's Amarone binge, the self-loathing in my soul, I thought of the delights of my dead father-in-law's cellar at Patience's house where we were to spend the late afternoon and have an early dinner. My stomach turned.

162

'I'll have a quick shower once I've finished and come and find you in the café,' I said, my face still in Dom's palm. He did not seem to want to let it go. 'Love you,' I said, and he released me.

Despite a shaky start, my training session went well. I could feel my confidence growing, and, yes, perhaps even my strength, or maybe it's simply the belief I can make my body stronger. I wondered if this was a trick of the mind. I didn't seem to have any power over the booze I threw down my neck, or over my ability to love the right man in the right way, so maybe I'd convinced myself that if I had agency over at least this one sphere of my existence, I couldn't really be the passive incarnate.

In this training session, we focused on my arms and chest: the biceps, triceps, the muscles behind my breasts and reaching towards my shoulders. I relished the heat, the sense of sinews stretched, tested, tearing only to begin to heal stronger; hardening cords, forming unseen under my body fat, something secret only I could feel or know. Perhaps, I thought, if I did drink later it would be because I'd felt I'd earnt it, not because I wanted to wipe myself out.

When I found Dom in the café after the session, I downplayed how much I'd enjoyed it, and what I felt I was achieving with Jordan's direction. This was probably my guilt over Gabriel coming to the fore once more. I didn't want to give Dom any cause for suspicion because I deeply enjoyed time with any other man bar him. It was probably the same force that drove me to turn down Jordan's offer of the warm-down stretches I'd enjoyed so much in my first and second session too.

'Thank god that's over!' I bent to kiss Dom's cheek, him sat at a table, the baby in a borrowed highchair.

'You didn't enjoy yourself?' Dom asked.

'I'm not sure *enjoy* is the right word.'

'So quit. I can already see you're getting smaller.' Dom inserted two fingers into the waistband of my jeans in the middle of the crowded café. 'You don't need to do that.' He pulled my jeans away from my frame, frowning with dissatisfaction, while I shook slightly on my feet. A woman on the next table caught my eye. She looked confused, then a little worried. I smiled back at her. She returned my grin uncertainly and took a sip from the coffee cup in front of her, still watching Dom.

'Darling,' I said, putting both my hands on the hand tucked into my waistband. 'I want to get stronger, be fitter; live long and healthy with you forever.'

Dom removed his fingers from my clothing and left his seat.

'Well,' he said to the baby, 'as long as she doesn't disappear from us altogether, I suppose we can't stop her, can we?' Dom turned to me. 'Shall I make sure you two get to the park OK?'

'I think we're good. You get on and do your work so you can relax later.'

Dom brought me in for a hug and kissed me. 'You sure you're going to be OK with Agatha? If she starts acting up, she's really into those new teething beads I bought. I also packed some blueberries and carrot sticks, so go ahead and use them if you think she's hungry. Oh, and there's rice cakes in the changing bag, but I wouldn't bother, I don't think she likes the texture. And when you get to the park, stick to her like glue if you take her out in the sandpit; she'll eat a handful the second you don't pay attention.'

'OK. Thanks for the tips!' I felt like a teenaged cousin doing a spot of babysitting for pocket money; someone with no idea how to look after a child, someone who'd had very little experience of it, before realising I was both of the latter things. A knot formed inside me, one I could only release by thinking about Hugo's vintage Chablis at Patience's house later.

I pushed the baby towards the park in her buggy feeling like a fraud, an actress playing a part. Each time she gurgled, I had to stop to check she was OK. If she went more than a minute without a sound, I halted, needing to make sure she wasn't choking or dead. I must have looked quite mad.

We reached the main gate into the park and started the walk towards the playground, me unsure, nervous about the prospect of the baby eating sand and having to tell Dom he was right to try to micromanage my afternoon with my daughter. We passed the playing fields; older men playing a sluggish game of football that made my mind turn to what Dom will look like when he's fifty, sixty, seventy, and then what state I might be in by then. What will my life look like? I wondered. I imagined old–lady me, decades into married life, maybe I have another child, more children I didn't quite know what to do with when they were small, and also when they were grown, seeking my guidance on the life ahead of them, my own life spent uselessly behind me. What could I teach them? What kind of role model might I be? My legs took on a sudden weight, my stomach too.

I walked on quickly, passing another playing field, one where younger men, teenagers, perhaps, were playing rugby. A flash of recognition: one team were wearing the colours of Sal's boys' school. Sal wouldn't be far away. I turned the buggy from the path onto the grass, looking for Sal's friendly face, telling myself I didn't need to tell Dom if we spoke; I'd only happened to bump into her.

'Oi! Cotton! Over here!'

And there she was. Sal looked so much like herself, so in possession of who she was, you would never know about the issues Dom had told me she and Tim were facing. She was fixed on the game, in her sunglasses, hands shoved in the back pockets of her jeans.

'How they doing?' I walked over to join her and tried to track Sal's sons within the blur of bodies running up the field.

'Hello, gorgeous monkey,' Sal cooed at the baby before speaking to me. 'The boys aren't doing too shabbily, for a couple of kids with an educational guillotine poised to drop on their necks.'

I did my best to look at Sal with quizzical concern.

'Jesus, mate, leave it out. I know Dom-Dom will have blabbed. I bet he couldn't even wait till you got home, could he?'

I abandoned any pretence I didn't know what Sal was talking about. 'He's really worried about you guys,' I said by way of apology for my husband's indiscretion. 'So am I.'

Sal took a deep breath in, swallowed, and pushed a finger behind her sunglasses where she looked to be wiping away a tear.

'Oh Sal, I feel awful. I had no idea. You didn't say anything, but I didn't ask either. And I'm so sorry I haven't been around this week.'

'That's OK. One of us should be getting their kicks where they can.' Sal sniffed.

'I don't follow,' I said quietly, plastering another puzzled smile on my face I already knew was doomed to fail me.

'Elle. I love you and I know you. There's a little spark between you and the hot new comms dude, and you should know, it's OK with me.'

'He's . . .' I struggled to think of what I needed to say. 'He appreciates what I do. There's not much more to it than that. Nothing's happened, by the way.'

Sal shrugged.

'And nothing's going to happen.'

'The Marriage Rule,' Sal said, exhaling.

'What about it? I didn't really think you were serious, by the way.'

'It wasn't exactly coming from where you thought it was, Elle.' Sal glanced at me through her sunglasses. 'You and Dom all hunky-dory? He seemed pretty tightly wound last night.'

'We're fine.'

'Of course.' Sal stepped back from the white line of the pitch as a cluster of grappling bodies swung in close to where she stood.

'So, are you going to tell me where your Marriage Rule is really coming from? Is Tim, I don't know, being a bit full on with you, maybe because he's looking for comfort away from the money stuff?' I asked, but not because that's what I truly imagined Tim would do, but because I could so easily see Dom doing this.

Sal scrunched up her mouth. The last time I'd seen that expression was when Zak and Lewis were being bullied at their old school. 'Tim hasn't come near me in almost a year. Or maybe even before that? Some midlife crisis bullshit. Whatever.'

'Oh Sal.' It was all I could think to say. Meanwhile, my mind immediately bounced into how liberating it would be if I knew Dom didn't want to come near me, for a year, or even longer than that. The guilt and dread at this thought and what it could mean for my future sent my hand to the baby's head. I felt the silkiness of her hair between my fingers, never wanting to be away from her but wishing she'd come into being by some other means than she had.

Sal tutted. 'Sorry, I didn't want to bring it round to my shit. The Marriage Rule.' Sal paused and spoke her next words slowly, almost tentatively. 'That was me trying to make the point that staying married is about being on the same page. Me and Tim aren't right now. Would you say you and Dom are?'

'You're not serious? You and Tim, you're a proper team. You . . .' I felt suddenly choked. 'You guys love each other,' I said and thought of how the pairing of Dom and I did not always seem to clear this basic threshold for a solid marriage.

'I've asked him to get help,' Sal said, 'but it's a no-go for Tim. I've told him I can't live in a sexless marriage. So, there we have it . . .' Sal's words drifted before she reset. 'Listen, I really don't want to talk about me. I want to know how you're doing. How are things with Dom, really?'

'I told you. I'm fine. We're fine.'

Sal paused again, gave me a sideways glance, as though disappointed with my answer.

'How come you've been let out for the afternoon? Not like Dom to let you loose on a Saturday. You been following the Marriage Rule like a good girl then?'

'No.' I lied. Because that's exactly what I'd been doing, all that week when I thought about it. 'Dom has to work.'

'Of course he does. Fighting crime, one desperate bastard at a time.'

'Something like that,' I said. 'What are you going to do?'

'This afternoon? Or about my lack of dough or my kaput husband? Not much, in all likelihood, on every front. And what are *you* going to do?'

'About what?'

Sal tilted her head at me. 'About nothing, Elle.' She scrunched her lips together, then turned back to the game. 'Looks like there's no choice but to carry on, hoping one day soon something or someone comes along to switch things up.'

I nodded though I wasn't entirely sure if she was talking about my life or her own. I used the opportunity to make sure we focused on her. 'The things we need come and get us when we need them sometimes,' I said, imagining her relief when she found out the boys' fees had been paid.

'What, like Dom?' Sal asked. 'Or like Gabriel?'

I meant to dismiss what Sal was saying but all I could muster was an unconvincing huff. Seeing me struggle, Sal generously changed the subject.

'What you doing for the rest of the day? Can we do something, seeing as how you're free for once?'

169

'Oh, we're going to Dom's mum's shortly.'

'On the hook for dinner Chez Pattycakes?' Sal gave a theatrical shudder. She and my mother-in-law have the same awkward chemistry she has with my husband, only a whole lot worse. Patience is resolutely opposed to anything even on nodding terms with the kind of barbed humour Sal defaults to around most people, but especially when she applies it to her and Dom. 'Be sure to say hi from me,' Sal said, tapping two fingers to the side of her head in a military style as she did. The gesture made me think back to my wedding day, when Sal tried to set Patience straight on my behalf.

I'd confided in Sal about the awful messages Dom had showed me from his mother about me; and then the appalling attempt to persuade me to get out of her son's life just a couple of days before the wedding. Straight after the ceremony, Dom had gone to track down our wedding car, leaving me alone with Patience and Sal outside the registry office.

'So, Patience,' Sal began, and I could immediately tell from her tone we were in for trouble, 'your new daughter-in-law tells me you tried to get her to sling her hook?'

Patience's eyes widened. I don't know who was more rattled, me, or Patience, who appeared stunned, shooting glances from Sal, then back to her son, who was on the phone a few metres away. She was petrified at being caught out.

'It's alright, Patty, you don't need to say anything. I'm sure now she's married to your son you'll give Elle the respect she gives you. That right?'

Patience went to speak, but Dom had returned. She closed her mouth and looked to the pavement.

170

'He's five minutes away, apparently,' Dom said, ending the call as he rejoined us. He looked up to see Patience clearly out of sorts and threw one arm around her. 'Come on, Mother, buck up! We all wish Dad was here, but this is a celebration!' He brought Patience into a vigorous sideways hug, one that was neither wanted nor reciprocated, his mother's body stiff to her son's embrace. 'Am I right, Mrs Graham? . . . Mrs Graham?'

Dom was calling me by his mother's name. I looked at him dumbly. 'I mean *you*, wife of mine.' Dom dropped his mother and surrounded me with his arms. It made me feel very small; my name, my sudden and immediate blooding as a 'Mrs', a 'wife' monumentally huge; me and it felt desperately mismatched. When Dom let me go, the smile I had attached to my lips could not hide from Sal how sick I suddenly felt. She reached for my hand and surrounded it with her warmth. It felt as though she was trying to channel her strength into me. Back on the rugby pitch sidelines, it was time I finally returned the favour.

'Sal. Don't change the subject. I want to talk about you. I want to be here for you,' I said, then remembered the pledge I'd made to Dom to cool off from Sal for a while. 'As much as I can be, I'm yours.'

Sal sighed before speaking again. '*I* am here, Elle. I'm so sorry I dobbed you in to Dom about Gabriel. I don't know what I was thinking; I never should have done that. I was just . . . He's just so . . .' Sal gritted her teeth for a half a beat before shaking her head and moving to squeeze my hands in hers. 'Whatever you need, whenever you need it, I have your back, you got that?'

'I . . .' I stumbled, not understanding why or how the conversation had come around to me needing her again. 'Thank you.'

'So, I'll see you for lunch on Monday? Pret's not the same without you. But, hey, if you do get a better offer, please, for the love of all that is good and holy, blow me out.'

'There is no better offer. There will be no "blowing out",' I said wearily.

A whistle blew. The game was over. Sal dropped my hands to pick up the brace of bags at her feet. 'Sure. See you Monday. Oh, and do send my warmest regards to Pattycakes.'

Chapter Eighteen

Day twenty-one, Saturday

'Yes. I'm going to get you out of this, Elle.'

'Oh Dom.' I have never been more grateful to my alpha, problem-solving planet of a husband than I am in this moment. And I'm not sure I have ever loathed myself more; not only for the nightmare I've brought him into, not only for the betrayal with Gabriel, but for never loving him enough until this second. 'I don't deserve you. I never did.'

Dom gives an odd, whimsical smile I can't place and don't need to. He still loves me, and he's going to provide my only hope of getting out of this room and seeing my baby again. He laces his fingers together in front of his face, the two index fingers touching his top lip.

'So,' Dom breathes, his eyes closed as he gathers himself before opening them with an almost perceptibly sharper focus. 'We don't have long before we need to call the police, because we *do* need to do that.'

'Yes, of course.' I don't know why I ever imagined it would be any different, but my heart falls at this. I suppose I was hoping my husband could pull off some kind of miracle, just as he had when he freed me from my old house share and the third-of-life crisis I seemed to have got myself into three years ago.

'But we need to establish some facts beforehand,' Dom continues.

'Yes,' I say. 'That's what I've been trying to do.'

'Sure, sure, but you're in shock. I'm shocked, but I'm probably in a better position than you to take a degree of control here, so maybe let me lead from now on.'

'Of course.'

'OK. So, let's get up and let me take a proper look at you.'

'OK.' I allow Dom to lift me to my feet before leading me back into the bedroom.

'Take everything off and lie down for me.'

'Dom, I— Oh god, Dom, I don't . . . I mean, we should really leave that bit to the experts, shouldn't we? I can't bear for you to see, to look at—'

'The experts are the ones who'll be looking to incriminate you, slap a murder charge on you and take you away from me and Agatha. So, I strongly advise you listen to me, take off your clothes and lie down.'

'I—'

'Elle. Do as I say. Please, you just agreed was the best way out of this. That's right . . . go on . . . everything.'

'I don't think I—'

'*Elle*. Lie down. Here. I have to take a good look at you.'

'OK, OK. But please, be gentle. Please, do whatever you need to do quickly.'

'Right . . . what do we have here, then . . . Well, I can't see any bruises on your thighs.'

'I have broken fingernails. See? Dom, take a look.'

'Open your legs.'

'I have bite marks. Look, up here.'

'Open your legs for me.'

'I don't want to do that.'

'But you want me to help you.'

'It feels sore down there. I'm pretty sure the police will see—'

'Whatever the police will see, we need to see it first. If you want me to help you, open your legs. Now.'

'Jesus.'

'Hmmm.'

'Oh, god. What is it?'

'Ri–ght.'

'*What*?'

'Everything looks fine. Let me take a closer look. A little wider please.'

'No, Dom.'

'Just relax.'

'I want to stop this now.'

'Hmm. There's no . . . I can't see any damage whatsoever.'

'It hurts. It really, honestly hurts.'

'But you don't look like you do. I can't see any evidence of violence: no obvious tears, no blood.'

'But I'm in pain.'

'I'm sorry to say, Elle, whatever happened here last night between you and your boss . . . it looks like you wanted it.'

'No. No, I honestly can't imagine I'd—'

'And that means, if we're going to at least get this reduced to manslaughter or even get you out of it entirely on the grounds of self-defence, we need to make it look like rape . . . It's OK, Elle, don't cry. Don't worry. I'm here now. Everything's going to be OK now you have me with you.'

Chapter Nineteen

Day seven, Saturday

It was after five when we arrived at Patience's home. Pulling into the drive, I thanked God for Hugo's extensive cellar before I found my thoughts turning to the man himself, someone Dom barely talks about, I'd assumed because of his unwillingness to process or display difficult emotions. I thought too of my own mother and stepdad with a pang of sadness that struck me with an unexpected power. It wasn't all terrible, my childhood, was it? Not brilliant; disappointing and hurtful when my mum seemingly put my stepdad before me. It was knotty, challenging, but not *bad* bad.

Was there a chance I had reached a stage in my thirties, around the same time I met Dom, that rather suited me to blame the people who brought me up for my shortcomings and my lack of fulfilment? There have been many times, perhaps even more recently with Gabriel, when I'd struggled to explain exactly why I went low-contact with my mum, stepdad and half-brother, why I did not want them at my wedding; times when I have had to stop myself from picking up the phone and seeing how they are for no other reason than to hear my mother's voice, even my stepdad's and my little brother's.

'Do you often miss your dad?' I asked Dom as he retrieved his phone from the charge point below the dashboard.

'Pa? I mean, yes, I suppose, but . . . well, he was Pa, so . . .' Dom frowned and seemed to shake off the notion of missing 'Pa'.

'Were you not really all that close?'

'Look,' Dom said, biting his upper lip with his bottom teeth, 'don't listen to Ol, if he's said anything.'

'Oh, no, it's nothing like that.'

'My big brother has a bit of a narrative about Pa, but he was . . .' Dom struggled to find the right words. 'He was a tough guy who liked everything to be the best it could, the business, the family. He was like me.' Dom checked his hair in the driver's mirror. 'And maybe Ol was a bit soft around the edges for Pa and I pulled a bit of focus from that and for whatever reason, Ol's always been, frankly, soppily grateful to me; even before Flic.'

'Oh, I wasn't implying anything—'

Dom gave a tight smile and dug one side of his chin into the air. 'Yeah, but you kind of were, so could we just drop it?'

I felt scolded as he left the car to retrieve the baby and her changing bag before I had time to respond. This chastisement made that dull ache for my mum even more emphatic. I decided I would think of a reason to call her that night, perhaps when Dom was bathing the baby. I wanted to speak to someone who knew me, who had a deep knowledge, not just London/work-me as Sal did, or as Gabriel perhaps thought he was beginning to; I

178

recognised I was also longing to speak someone whom I knew fully too. My husband, with his closed manner, his weird dynamic with his mother, as well as something seemingly uncomfortable with his father and Ol, was not that. Perhaps this was part of my problem: how could I ever love Dom fully if he wouldn't share all of himself?

We entered Patience's house and walked through the gloomy hallway; wood panelling; Victorian watercolours; a tall vase of purple thistles and stalks of grey-blue eucalyptus on an antique chest of walnut and inlaid cherry wood, which I believed had been handed down through generations of Grahams. The whole house could feel like Hugo's mausoleum, especially when it was as quiet and still as we had found it. Dom went ahead and checked the dining room and the kitchen, with the baby on his hip and me trailing behind, but Patience was not to be found.

'Mother!' Dom called, moving to open the back door from the kitchen, where there was evidence of lunch being under control: the Aga on, stacks of clean plates ready for warming, serving dishes awaiting their vegetable contents, which were at that stage bubbling gently on the stove. Still holding the baby, Dom stepped out into the garden. I followed.

I disliked the atmosphere of Patience's garden even more than I did the brooding ambience of her home. The garden was like the woman herself, like the Grahams altogether: defined by height, discipline and never quite being able to achieve an unobscured vista. It was technically aesthetically pleasing, the palette of greens, white and creams with only occasional splashes of blueish purples, and was almost excruciatingly

179

tasteful. It did, however, appear to have been designed with a system of miniature and side gardens conceived of for the sole purpose of wrong-footing the garden visitor. There were tight paths winding this way and that, some leading nowhere, some taking you in an unexpected circle through another corridor of architectural shrubs and perennials, many of these blooming as high as me, some taller than Dom, a great many with large leaves that rendered the way forward dim and indistinct, confusing the eye by playing with the depths between zones. You might crave light and follow a path you thought might lead you there, only to find yourself in yet another oppressive cranny. There were only the briefest of respites in Patience's garden, the odd patch of lawn in a spotlight of sun, a jagged patch of paving. It would be so easy to lose the baby in there. It had proved easy to lose Patience.

Dom, the baby and I followed another turning into another dead end, Dom cursing under his breath, me keen to get out of the briar-like density of this controlled, mystifying orchestration of nature as soon as possible.

'Jesus, no wonder Dad keeled over out here,' said Dom. I dared not query further for fear of being reprimanded for some mawkishness or pursuing any kind of detail on his father that Dom did not relinquish voluntarily. 'It was right here,' he said, looking around at the ghostly white heads of the giant hollyhocks encircling us. 'Or was it back there? This place is a fucking maze, it's enough to give anyone a heart attack . . . Mum!'

'I'm right here, Dominic,' Patience said from nearby, only she remained invisible.

'*Where?*' Dom said, not bothering to mask his impatience.

'Here. To the left.'

We both angled our heads only slightly and there, perhaps only a metre away, was Patience, her cream and grey tones only just distinguishable from the dappled shadows, pale petals and dark foliage. She stepped around the path on her side of the hollyhocks and joined us in the light.

'Incredible how easy it is to hide in plain sight,' Patience announced.

'It is when you've planted a jungle out here,' Dom said. 'Reminiscing were you, Mother?'

'I was removing unwanted things.' Patience referred to the basket of defeated weeds, roots exposed, stems broken, a pile of them, soiling the flat rattan basket on her arm. 'Utter balsam for the soul to be rid.' And I knew, of course, she was directing all of this not to the weeds, but to me.

I smiled as widely as I could. 'You make such a beautiful job of it, Patience.'

She shrugged. 'It's easy. You only need to know where to look.' At that, Patience placed the basket on the ground, pulled out a small pruning knife with a wooden handle and a mean-looking hooked steel blade, reached down and yanked on a strangle of bindweed that had reached, practically unseen to the untrained eye, around the base of one her fine, tall blooms. She followed the line of its growth to the source in the soil and severed it with a brisk swipe of her curved blade. 'And of course,' she said, throwing the line of the conquered wildflower, its white trumpets, and heart-shaped leaves not at all unpretty, but unplanned and

181

unwanted, into her basket of limp, defeated garden invaders, 'one has to be persistent.'

I kept the smile on my lips and silently thanked god that Ol would be there soon with Cora, then took a moment to express my gratitude to the ghost of Hugo for keeping such a well-stocked cellar.

Lunch was even more excruciating than usual. Cora was getting over a cold that had left her uncharacteristically highly-strung. She wriggled and writhed in my lap, before hopping off to roll around on the sofa. She couldn't seem to get comfortable anywhere and was making her discomfort known.

'Here, let me take her out of here for a play or something,' Dom said, eventually.

'No!' Ol said more sharply than I'm sure he meant to. It was an odd kind of outburst. Dom looked to his brother perplexed. Then, his expression hardened into something else. Dom raised his eyebrows, as though waiting for Ol to backtrack on apparently not wanting him to take Cora away on his own. 'I mean, it's probably best if Cora settles herself. There's not much anyone can do for her, even you.' Ol grinned a little too widely for it to be natural.

'Suit yourself,' said Dom. 'I'd be a much better uncle if you let me.'

Ol didn't have an answer to this. He seemed to huff something approaching actual words, but none good enough to articulate. I tried and failed to catch Ol's eye. I assumed Ol's strange coolness was down to tiredness, general grief, having to deal with a sick five-year-old and running a business. He seemed unusually distracted and uncharacteristically tetchy with Dom, especially when he offered further help.

'It's time you let me babysit for you. Get out there. Flic wouldn't want you being like you are forever. And it can't be good for Cora, you being so bloody miserable,' Dom said to his brother as the afternoon wore on.

'I'm not miserable, I'm grieving.' Ol was trying to smile, to make his words sound anything but confrontational, because there was no doubt that he was challenging his brother's perspective, something I rarely, if ever, saw. 'And I think I know more than you on what Flic would want, Dom, *and* what's good for my daughter, so let me do it my way and you . . .'

'Me what?' Dom asked. 'Go on, *me what*, big brother?'

'Nothing, buddy, forget it.'

Patience had watched the entire exchange and only seemed to speak when she was confident Ol had nothing further to say. 'I think I'll serve dessert in the front room,' she said calmly and left her seat.

Dom's phone rang. An apparently urgent call from one of his investors. He left the room. I turned to watch him through the open dining room door taking the stairs in threes to his old bedroom/office up in the attic. Dom seemed to not want an audience for this particular development in his deal. My stomach fell over itself. I sensed he might be very cross indeed when we got home, possibly not in the quiet way I was used to. Recently, I'd feared the barrier between Dom's unspoken fury and the external world was thinning to little more than a membrane.

183

'Let me help clear these, Patience,' I said, standing up to reach for a half-emptied serving bowl, anything to distract myself from my now-churning stomach.

'No. You and Oliver should go into the drawing room. Cora can help me; Agatha can watch.'

'Great idea, Mum,' Ol said before speaking to Cora. 'You go with Grandma.'

It struck me as curious Ol was happy for Patience to take Cora but not Dom. The more time I spent with the Grahams, the odder the family was becoming. Ol went to the bathroom, and it was clear I had no choice but to do Patience's bidding and make my way to the formal room at the front of the house. I took my last glass of wine with me and tried to ignore the heavy feeling in my abdomen.

Alone in the front room that Patience rarely used, I noted the various items of dark antique carpentry, a very expensive if aged Persian rug over the polished floor and a somewhat chintzy drinks cabinet which I went over to inspect in case I ran out of wine and didn't want to make a big deal of getting it topped up. I wondered if I might make do with some throat-burning sherry if needs must. Adjacent to the cabinet was a bookcase. At the same level as the cabinet, there was a row of anonymous-looking book spines, ending in that of an outsized book. A tome in blue-grey suede, it protruded from the rest as though inviting discovery. Alone still, I tugged it free.

A wedding album, Ol and Flic's. The date told me their anniversary was imminent. It was little wonder Ol had seemed more unhappy than usual. At first, as I turned the album's cover, I felt like a voyeur, an intruder, but I told myself that was Patience's voice speaking. I might not have been part of the Grahams back then when Ol and Flic got married and though I never got the chance to meet my sister-in-law, I felt connected to her somehow and I definitely cared for Ol a great deal. I loved Cora. And, of course, I was married to Dom. Like it or not, I was one of the Grahams. The leaves of the album cracked as though undisturbed for some time. Perhaps it had proved too painful for the rest of the repressed Grahams to allow themselves to remember Flic at all.

After some group shots on the steps of the church, there was the loveliest portrait of Flic, in a crown of slightly hippyish woven delphiniums and ivy. She wore a simple, sleeveless ivory gown. Behind her, his arms around her waist, hands clasped around hers and resting on her lower stomach as though inviting the child they'd soon make together, a fresh-faced Ol. Beaming, Ol only has eyes for his new wife, not in any way that suggested possessiveness, a deal clinched – the way it struck me Dom looked at me in our wedding portraits – but in a way that says: *You, us, we're really together now.* Flic gazes back at her groom in a way I knew I did not in my wedding album. The look she gave Ol said: *I'm so happy it was you.* They looked perfect, as though they really knew and saw all of the other person and loved what they had found inside the other. I swallowed the gourd that had swollen in my throat and turned the page.

Ol and Flic's wedding was obviously a much larger and far more lavish affair than mine to Dom with many more guests and, of course, their father. I focused on an image of Patience and

Hugo either side of the bride and groom; Hugo looked to be a slightly shorter, grey-white version of Ol. He appeared oblivious to the heart condition that would kill him not two years after the wedding. Something about the way he held himself with such overt confidence reminded me so much of Dom. Hugo's smile was so much like Dom's too — it seemed one less of pride in his son, the way his chin was turned up and the jaw jutted out spoke more of pride in himself as founder of the feast. Patience. While appearing as redoubtable as ever, in a white-and-navy ensemble of a skirt and frock jacket, both cinched tightly at the waist, and a large-brimmed white hat, in this one picture, she is smiling. She looked upon her eldest son and the wife she approved of as if she was irrefutably, if momentarily, happy. She looked quite unlike the woman I knew. Next, a portrait of her, side by side with Hugo. Her smile is gone. She stares with something I read at first as defiance, then noticed the hardness of her jaw: defensiveness. She didn't want to be in that picture. I felt my time alone with the album was running out, so as much as I wanted to dwell on decoding Patience and Hugo, I turned to the next page greedily.

A different perspective on the happy day: a montage of images of Flic with a woman I guessed was her maid of honour. It was her, the cornflower-eyed, vivacious woman whose portrait had hung on Patience's wall the week before but, when I thought about it, had disappeared once more. Here, I could see that same attractive energy, and in those pictures of her with Flic she looked physically strong too; tall with athletic shoulders atop her sleeveless delphinium-coloured bridesmaid's dress. In the photos, she and Flic had their arms around each other in one shot, their heads thrown back in laughter in the next. It made me wish for Sal's company and wonder how I'd ever cope if Dom was really serious about me 'cooling things off' with her. I couldn't let that happen. But what would happen if I said I wouldn't go along with what Dom wanted? What would happen if I started to say no to him and kept saying it?

I took a large swig of my wine and turned another leaf. I saw Dom, posing for a shot with the maid of honour, arms slung around each other's waists. Jesus, I wondered, did she and him have sex that day, in that time-honoured best-man-shags-maid-of-honour tradition? Next, another image of the two of them dancing, looking into each other's eyes, in the background of a shot of Ol and Flic. Hugo, meanwhile, grips the hand and hip of a clearly uncomfortable Patience on the stretch of shined floor in front of a tuxedoed band. The closeness of Dom and the maid of honour, their inclusion in what looks to be the first dance of the wedding made me seriously wonder if it was more than a one-night stand? Was this tall, lean, striking specimen the prized hollyhock Patience would have approved of in her family garden, not the classless, invasive bindweed Dom had allowed to twist around him? Was that impressive type-A female 'the one that got away'?

'Oh, right.' Ol had joined me in the drawing room. 'You're looking at that.'

'Yes, sorry,' I said, detecting something unhappy or at least uncomfortable in Ol's tone. 'I just came across it, I didn't mean to . . .' Ol dropped himself down onto the small, overstuffed

187

sofa opposite my chair. He said nothing, only leant forward, and rubbed his eyes, sighing deeply.

'I didn't know your anniversary was coming up,' I said into another beat of silence. 'Ol, I'm so sorry Flic isn't here to share it.'

'It's OK. I mean, it obviously isn't, I'm not, but I'm a lucky man. I have my girl. I have you and Dom.'

I said my next words as carefully as I could through the bloom of booziness in my mouth and mind. 'Aren't we all lucky to have Dom? It's like he was born to be brilliant, at his business, at caring for people too: me, my baby, you.'

'You think that too?' He gave a short laugh and nodded. 'Some days I feel like I owe that guy my life.'

'And how he cared for your Flic too, that must have been such a help.'

'Yeah. Definitely. Of course,' said Ol as though he needed to overstate it to make it true. Or maybe he was so grateful for Dom he was inclined to drive the point home.

I flipped to another page of the album. It was a large image of Ol, Dom, and Hugo. Dom was standing tall between the two of them, with his feet angled towards his father, almost as though he's blocking him from his older, much humbler brother, whose expression carried a certain wariness of the father behind the frame of his 'Norseman' little brother. The dynamic I thought I could see before me made me dare to test a theory, to get closer to the parts of the man I was married to but did not know.

'And when you were small, Dom took care of you? Did he stand up for you sometimes? To your dad?'

Ol gave a little huff of a laugh. 'He's started speaking about all that? Finally.'

'Not in a manner of speaking,' I said, desperate to know what *all that* was, but that wasn't going to happen now.

'What's she doing with that?' Dom had entered the room, his work call finished. His presence had immediately changed the atmosphere. There was even more darkness packed into his voice than there had been back in the car when I'd dared probe on the subject of his father.

'It's fine, Dom. No harm done. Take it easy,' said Ol, rising to his feet.

Dom pushed a breath through his nose and glared at his brother, took another, less audible breath, and looked at me expectantly for my explanation.

'I didn't mean to pry or bring anything difficult up. I—'

My stomach dropped afresh. There was a tension sat behind Dom's expression I was becoming used to recognising, the anger he worked so hard to repress was springing to the surface. Patience arrived behind him, and then, the baby. She was pushing an old-fashioned, faded wooden walker contraption, with a set of bleached painted bricks, some of them missing. Another Graham family heirloom. Cora was at her cousin's side. 'Look! Agatha's walking!' she cried.

'Oh wow, look at her.' My hand went to my mouth. My baby daughter transformed into an older version of herself in a matter of minutes.

'Learning to walk on her own two feet,' affirmed Patience as the baby, looking suddenly like a toddler, stomped forward. *She is*

189

becoming a little girl, I thought; *she's growing up too fast*. She's taking her first steps towards leaving me, as I'd, effectively, abandoned my own mother, for reasons I couldn't seem to remember. I wished my mother could be there to see my daughter enjoying the feeling of height, of her own strength that had been waiting dormant in her legs until that moment.

'You *what*, Elle?' Dom asked me, referring to my earlier comment on the album I'd all but forgotten with the sight of my daughter taking her first steps. 'You didn't mean to pry but . . . ?'

'It was just there, Dom. Sort of sticking out, I really wasn't—'

'Why are people so intent on bringing up what's gone?' Dom asked Patience through gritted teeth, as though accusing her of placing it there to entice me into the family's history, past lives Dom felt best forgotten.

'That's my wedding album you're talking about, Dom. That's my wife,' said Ol.

'That's not what I'm—' Dom said, just as Agatha fell, bottom first, to the floor and gave a short, joyful giggle. 'Jesus, Mum, you're going to deform her. Her bones aren't ready to support her.' He snatched the baby from the polished wooden floor and took her into his arms, sending a thrust of anxiety from my lungs to my bowels. I wanted to take her off him, but Dom had already left the room and was heading to the dining room where I knew he'd left the baby's changing bag. I rushed to follow him and the baby out of the room, whispering something like an apology to Ol, then Patience, my eyes on the baby over Dom's shoulder throughout. By the time I reached the hall, Dom already had the changing bag slung on his shoulder and was making his way down the hallway.

'Don't you dare say, *you didn't deform me*, or I swear to god,' Dom said to Patience, by then in the doorway of her drawing room, watching her son leave.

'No, Dominic,' Patience said, looking to me as I tried to smile politely as I rushed past her and out of her house, sticking as close to Agatha as I could. 'I wasn't going to say that.'

Chapter Twenty

Day twenty-one, Saturday

'No need to cry. I'm going to make love to you,' my husband tells me.

I find I cannot speak. This sounds less like a strategy to get me out of here with something like my life intact, and more like torture. Also, how could it look to anyone that I *haven't* been assaulted? I know I have. Then, I think about the many service users at my charity who aren't believed when they've said they were in danger and needed alternative housing, the horrifying scale of the women subjected to rape every day that the justice system has effectively decriminalised through dirt-low conviction rates and sky-high thresholds of proof.

'It *will* be an expression of my love,' Dom continues. 'But I am going to have to be rough with you and you're going to have to pretend; you're going to have to make it out like you don't want it, don't want me. You're going to have to fight like hell to get me off you, but you are going to lose.'

'I don't want to do that,' I tell him. 'Is there no other way?' I push the palms of my hands into my eyes for a moment before looking back at Dom. He is pursing his lips, as though deciding how best to bargain with our baby over letting him wipe her face.

'Take a look around you, darling. You're in need of some pretty radical thinking to get out of here with your life, with *our* lives as we know them. Besides which, it shouldn't be too out-there to imagine you could get through a little rough-play with your husband, should it?'

'Dom, there's a dead body, the cold dead body of Anton behind me. The idea of having any kind of sex now, least of all . . . what you're describing. Forgive me if the idea does not fill me with delight.'

'But you agree we should do this?' Dom asks and I realise I am still naked on the floor after his examination earlier, sat holding myself, my knees, and my own arms the only things protecting what's left of my dignity.

'I don't know. I hate all of this and I just don't know.' Tears break through again.

'What if it's the only way you're going to get to keep being Agatha's mother, be in her life in a meaningful way, avoid prison? Isn't that enough to convince you? I mean, I'm racking my brains here, but this is the best I have. Do you have anything better, any other brilliant ideas you've been keeping to yourself?'

'No. No, Dom. I don't.' I drop my hands to the floor, my exhaustion, my filth and my hopelessness flooding my bones. I would like very much to put my clothes on, leave this room on my own and return to my old house share. I would love to take a long bath like I used to, in the bathroom at the top of the house near my room that had no shower and only said bath, and because of this, no one else used but me. I would spend evenings between dates or nights out in that room, luxuriating in my own company, in my fantasies about what my future might still hold. I would emerge from my soaks feeling so clean and supple as to be renewed, restarted, ready for whatever tomorrow might deliver; that's until all my tomorrows began to take me further away from my youth, but no closer to my future. I want to go back to the days before those, before I was desperate for change and I clung onto Dom like he was everything my life depended on, because I didn't think quite enough of myself.

'So, is that a yes?' Dom says, back in the hotel room. 'You agree my plan is the way to go and that we should do as I have suggested and that you understand what that means?'

I look to my husband, confused. He sounds as though he's asking me to agree to terms and conditions, as though he is asking for my consent.

I take a breath in, imagining how things appear in this moment, with no conclusive proof, apparently, of sexual assault, but with the undeniable evidence of Anton's murder and a three-year backlog of incriminating messages, emails, and conversations in which I have wished him physical harm and worse. And then, I imagine how it could potentially appear in a world where we could convince others I was bullied, then raped by my abusive boss, a world where what I have done to him is somehow excusable. And in that world, I get my baby back.

'Yes,' I breathe.

It happens so fast.

Before the air of my last breath has left my lungs I am slammed, hard.

Before I can understand what is happening, my back is on the floor, my shoulder blades pressed deep into the carpet so that I can feel the solid surface beneath the thin underlay. And then, I cannot breathe at all. A hand over my mouth, fingers long and strong, a deadening mask. I scream, or I make the noise of a breathless scream. Terror. Next, a tremendous pressure to my shoulder, disabling my arm. Still, I fight. His free arm pins mine to the floor above my head, a knee, powerful and relentless, pushing against the space between my thighs. I press my legs together so hard, to not allow the knee to create that void it seeks, to keep my thighs aligned and steady. But the knee is too insistent.

He is so powerful as to be unnatural, as to be fevered. He separates my legs and I silent-scream once more, not making a screech, but a basal, primal noise that hums through my body, pointlessly dissipating into the compressed air between his fingers. I move to turn my hips so he may not access me, but he is too heavy, too determined. With my free arm I thump him. I strike him again and again, as best I can do, which is not much at all; the pointless close-fisted taps on his back he may well be taking as encouragement. And then, despite doing all I can to strain to move away from him, he accesses me. He is hard, outside-of-humanity unbreakable. I cry out again behind his death-mask fingers. I am howling, but no one can hear.

And then, a kind of terror takes over that tips into something else: self-preservation.

I stop fighting.

I make my body go slack, and send my mind back to my old body, the one in the bath at my house share, into the body of Elle Cotton.

'Why have you stopped? Fight me,' he says as he thrusts agony into me. 'Come on, show me you don't want me.'

I do not move. He takes his hand off my mouth and removes himself, only to unwrap a condom, roll it onto himself, then turn me onto my stomach, heave the corpse-woman onto her fours.

Elle Cotton, meanwhile, sinks her head below the bubbles in her bath to rinse her hair, then see how long she can hold her breath without panicking. Elle Graham remains a rag doll as he gathers her hair into his fist and pulls it so tight she cannot help but gasp with the pain. And then, she breathes into it, moves through it, second by second, minute by minute, as she had done so many times when he was inside her; many moments Elle Cotton had to get through in the long series of moments that made up a day of being Elle Graham. The pain, as he pushes her harder, splits her wider until he comes, that is Elle Graham's to own. And when her hair is clean and she can breathe again, Elle Cotton steps out of the bath and reaches for her towel to pat herself dry gently. She returns to her room, where she will sleep undisturbed, ready for another day, perhaps one where she might finally get closer to her future.

He flushes his condom down the toilet before putting his clothes on, while I pull my leggings and vest back on. When he returns, he tells me what I should say about rape and self-defence when I go to the night manager, then the police, and then the solicitor he is going to arrange for me. He tells me he is going to leave soon, escape back through the window and into the creeping dawn, until such time as he can come and get me from wherever it is I will be taken.

He tells me again how everything is going to be OK. He does not care to know it never will be again. He says to me again that if I stick to his plan, it will be fine; he does not care how deeply I doubt him. He says that he forgives me for everything and that I will be home with him in no time. But wherever he is will never be my home again. He tells me I should not call the police myself, but stagger, bewildered to reception where I can tell the night manager what has happened so that she might call the police at a time when he is sufficiently distant. He can never be far enough away from me.

He wants to watch me leave the room before he departs himself, unconvinced, perhaps, that I am ever going to. Maybe he imagines, correctly, I would prefer, in this moment, to join Anton on his deathbed where we both might rot to nothing, turn to a putrid mush of blood and thread together. That is how I feel. As he talks, I pray for my death, and also for his, so that the baby will not be touched by him again, and will instead be raised by Ol, with Cora as her sister. Yes. I can die, if not happy, if not with a clean conscience, then not in abject fear of the future that lies ahead for my daughter if she is to have her life overseen by the man who fathered her.

'I love you so much, Elle Graham,' he says, waiting to make sure I leave the room. 'You can do this. Do this for me. Do this for Agatha,' he tells me, poised to disappear via the open window.

I step towards my hotel room door. I want to show him I will leave the room, but only so he will leave me now. My hand is on the door handle. I take one last look at him, at Anton, at the room where my world ended, and prepare to step into the new and hellish reality beyond its door. My husband watches me all the while.

'Wait!' he nearly shouts. 'Sorry, I mean, do me a favour and wait there for a second. Don't move; I need to quickly check one last thing. Just . . . just stay right where you are.' I hear the rustle of his overshoes reaching the floor in the room once more.

If he won't leave me this second, then I must leave him.

I pull the door wide open to see the corridor beyond.

A woman.

A police officer, her knuckles in front of my face, suspended.

She was about to knock on my door.

I know her, I think, though in this moment, I don't remember how. She stares at my face, then peers past me. She opens her month to speak.

'Dom?'

Chapter Twenty-One

Day nine, Monday

I meant to meet Sal for lunch today, truly, I did. But the universe had different ideas. Getting the bus to work took twice as long as cycling, and I was still not quite sure what margin of error I should give. In truth, this morning I was so hungover, I cancelled my training session last minute, a post-alcohol sickness in my mouth and blood accumulated over multiple days and nights, with a headache that would not shift from my temples and sockets that felt somehow puckered, too small for my eyes. I had a thirst that would not be slaked and a dull, concerning strip of pain in my lower back, which I ascribed to my kidneys objecting to being required to deal with their poisoning-upon-poisoning. I should have left the house earlier than I did. I had no excuse but the booze.

The slow sousing began on, or perhaps only continued from, Saturday night, following Dom's outburst at his mother's. At first, he was silent as he wordlessly unpacked the changing bag, then began prepping the baby for her bath by taking off her outer layer of clothes and throwing them into the utility room.

'I can bath her tonight,' I said, following him, aching to have some time with the baby and get her away from Dom when I knew he was so cross. I wanted to drink more, but I did not want to be any more muddied should I get to bathe my child, so, at that stage, I did not sip from the goblet of Amarone Dom immediately poured for me when we got in. I took tiny sips, so as not to upset him any further, but was determined to remain sharper than I might have otherwise.

'Dom,' I said to him as he all but threw a dirty bib into the pile of baby clothes on top of the washing machine. 'Why don't you take a break tonight? You do so much. Let me bath Agatha.'

'I am perfectly capable, thank you very much.'

'Of course, you are,' I said, quietly, daring to reach out, placing what I hoped was a soothing hand on his back. He shook off my palm.

'Please. I've had enough of being treated like some idiot child today.'

'I've said sorry about looking at the album,' I said quietly. 'I never meant to upset anyone.'

'Would you forget about the fucking album.'

I had never seen him like this. I have sensed my husband's anger, like one of London's underground waterways that once carved the landscape but were now buried, invisible but nevertheless pumping relentlessly below our lives. Was this his anger finally resurfacing, its source swollen by my stupidity, my inability to do the right thing, be the right woman for him?

'The deal. The *deal*, Elle. The lawyers. They're being fucking pricks. Tomorrow, they're going to advise the supermarket to put the deal on hold while they *look into a few things*.' He turned to grip the kitchen island with his free hand, the other, holding the baby's leg on his hip. '*Cunts!*'

Dom's shouting made the baby suck a single, prolonged breath from the air and convert it into the most heart-breaking cry. I needed to take my daughter from him but was afraid that if I tried to do so she, and he, would only get more upset, maybe even get hurt. I imagined his long, hard fingers pressing deeply into her flesh and it squeezed the breath I held in my lungs.

'Fuck!' Dom grimaced; his head angled away from the baby. 'Fuck,' Dom said again, this time more quietly as he gently touched the baby's face before holding her more closely. 'I'm sorry. Daddy's sorry. Daddy's sorry,' he whispered into her ears, swaying her with his eyes closed.

I watched them like that for a moment until Dom opened his eyes. They were full of tears. 'I'm sorry,' he whispered, his voice curiously high and boyish. And, as my tiny baby continued to grizzle because of an uncontrollable, aggressive outburst from her father, he appeared to be infantilising himself. It was profoundly, sickeningly unattractive.

'She doesn't need a bath, not tonight. Let me put her down,' Dom said.

'OK,' I agreed; anything to get her away from him in the state he was in.

'I'll give her a bottle. Why don't you go to the guest room and wait for me?'

'Dom, it's been a big day, I'm not really—'

'Please. Go and wait for me in bed. I need you.'

Drink stultified my awareness of my life on Sunday, deadened if not my desire to, but my ability to call my mum. By Monday morning, it had thickened my blood, my thought processes, my ability to view my life with any clarity, and move through the time of which it comprised. Because I'd got the bus later than I should have, I hit the worst of the rush-hour traffic and was going to be inevitably and significantly late.

When I finally reached the office, Anton was at his desk, headphones in, his revolting upper incisors worrying his protruding lower lip. Gabriel appeared to be on the same Teams call and was nodding darkly at his screen. He sent me a pensive smile. Anton spoke.

'Well, she's here now, perhaps there's an opportunity to understand the lessons learnt. Elle, you ready to jump on a call with Steve? I sent you the invite this morning, but it seems like you've struggled to get here today.' Fuck, Steve, Financial Director Steve. 'He's working on the annual report and we need some narrative explaining why we think donations were down on the campaign you worked on last year. Hoping you'd be able to shed some light on why it failed to deliver.'

I felt sick. My head was no longer in pain but felt as though it was floating above the rest of my body. I fell into my seat, rushed to log on and join the Teams invite Anton had only just forwarded. I was a sweaty mess, completely out of control. Steve – another exile from the private sector known for importing the same level of ruthlessness he had exercised at the multinational bank that was his previous employer – was likely to decimate me. I had no choice but to prepare for the worst.

'Elle,' Anton said, 'glad you could join us. So, is there anything you can tell Steve that he can cascade to the leadership team about the outcome of your campaign? What can you tell us about preventing further efforts from delivering such low return on investment?'

Low return on investment. That was me all over. It seems like whatever people pour into me, I give them so little back: my mum, my best friend and especially my baby, and all of my connections are turning to shit around me because of it. A strangle of pressure wrapped itself around my windpipe, adrenaline shot through my neck, my saliva glands spurting under my tongue.

'Um . . .' I swallowed. *Come on, Elle.* 'There's not a great deal to say, really. I tried, as I always do, to craft words for all of the campaign collateral – the website, the placed articles, email marketing, the social – based on what the research told us about the obstacles and opportunities we faced.' I made myself look away from the scarlet square with my face in it and met the expressions of Anton and Steve, too ashamed to let myself check Gabriel's reaction. Anton's incisors rested on his lower lip as he failed to dampen his relish at seeing me squirm. Steve, meanwhile, appeared deeply unimpressed. Still, I had no choice but to stagger on. 'As usual, creating copy that resonates with people, I guess it's art and science, only it's not that scientific and sometimes, things just don't land, so . . . I don't know. I'm trying really hard this time with the agency project; I mean I did last time too . . . I-I'm sorry I let everyone down.' I shook my head, before smiling at Steve and Anton in turn to show I was still optimistic, still fit to work and not requiring some kind of performance intervention, though I probably looked unhinged.

'If I may say something?' Gabriel had spoken up. 'Just coming back on the return-on-investment point earlier. I had a look at the figures; in terms of marketing spend, Steve, am I right in thinking you'd cut the budget?'

Steve paused for a moment. He seemed to suspect where Gabriel's line of questioning was heading and did not like it. Meanwhile, as Gabriel effectively had the floor, I had no excuse not to give his face my full attention; the way some of his curls had fallen onto his forehead, how delightful it would be to move those strands away, to appraise his face intimately, the intelligent line of his lips.

'In fact, didn't you sign off on a fifty per cent reduction in year-on-year marketing spend?'

'We were under pressure to find savings,' Steve replied.

'Totally,' Gabriel said, nodding. 'I guess a couple of things strike me: one, while cutting marketing spend will make expenses look tighter in the short term, in the longer term it could be a false economy. And, actually . . .' Gabriel looked at a notepad he was scribbling on '. . . given the reduced budget on the marketing, the return on Elle's campaign was pretty robust. I mean copywriters, even of Elle's calibre, are always learning, but we need to view what creativity is capable of in context, and for this campaign, that was reduced exposure to potential donors.'

I hadn't even thought to look at the spend, and it looked as though it wasn't my failure to connect would-be donors with our messages, it's that they didn't have the opportunity to see them in the first place.

'Thanks for bringing that granular level of transparency,' Anton said, because he'd rather deploy *granular transparency* than bring himself to say the words: *You're right* to Gabriel and *I'm sorry* to me.

The rest of the meeting was undramatic. My breath and pulse levelled; my nausea subsided. When Anton and Steve directed their request for an update on the agency project at Gabriel, he said, 'I think Elle is best placed to answer that. She's the creative force; I'm pretty much facilitating.' There are few things more arousing to me than a man who insists a woman is given the appropriate space to accept the credit she is due. I couldn't imagine any point in Anton's career when he had been that man, and, honestly, nor could I ever envisage Dom acting as Gabriel just had.

When the Teams call was over, Gabriel and I were due to meet ahead of a get-together with the ad agency later. We entered a conference room together, one down a corridor and away from the rest of the office.

'Good weekend?' I asked, before being struck with a sudden horror. Weekends when you're single are for dating, booty calls, and one-night stands. I couldn't cope with the idea of Gabriel even hinting at his. I closed him down before he could speak, blurting out, 'Wait, before I forget, thank you.'

'For what?' he said, the most delectable smile reaching deep into his eyes.

'For taking on Steve; for deferring to me on the agency work.'

Gabriel shrugged as he took the seat not opposite me, but right next to me at the table. I savoured being this close to his

205

skin, so different from my husband's, a light smattering of dark hair across tightly packed sinews cloaked in a tan that seemed to deepen every day. He opened his laptop in front of him, though his gaze was on me. We were not very far apart at all. It would be so easy to lean in, tilt my head and take the feel of his lips for my own. Then, I remembered my boozy breath, and my husband – how little I wanted him – and the mess of my life poured into the gap between Gabriel and me.

Last night with Dom was appalling. In the spare room, he buried his head in my stomach as I lay on the bed and cried before fucking me with a force that bordered on painful. He needed to lose himself in me and I couldn't not let him do that. While it was happening, I thought about what would happen if Dom knew I was only going through the motions to make him happy. How would he feel if he knew I was planning to get through my life with him using a combination of zombifying booze and the enlivening peril of time spent with Gabriel, and perhaps men like him into the future until men like him didn't want me anymore. I would truly destroy Dom.

The truth was, I could too easily see Dom threatening to harm himself if he knew my true feelings, about the sex with him, the whole life with him. I couldn't do that to Dom, or to the baby, not after everything he'd tried to give me and all he'd done for her. It wasn't Dom's fault I didn't want him; he wasn't to blame. I'd agreed to marry him, to bring a child into that marriage when I didn't love him as much as he did me. The best I could hope for, the best I deserved, was successfully hiding from Dom how I'd only ever be hovering above my life's flatline, maybe only long enough to see my daughter into adulthood. Maybe until my own body matured into something he no longer wanted, and whatever might remain of my soul turned into something he no longer needed. Yes, this would ruin me, but no more than the guilt were Dom to hurt himself if I left him. So I would, instead, have to find a way to swallow the nuggets of guilt and self-hate that accompanied my self-medication with booze and flirtation with men like Gabriel.

'What I did, if I *did* anything,' Gabriel said, back in the meeting room, 'it wasn't a choice. No one could stand by and let Steve try to shunt the blame for his short-sightedness onto someone else.'

I fiddled with the edge of my laptop and took a deep breath, inhaling the intimacy, the care in Gabriel's words. When I turned to him, he looked into my eyes for a moment, before his gaze drifted lower, to my mouth, viewing my lips with such seriousness, such intent that I would never be able or want to lose the image of that intensity as long as I lived.

'And how was your weekend? Any dates?' Gabriel asked me after two or maybe three delicious beats that made my breath stall, his voice slow and deliberate.

'Dates? Hardly,' I said quietly. And this was yet another juncture where I should have told Gabriel about my husband, and about my baby girl; confess, perhaps, the horrible bind I was in, request that instead of being a lover, he might want to be a trusted colleague and supportive professional friend.

'God, if I ever saw you on one of the apps I'd—' Gabriel halted mid-sentence and took an audible breath. 'Sorry. I have to stop doing this,' he said, but he did not move his face, which was moving by delicious, tiny increments towards mine.

'What if . . .' I whispered.

'What if, what?'

'What if I don't want you to stop? What if I only want it to go on and on?'

Another breath I could hear, this one short, urgent.

'I would like,' he said, reaching into my space with his face, those lips I ached for parting, 'to kiss you very, very much.'

And then, it happened. Contact. Breathtaking, full-lipped, open-mouthed contact. Our tongues dancing as we pulled each other closer, my hand behind his head, drawing him into me more. We kissed as though we were ravenous, as though we were born to fit together like that. Individually, we are proficient kissers, of that I was sure, but together, we defined the essence of kissing, the intuitive move of the head, the repositioning of the lips to explore some new millimetre of the other person. I had thought as I'd edged into my late thirties that perhaps I'd grown out of kissing. I hadn't. I'd only grown tired of indulging the artless stabs of the tongue my husband gave me near the climax of his sex. This, what Gabriel and I were doing, was better than sex, more erotic, more profound. Our kissing was operatic, symphonic. But it had to end.

'We have to stop,' I said, forcing myself to move back and away from Gabriel.

'Fuck.' Gabriel's head fell into his hands. 'Fuck. That was . . .'

'Unprofessional? Inappropriate? Insane?' I breathed, leaning back.

'Incredible.' Gabriel shook his head. 'Listen, let's get through this –' he gestured to the open document on his laptop '– and then, let's take a ride away from here, together, at lunchtime.'

'OK,' I said. 'Oh, but I can't cycle. My bike. It got nicked.'

'Shit. I've been wondering why I haven't seen you locking up in the morning. I've been lurking down there, waiting for you, by the way.'

I took his hand. He kissed it. It felt so beautifully tender; so natural.

'Where was it stolen?' he asked.

'Oh,' I flustered. 'Outside my gym. Such a pain.' I shook my head. 'I don't think I'm going to bother anymore.'

'No! That's too bad. Let me sort you out with a bike.'

'It's fine. I think I'm done with it for the time being.'

'Why? Let me help you out. You'd be helping me. At any one time, I have at least four pissing off my flatmate in the hallway.'

'No, please, Gabriel. You keep your bikes.'

'Ms Cotton,' he said, and my heart jumped at how sexy he sounded, before plummeting on realising afresh both that I was a married woman and how dishonest I was being, not only to him, but to my husband too. I truly deserved ruin. 'I would like it very much if you could understand that whatever it is you want from me, it's yours for the taking.'

I wanted to fall into him right then and there; I wanted for us not to be in a meeting room but in a hotel room, where I might keep Gabriel captive for as long as I needed to exhaust every curiosity I had about his body, and for him to explore all of me.

That lunchtime Gabriel and I walked until we found somewhere we could kiss without an audience. It was a railway arch, dark and musty, lacking any softness, any romance at all. It didn't matter. The sweet release of the deeply felt need for more and more of each other could have happened anywhere. We could not go much further than our kissing. Perhaps we never would. And perhaps that's the best possible outcome. Because I have a baby. *I have a baby.*

'I want to see you. Tonight?' Gabriel said between kisses under the arches.

'I can't,' I said honestly, then thought on my feet as to why this would be the case if I was single. 'I don't know how we can keep doing this. It could ruin both of us at work. We have to be discreet, even doing this. And, Gabriel, I think this is all we can do.'

'Is this really all I get of you? It's not enough. I can't ignore my feelings. Can you?'

I didn't answer. He kissed me again, his fingers in my hair, making the new growth below my dull, postpartum outer casing tingle, sending my entire body into the most exquisite ache. I savoured the feel of his erection, hard in his jeans, pressed into me, his fingers daring to inch under my T-shirt, my back against the brick.

'Let's take each day at a time. I can't commit to anything, not right now,' my mouth said, the rest of me lost in thoughts of exactly how incredible inching him into me would feel.

'Fuck, Elle. This thing, *you*, you're taking me over. I'm losing my fucking mind here,' he said, in between kisses on my neck.

'Me too. Which is why I need you to understand that I need to take it slow, as much as there's a huge part of me that really doesn't want to, doesn't know how I'm going to do that.' I was lying to Gabriel about many things, but this, at least, was true.

We walked back to the office, he wanted to go arm in arm, but I had to rebuff him.

'Gabriel. What if Anton, or Caleb, or anyone, saw us? We can't risk that.'

I was in a great deal of trouble, sliding over the event horizon of my emotional black hole; soon, it might be pointless to try to resist its unstoppable force. The only thing keeping me in the space and time of my existence was my baby.

I was so glad I was able to rearrange my session with Jordan after work, having cancelled on him that morning. It was almost impossible to imagine how I could interact normally with Dom, and also Patience if she'd decided to stick around after taking care of the baby that day, having done what I had done, feeling as I did about another man. I could not wish away fast enough the seconds until I could see Gabriel again. I wished I did not have to spend even one of those seconds with my husband and his mother. I found myself fantasising about returning to another home, my own. I'd pick up the baby from nursery along the way, and we'd go home and lock the door on our little flat to the rest of the world, have a bath together and sleep soundly.

All of these thoughts were thundering through me when I let

myself into the house I actually live in after my training. It was at first a shock, and then something of a relief to see Sal there. She was hunched over the table in the kitchen/diner, Dom on the chair next to her. In between them, several balls of scrunched-up kitchen roll, an open bottle of wine and two glasses, half-filled. It took me a second or two to work out what was going on.

'Sal?'

'Hey, love,' she said, accepting a piece of kitchen roll Dom had just torn off for her, before pressing it to each wet eye in turn. 'I didn't know what else to do, sorry for busting in on your evening.'

'Don't worry about that. What's happened?'

She turned her swollen eyes to Dom apologetically; he'd clearly just heard it all. I felt an odd stab of jealousy at Sal taking Dom into her confidence before she'd had a chance to share her crisis with me.

'Tim and me, we had a massive fight, like, *huge*. I said a lot of stuff, things I know I probably shouldn't have. He's gone to stay with his mate. I don't know for how long. Worse than that, I don't know if that's a bad thing. I don't know if it's right my marriage is over.' She stared out in front of her, bewildered at her own words, then focused on me, as though I might be able to offer any kind of clarity. 'I mean, what the fuck? What the actual fuck?'

'Sal, I'm so sorry. How did it all kick off?' I asked, moving to take a seat, but before I did, I quickly retrieved a glass from the open cabinet behind me, topping up Dom's and Sal's glasses before pouring myself a measure I already felt was far too shallow. After the day I'd had, arriving at my home to see Dom and Sal as they were, rather than the two of them sparring with each other, only added to my discombobulation.

'A miracle. A fucking miracle is what started it,' said Sal. Meanwhile, Dom pursed his lips and raised his eyebrows. He caught my glance, and his mouth made the shape of a shush, unseen by Sal.

'We were this close . . .' Sal gave the air in front of her right eye a tight pinch. '*This* close to calling the boys' school, explaining, *begging* for another impossible extension to the grace period for settling last term's fees, never mind this one, when the bursar calls us.' Sal shook her head in mystification.

'Saying . . . ?' I urged Sal, Dom giving me the smallest nod of approval at my acting dumb to where I knew Sal's story would be heading.

'Saying they'd just received an anonymous boost to the hardship fund, telling me they *were pleased to say this could be used to settle the boys' fees for the entire year.*'

'Wow. That's . . . *wow*,' I said.

'I know, right? So, I call Tim to tell him the good news, and he's like: *Let's discuss it first.* And I'm like: *What the fuck is there to talk about?* This random donation has saved our boys' arses, saved ours. And when we got home he's like: *My sons aren't a charity case; my family, me, I'm not a good fucking cause, I'm a successful man and I don't need to rely on handouts.*'

'And you said?' I asked.

'And I said . . .' Sal swallowed. 'I was pretty angry he was putting some male pride bullshit ahead of reality, before what's best for Zak and Lew, so I told him it's OK to get help when you need it, when it's offered. And he said he didn't need any help with anything, ta very much, and then I said some stuff; stuff about some other places I think he should be asking for and getting help.' Sal chewed her lip guiltily. 'You know, the stuff I mentioned about some problems we've been having,' she said. Dom peered through the large window into the garden, as though he wanted to pretend he wasn't there. Had Sal shared with Dom about her husband's sexual dysfunction? I couldn't imagine them conversing so intimately, but then, Sal did seem desperate.

'And things got worse from there?' I asked, reaching across the table for Sal's tissue-clutching hand.

'They got much fucking worse. It was awful; it was ... ugly.' Sal closed her eyes and breathed through the top of the next surge of tears. 'I don't know how we're going to come back from it.'

'Oh, Sal. I'm so, so sorry. Do the boys know what's going on?'

'They know something's up.' Sal checked her phone, ostensibly for any communication from Zak and Lewis, but gasped when she saw the time. 'Fuck, I gotta go. We can't have them malnourished on top of being emotionally destroyed.' Sal allowed herself a quiet half-laugh at her joke. I was about to offer to go home with her and cook, as Dom moved to show Sal out ahead of me, when an uninvited voice joined the conversation.

'Someone once told me . . .' Patience was in the doorway to the kitchen, the baby, damp in a hooded towel, on her hip. I wondered how long she'd been standing there, and also how long she had left Sal and Dom alone. 'The secret to staying married a long time . . .' Patience walked over to where Dom

214

stood and held the baby out for him to take off her '. . . is to not get divorced.'

'Thank you, Mother,' said Dom. 'If we want unsolicited marriage counselling then we'd . . . solicit it,' he stumbled. 'I apologise, Sal, on my mother's behalf.'

'What's your point, Patience?' Sal said.

Stood together, Sal and Dom almost appeared as though they were squaring up to Patience. Still sat at the table so I could steal another gulp of wine as Dom had been escorting Sal away, I had the most peculiar feeling of being an intruder in my own kitchen, my own life.

'Isn't it clear?' Patience said to Sal. 'As long as you can tolerate whatever your spouse inflicts upon you, you can remain married for eternity. If you're not prepared for that, then it won't happen.' Patience turned her attention to me. 'Will it, Elle?' She gave a strange cock of her head, thrusting abject panic into my chest. What if Patience had taken the baby for a stroll by the river that sunny day; seen her daughter-in-law losing herself to another man?

'If you say so, Patience,' I said, raising my eyebrows and offering Dom a whimsical smile that I hoped communicated to him: *What is your mother **like**?* and my ultimate solidarity with him in trying to put Patience in her place. But she had more to say.

'I wonder, how many people really believe they have found the one person who they hope are as perfect for them as they seem, but are ultimately deeply disappointed.'

'Mother! You make it sound as though you're talking about you and Pa? Don't tell me that's what you two were all about?' said Dom, semi-outraged.

Patience viewed her son coolly. 'I thought you'd heard enough of my perspectives on marriage.'

Dom reached back to the dining table, specifically, the nearby chair, where Patience had hooked her cardigan and handbag earlier that afternoon. 'Well, thanks for everything, Mum.' He handed his mum her things.

Patience placed her bag on her shoulder and folded her cardigan over her arm. She stood for a moment longer, as though daring Sal or Dom to say something further. I was reminded of the inner steel I saw shimmering through the images from Flic and Ol's wedding.

'Don't let us hold you back,' Dom said, all but bustling Patience to the door by this stage. 'I think you've done enough for one day.'

'Catch you on the flipside, Mrs G,' Sal chimed in, backing up Dom's dismissal of Patience in a way I found difficult to watch.

'Actually, Sally . . .' Patience turned the full force of her lofty glare onto Sal. 'There was another thing I might say to you.'

'Oh yeah?' Sal tilted her head. 'Let's have it.'

'While the saying suggests you should never look a gift horse in the mouth, I'd argue that's precisely the only way you can establish the true cost of said gift.'

Sal appeared bewildered and then stunned. It was clear Patience somehow knew something of how and by whom the boys' school fees had been paid. How, I didn't know. I couldn't imagine Dom would ever discuss the bail-out of another family with Patience, a woman who seemed wholly indisposed to charity. Perhaps she'd overheard him making the call, or perhaps she knew her son better than he imagined. Because behind every philanthropic gesture is power. You give because you can. You take because you cannot say no.

'I'm sorry, what—' Sal began.

'Come on, Mum, I'll walk you to the door.' Dom stood squarely between Sal and Patience, but his mother would not be deterred; she was not finished.

'Nah, it's alright, actually,' Sal said. 'I'm out of here. Thanks for the wine, Dom. Call you later, Elle.'

Patience watched Sal as she passed. 'Looking that gift horse in the mouth, Sally, is also the only way you can tell if your new steed may bite.'

'*Mother*,' Dom said, his head in his hands.

'It's alright, Dom,' Sal said as she stopped and then spoke back to him. 'I've got this.' Sal then turned to Patience. 'I don't know what your problem is, with me, with Elle, but truly, Patience, today is the day I feel well within my rights to finally say to you, from the bottom of my heart: *Fuck. You.*' Sal turned to Dom and me, a saccharine smile plastered on her face. 'Nighty-bless, guys.'

'*Sal*,' I said, making it clear I did not approve of how she had spoken to Patience, as I finally left my seat. 'I'll call you in a bit, OK?' I added, stepping to her to hug her goodbye. 'And let's definitely do Pret tomorrow,' I said quietly as we embraced.

'Hey, no pressure.'

Sal left. The air seemed to pulsate with silence for a moment. I waited for Dom to say something, or Patience. But they said nothing, only stared at each other. It felt, very much, like a contest. It was utterly unbearable.

'I'm so sorry about what Sal said to you,' I ventured to Patience. 'She doesn't speak on my behalf, really.'

Patience calmly turned to me. 'Yes, she does. That's exactly what you'd like to say to me. If you had the bravery. But you don't. Not yet.' She assessed my reaction, shooting a look at Dom, who by now was gripping the top of one of the dining chairs closest to him, his knuckles bone-white.

I went to speak, to make some pointless, unfunny, meaningless joke, but the words faltered before I could form them. Patience spoke again. 'Well, I should think that *is* enough for one day. Good night, Dominic.' She turned and approached me. She leant into my space, so close I could smell the soap-Bergamot fragrance of *Je Reviens*, so close I had to fight my instinct to flinch. Patience moved closer. And she held me. Then, she hugged me more tightly, and then more forcefully still. The physicality of it was extraordinary. But it didn't feel like affection; it felt, very much, like a show of strength.

The drama with Sal and Patience was an all-too-welcome distraction from the terrible, duplicitous, murky things I had done and felt that day. We opened and finished a bottle of Amarone, of which I believe I drank three-quarters as Dom settled the baby. I was on course to blast through a case of fine wine that should have lasted months in a couple of weeks. I'd wanted to be the one who got the baby to bed that night. In the end, I was too ashamed of my booze-red cheeks, the alcohol on my breath and the chance I might accidentally harm her to even ask Dom if I could.

After dinner, me and Dom headed to bed early. I was hopeful

the emotional ups and downs of the evening would be enough to dampen his usual desire for sex. I was practically joyful with relief when I returned from brushing my teeth in the en suite to see he'd turned his bedside light off and had his eyes closed; a sign, I knew from experience, that meant I would be left alone that night.

I crept into bed, careful not to disturb the baby, or Dom, and killed my own bedside light.

'You must be exhausted,' Dom whispered, sleepily. 'Tonight; your training; work.'

'What about you?' I said. 'You've had a full-on day: your mum, the baby, deal stuff. You didn't say if there were any updates after what you'd heard about the lawyers—'

'Deal stuff is fine, really,' Dom cut me off. 'I'll sail through. It's easy street, not like what Sal said you were handling.'

Though the lights were off, I feared my husband might still see the rush of guilty blood to my face. 'What did Sal say I was *handling*?'

'She said you were facing an uphill struggle trying to keep your new project under control.'

'Oh,' I breathed. 'She did?' *Why was Sal lying?* 'It's really nothing as dramatic as all that.'

'No? Sal seemed to think you were having it pretty tough; said she wouldn't be surprised if you had to pull a few late nights.'

Was Dom testing me? Had Sal said this? If so, I guessed she maybe wanted to give me more freedom in the evening so that I might see more of her, or, when I really thought about it, more likely so I might spend more time with Gabriel. Then, I heard myself ask: *Does she want me out of the way?*

'I may have to put some extra hours in, but there's nothing planned right now.'

'You know I never believed her, by the way,' Dom said.

'Believed what?'

'What Sal said last week, about you and the *young buck* working on your project. I'm not so insecure I have to stop you from working late.' Only his voice, tighter, higher, sounded like the needy version of my husband, the iteration of him that's on his way to explosion, the version of himself he struggles to hide from me and keep away from the baby.

'Sal didn't really imply anything like that,' I said, heat surging into me.

'Not in so many words. It doesn't matter anyway. I trust you implicitly. Because there's no reason not to, is there?' I could hear more upset entering Dom's already heightened tone.

I let the words hang in the air, as did he.

What could I say to him that would not betray me; that was not as incriminating as any spoken response would be? What words would mask my guilt, assuage Dom's insecurity and keep him calm? There was nothing I could say. So instead, I removed my vest, slipped free of my pyjama bottoms and pressed my body against my husband's.

Dom breathed. 'I thought you were exhausted.'

'*You* said I was. I didn't.'

I straddled my husband, lowering myself to his face to kiss him, trying to banish all thoughts of Gabriel, until the thought of him was only thing that could get me through.

Chapter Twenty-Two

Day twenty-one, Saturday

'There's a body,' Dom blurts out, as though this might make me ignore the fact the police officer at my hotel room door has just indicated she knows my husband. As if him saying this would somehow detract that he's about to leave a murder scene through an open window. 'There.' He points at the bed. 'That man raped my wife.'

The police officer returns her attention to me, her eyes wide. That's when I recognise her: she's the maid of honour from Ol and Flic's wedding. My mind, already overloaded, feels as though it might implode with this extra bafflement. But I can't allow it. Not now. Not when I know with absolute certainty that my husband, the man who has just violated me, is the last person in the world able to keep me safe.

'Who are you?' I ask the police officer, my voice quiet and low.

Her hand slowly reaches for something. My mind races with what it might be. I've had zero dealings with the police. Is she getting ready to defend herself in the face of people who may well be murderers; or turning on the body camera I can see attached to her stab vest to capture what's about to unfold; or maybe she's about to neutralise me with a Taser.

The police officer pulls out a mobile phone.

'Hello,' she says, her voice faltering as she makes her call. 'This is Special Constable Thea Stubbs, calling for immediate assistance. I'm at the Parkview, Mayhew Way, and . . . it's a murder scene; there's been a suspected murder. I . . . Can you send someone quickly because there's been a murder. Thanks. Thank you. Did I say— I'm at Parkview.'

She slides the phone slowly back into her pocket, swallows, takes a breath. Dom climbs back into the room.

'Sir,' she says quietly, then clears her throat. 'Sir. I'm going to have to ask you to . . .' She scans the room for something or, perhaps, somewhere. 'I'm going to have to ask you to step into the bathroom and close the door and to not touch anything inside.'

'If you'd just let me explain—'

'No, sir. If *you* could just—' She holds out an open palm in the direction of the bathroom, her head bowed as she waits for Dom to remove himself.

'Thea, I know what this may look like but this is really quite ridiculous.'

'If you'd just do as I've asked, please. I'd ask anyone else in the same situation to do the same thing: requesting you step into another room is so I can give both of you the opportunity to explain your involvement or non-involvement in the incident here, so the information you provide can be as accurate and complete as possible without any omissions or distortion.'

'Jesus, you sound like you've just swallowed some kind of

police manual. Medicine not work out for you?' Dom says, staring hard at Thea, who I can see does not meet his eye. 'Your doctorly instincts not all you thought they were cracked up to be after all? Figures,' he sneers. There is deep history between them, real bitterness too, on his part. Who left whom, I wonder for a split second before I know with absolute certainty that she dropped Dom. I've known her for seconds, but I already know she is far, far too good a person for him.

At Dom's last comment, something seems to have switched in Thea's entire demeanour. She comes deeper into the room, walks to where Dom stands, steps so she's very close to him.

'Move. Now.'

Thea turns away, assured her words have been heard. Over her shoulder, Dom shoots me a warning look, though I have no idea which element of peril I'm being cautioned about: is it 'our story', which surely he can see is now in tatters, with a police officer having witnessed my husband about to leave a murder scene through an open window dressed like some kind of contract killer? Or is Dom warning me not to ask Thea how she knows him? Thea takes one step away from Dom and swiftly turns around again to him as though she's forgotten something. She catches Dom's dark, furious expression and when she does, he freezes.

'Actually, sir, if you could hold it there for just a second.'

She takes out her phone again and begins to capture images of Dom: his face, baseball cap, his hands back in their latex gloves, feet in overshoes.

'If I could just explain something, or I'm sure my wife will explain, this really isn't—'

'Turn around.' Thea takes more pictures; of the torch in his pocket, which she then, having removed a pair of her own latex gloves and put them on, slides free of his pocket and slips into a clear, plastic evidence bag.

'Turn to me please.' I can hear some of that strength and vivacity I had seen in the photos of her at Ol and Flic's wedding in her voice.

'Thank you. In there now, please,' says Thea, her voice pointedly level, as though she knows there are few things Dom finds more disturbing than a woman in control.

Dom huffs but ultimately does as he is told, and heads into the bathroom, apparently too wary to send any further looks my way.

'Stand there for me please, madam.'

'Just here?' I point to the ground below me, feeling stupid, feeling dirty and small next to her steel and purpose.

'That's right.'

She moves past me and towards Anton's body. She uses her phone yet again to capture the bed, the blood, the spurt patterns behind her on the wall. She may be running through the protocols of a thorough police constable, but something about the halting, semi-improvised way in which she's finding new angles to take her pictures, pausing while biting her lip feels strange. There's something suspicious, or perhaps only oddly amateur about her demeanour. She's acting like she's never attended anything like this before, a murder scene. Wait, didn't she say she was a *special constable*? They're volunteer police, more used to dealing with minor disturbances, drunk people in town centres. She's no more used to what's happened in this room than I am. And seeing Dom in here has clearly only added to her shock.

'I'd like to take some photographs of you. Are you OK with me doing that?'

'Yes. Yes of course.'

Thea comes to me, takes images of my face, neck, asks me to move my hair up so she can record the skin around my ears, across the punctured stretch of my collarbone, where, when she reaches the bite marks, she winces. I feel utterly ashamed. Thea notices.

'I'm sorry, it's just they look a bit nasty. Are you in pain?'

'No,' I tell her. 'Yes. Actually, yes, I am.'

Thea swallows. 'He hurt you?'

I regard dead Anton shrouded in the bloodied sheet behind Thea. 'Yes, but look at him now,' I say, my guilt and my tears cracking through.

'Not the deceased.' Thea raises her chin and waves her head towards the bathroom, in the direction of Dom.

Chapter Twenty-Three

Day thirteen, Friday

Friday the thirteenth day of my so-called boozer's log. Shall I deem this the luckiest or the unluckiest day so far? My whole life feels as though it's in a *lucky-for-some* hinterland. A tall, attractive, rich husband, a big house, a baby, the option of walking away from my awful boss and the daily grind, the very definition of 'lucky' for some women. But that life seems to have cost so much more than it can ever give me: my sense of self, my autonomy over my body, my future as I truly saw it; my true happiness. As for my lover and what we did today, once more in the railway arches, it may have rendered this Friday a red-letter day, or one I should banish from my memory in shame. I may have been doing the best thing I could for the baby by stepping over a point of no return towards a future without Dom. Or I may well have ruined her life.

Because this time, I brazenly planned my encounter with Gabriel. I wore a loose-fitting, button-down dress and informed Gabriel I'd left my underwear at the gym that morning. We hurried together to our dark, quiet kissing spot, off the beaten tourist track of the Southbank, with only the occasional passer-by causing us to halt, but only for a moment, eyes still closed, hands and fingers returned to half-decent places. This time, he was able to work his fingers through a gap in my dress and reach between my legs, tentatively, a little clumsily at first with the odd angle and the fact he could not be seen doing what he was doing, but when I tilted my pelvis towards him, the touch of his fingers became firm and insistent. I kissed him deeper and harder, and I came; I came, standing up in a dirty railway arch, forgetting, not caring that at any moment, a lost tourist might stumble by. That orgasm was my timeless black hole folding in on me, reducing me to nothing and expanding all of me to everywhere simultaneously. I felt as though I may be killing myself with the one thing that allowed me to feel alive again.

I walked back to the office full of my own life, my own pleasure, but overcome by the most sickening anguish. What would my daughter think if she were to ever know what I had done? How would Dom ever react if he found out? Sole custody, seeing the baby only in the tiniest of supervised doses. He could do that, if he wanted to and if he found out what I had done, perhaps he would. I also had to worry about how to keep coming up with excuses as to why I couldn't see Gabriel in the evening. I was glad for that day at least, I had something I could tell him that was in part true.

'I'm babysitting for a good friend tonight. He's a widower. It's his first attempt at getting out there since his wife died.'

Only, even this turned out to be another falsehood.

Because we didn't know how late I'd be home, depending on how well Ol's first date went, and the fact Patience was going to be out with her *Propagators,* Dom planned to take the baby over to Patience's place for the night. This way, he could work and there would be no danger of me disturbing the baby, who had been extra hard to settle these past few nights due to her teething. I think Dom also wanted to make it clear to Ol that now he was finally 'getting out there' there was no reason not to make the most of it.

'I made you a care package,' Dom announced just before he left for his mother's. He reached into the fridge and retrieved a small straw hamper that would have taken up an entire deep shelf and a bottle of Amarone. He placed both on the kitchen island with an expectant look about him.

'What's this?' I asked.

'Oh, just a few treats to say thank you for letting my bro get back on the horse without having to worry about Cora. I don't know if you've noticed, he can be a tad protective, a little paranoid about other people taking care of her.'

'No, not really,' I lied because when I thought about it, there have been times, a few times, when Dom had offered to look after Cora and Ol had come up with some excuse. Was it because Ol worried Dom would be better than him at caring for Cora, as well as everything else he shined at? If so, did that make me the relative least likely to outshine him on the care-giving front? My mind boggled while I turned my attention to Dom's package for me. 'A few treats?' I said, picking up the box, heavy with whatever was in there. 'There must be enough to feed a family of four in here.'

For a second Dom appeared crushed, then I saw a flash of

anger, which he blinked away. 'I was trying to make sure you had something you like, something that perhaps might prevent you from wasting away. I'm struggling to understand why I'm paying for my wife to be rendered down to nothing.' I must have looked startled at his outburst. He flicked his internal switch once again and set his mouth into a smile and shrugged. 'But hey, what do I know about what's fashionable for women these days?' He paused for a moment. I waited for him to speak again. 'I guess you get your fill of sweet things at Pret with Sal.'

'I'm sure whatever you've got me is better than anything you can get in there,' I said, opening the box, hoping he didn't see the lies written all over my face. 'Oh wow. Salted caramel cookies,' I said. 'What else?' I riffled through the indulgent hamper, its boxes of truffles, wrapped cheese and other fattening foodstuffs.

'Did you go there today?' Dom asked.

'Go where?'

'Pret.'

'Yep.'

'It's the one right by your office, isn't it?'

'Yes,' I said, peering at him with what I hoped looked like the natural confusion of an innocent person. 'Why?'

'No reason,' Dom said, but his eyes appeared to shine with purpose, one I did not like at all. 'Let me give you a lift to Ol's.'

'Oh, I'm not quite ready yet. I was going to walk.'

'But you're going to be overloaded, aren't you, if you take both laptops, work and your own, and all your goodies in the hamper and everything else – it's too much. I'll give you a lift.'

'No, as in, no, I'm leaving my laptop here.' I eyed my personal laptop, at that moment, sitting on a low shelf in the living room. I had wanted to spend the evening back-filling my diary, but now, I'd have to leave it there. 'And you know me, I pack light. I can manage, honestly.'

'And you're going straight there?'

'Where else?'

Dom waited for a second, then said, 'Nowhere. With no one. You're leaving shortly?'

I looked at the clock on the kitchen wall. 'In about five minutes.'

Dom came around to my side of the island, slipped his arms around me and brought me to him for a kiss that shocked me with its intensity and force.

'I'm going to miss you,' Dom said.

'It's only for a night.' I gave him a quick peck before escaping his grasp to go towards the baby, planning to pick her up from her playmat and give her a goodbye cuddle.

'Best not do that, Elle. We don't want her getting unsettled before she has to leave you.'

Dom went to her and picked her up himself.

'See you,' he said, turning and leaving with their overnight bags without any further ceremony.

'Goodbye, darling,' I said to the back of Dom and Agatha, disappearing into the hall. 'Love you,' I said quietly to my daughter as the front door closed.

It felt strange to be alone in the house, something that never usually happened. I expected I might have relished such moments of solitude, like I used to back in my house share when everyone was out and I could have one of my sessions languishing in the upstairs bathroom, but it didn't arrive. I realised this house would always be my husband's; I'd always felt as though I was somehow borrowing my space here. It could have been because he'd bought the place before I knew him and it's only in his name. Or maybe it was because deep down, I'd only really wanted Dom's occupation of *me* to be borrowed, temporary. I left the place as quickly as I could. When I was far away enough from the house and there would be less chance of discovery, I tipped the contents of Dom's 'care package' into a litter bin, though I retained the Amarone.

Ol had requested my babysitting services on Monday night, via Dom, perhaps a little embarrassed about the date, and maybe not wanting to ask Patience in case she proved over-interested. I really wished I'd been able to take my personal laptop with me, so I could record and darkly marvel at the journey my life had been dragged into those past thirteen days, but, as I walked over to Ol's, I began to wonder if my misadventures actually began the night I met Dom.

It happened at yet another leaving do for a housemate, one of the girls I'd grown quite close to, bonding over stalled careers and bad dates. But Tanya had turned it around; her lucky day had come. She'd left her law firm to work for its rival at a much higher salary and in an elevated position; around the same time, she and her boyfriend, who also worked at her old firm, had got serious. Leaving her old job meant she could move in with him, and that meant I was required to watch yet another person, another woman in her thirties, leave the house share to start her future.

To say farewell, Tanya had planned a night out with me, some of the other friendly housemates, her colleagues and mates at a pub in her new neighbourhood. It was farther out than we'd normally go, on the outer reaches of Zone 3. I treated it, I suppose looking back, as a bit of a joke: a night out in the 'burbs. The drinkers in the pub, in a smart area of low-density housing and Teslas, were different from the young professionals at our usual haunts in town. When we got there around six, there were tables of young couples, bumps and babies everywhere. The place seemed to have put people around my age in some kind of time shift; only, while everyone around me was moving through time, I was stuck and had no obvious means of moving forward. I wasn't in an out-and-out crisis, I wasn't rebounding from a bad break-up, though I was smarting from the promotion of Anton over me at work, but I wasn't desperately searching for love or anyone to rescue me. My life was merely suggesting it was perhaps time to do something different, though with a series of whimpers, not traumatically loud bangs.

But it was that night that the reality of my slow progress first properly struck me. Then, as though it might show that I was at least free to do whatever I liked in my responsibility-free existence, I soaked myself in drink. I got far drunker than Tanya or any of her friends. When closing time began to approach, I'd hit a boozy sort of mawkishness. I observed couples like Tanya and her man and thought of the young families behind the doors of the neat terraces lining the streets around the pub, and then of

232

my room at the top of the house share; perfect for the twenty-odd-year-old I was when I moved in, but probably becoming increasingly sad for a woman heading into her mid-thirties and in career stasis too. Most people in my party had left except for a few stragglers, and by then, I think I was well into the self-pitying stage of drunkenness as I prepared myself for the schlep back to the shared house and another weekend where I pondered how my pool of single friends was becoming vanishingly small, and how my immediate career prospects were thinning too. I distinctly remember trying to coach myself up off my seat and out of my torpor. That coming Monday, I told myself, I would resign, get away from my new 'boss' Anton, convert my reputation and the award I'd won into the next step up the ladder, earn enough to rent a place of my own, be the housemate to whom the others were required to say goodbye. Yes, I thought, taking a sip from the glass of water Tanya had brought for me, I would get myself home, and get myself together.

'Come on,' I said to myself, taking a deep, drunk breath. 'You've got this.'

'What have you got?'

A man. Behind me. Perhaps he had been watching me for some time from where he sat, alone just a couple of metres away. I turned. It immediately seemed to me he wasn't my usual type, though it also struck me, thinking back, that I didn't really think I had a type until I saw this man. No, he was not my usual kind of guy, but he was striking, and big, even as he sat. When he took something of my breath away as he stood up to reveal his full height, I had liked to tell myself it was the stirring of something special at first sight. In fact, it was what it was: he was an unambiguously, unusually tall man, and all his attention was focused on me. And when my stomach clenched as he approached, I'd taken to telling myself it was excitement at the prospect of this fine, well-dressed man coming over to me, coming down, it seemed to me back then, to my level. But I wonder, at the sight of all of him, set on coming towards me, occupying the space right next to me, too close, too presumptuous over the idea I would immediately accommodate his presence, was that anxious feeling something else? A warning, a sense of fear, perhaps, that I was drunk, miles from home and hemmed into my seat by a man who could easily overpower me if he wanted to. I recalled some other detail, in the cold light of the current state of my life: I put my fingers around the stem of the last glass of wine I intended to drink in that pub, and I pulled it closer to me. I had a notion I should be careful; a man like him might spike my drink.

'May I ask who you are?' he said.

It was such a deceptively simple opening gambit.

'I'm Elle. I'm with my friends.' I gestured somewhere but could not see anyone I knew in the smattering of bodies clinging to the bar or to each other. 'They were here a minute ago. I should catchup.' I cursed myself for slurring 'should', 'catch' and 'up' together and straightened my posture in my seat. Soon after, Dom retold that moment to me as I was doing my best to impress him, to not betray how pissed I was, but that's not what it was. I wanted to show him I was not weak, that I was not a soft target for whatever he had in mind. How wrong I proved myself.

'That's not it,' he said, narrowing his eyes, which I have told myself I could not meet because they were so entrancingly and startlingly blue. Looking back, in reality, the full beam of Dom's intensity made me uncomfortable. His eyes left me unsettled, not intrigued, not aroused.

'Who are you? I'd really like to know,' he asked.

And I suppose he said it kindly or sincerely enough that I stopped feeling quite so intimidated. Perhaps there was something else too; Dom was alone, like me, but I did wonder whether he might have been solo the entire evening. I think a part of me felt sorry for him.

'Who am I?' I said. 'I'm a nearly thirty-four-year-old copywriter for a charity. I'm kind of doing alright, I think, I don't know. Could do better. I had a three, no, two-and-half-star childhood, one sibling, my half-brother. Him, my mum, stepdad, they're alright, I guess. Could be better, could be a lot worse. No lasting psychological damage, not as far as I can tell yet. Yeah, that's probably the top bullets on the first slide.'

Dom waited a moment and did not speak. He seemed to monitor my face as though trying to assess everything that sat behind every word I had said. I felt as though I was being sized up, measured for something. It was extremely intense, so I did what I always do when I want to please the other person, make them like me, change their opinion of me for the better; I smiled. He grinned back at me before releasing a great guffaw into the echoing murmur of the pub. It too was unsettling. I think I was a bit embarrassed; perhaps he saw, because then he said: 'I have to go.' And the sudden withdrawal of his interest, his solidity in a night that had only served to show how flimsy my adult life was becoming, caused a bloom of minor sadness in my chest, which, again, Dom must have seen on my drunken, uncareful expression.

'Unless you want me to stay, unless you might want to know who I am too?' He offered me his huge palm and I took it. He squeezed my hand firmly, but stayed just below the threshold that would make someone afraid of getting hurt. 'I'm Dom.'

'So, Dom,' I said, 'who *are* you?'

We had another drink, then another, and I did not especially like how he kissed, and when he tried to make me laugh, I had to pretend I found him far funnier than he was, but I liked the glimpses of vulnerability I could see peeking from under his impressive exterior, and I liked how much he seemed to like me. It was this, more than any wine or spirit I drank, that was by far and away the most intoxicating thing I'd encountered all night.

The second bell had gone in the pub; the landlord was ordering us remainders to sling our hooks and go home. I was undecided whether I should go on somewhere else with Dom, though I was pretty tired by this point and the drag home seemed almost impossibly challenging on at least two night buses, or a prohibitively expensive Uber. Dom was returning from the bathroom. It was time to make up my mind. As he crossed the pub, a very slim, attractive young woman seemed to spring out from nowhere. She grabbed Dom's hand as he passed, pulled her back to him. She'd managed to position herself in front of him, and she rested her hands on the width of his chest. I felt immediately possessive over him at the spectacle. So, when he told her, 'I'm so sorry, I'm spoken for,' as he looked over at me with those Baltic eyes, I thought to myself: *Yes. OK. Yes.*

236

I went back to his house, the house I live in now, which was around the corner from the pub. And although he didn't set me alight in bed, I'm somewhat ashamed to say the package of him – his home, his success, yes, but more than this, how he bombed me with compliments, with a level of attention and interest that felt like love and made me feel exceptional in ways I had never experienced before in any relationship, won me over. It was this that made me imagine he could be more than the sum of his parts, that, perhaps he could be everything, if I could let us.

'Elle, it's you. You're perfect,' he told me, not even a year after we'd first met. 'Would you like to be married to me?' He held out a huge ring with a ridiculous diamond on it. It looked like something I would never wear.

'OK.'

'*OK?* Only OK?!' And there was that wounded, boyish expression I had come to know.

'No, I mean, yes. Yes please, *of course*. Thank you. Yes.'

I approached Ol's door, thinking back to that time, before my thoughts turned to what Ol and Flic's early courtship would have looked like. I imagined not the minibreaks at designer hotels in the Cotswolds, Paris, Seville and New York that Dom had organised in our first year, nor the endless extravagant bouquets and jewellery that I never asked for and always felt uncomfortable accepting. Instead, I imagined humble gestures, shared interests, *real* passion between two matched souls, paired bodies. I felt a pang of jealousy that Ol had that with Flic, and that he might, perhaps, begin to discover something like that again from that evening onwards. He's the sort of person who could and should

237

find another proud and robust love, one fit to withstand both external and, crucially, internal scrutiny.

I texted Ol to say I was outside his house, not wanting to ring the doorbell so as to disturb Cora. 'Hi,' I whispered when he opened the door. I could tell immediately he was out of sorts.

'Hey, Elle. Come inside.' He immediately turned away from me to walk into the house.

'You all set for tonight?' I asked.

Ol said nothing, only moved slowly to the living room at the front of his cosy, homely house, evidence of Flic on every wall, every surface, each and every corner. Of course, he wasn't *all set*. I cursed my lack of sensitivity as I took a seat in the armchair next to the sofa, where Ol had sat. He was wearing the sort of cargo pants he tended to wear when he was gardening, and a loose-fitting T-shirt that revealed a pale patch of chest below his tanned neckline. He didn't look as though he was going anywhere.

'You doing alright there, Ol?' I asked as gently as I could.

'It's been a strange week.'

I nodded, inviting him to say more, if that's what he wanted. His family might shut him down if he wanted to speak of Flic, their time together, how he wasn't ready to stuff his memories into the dark corners of their lives and move on without looking back, but I wouldn't do that.

'That difficult client I mentioned to you at Mum's, well, we're still having issues with him. So, I suggested I come in for a meeting to sort things out on Monday.'

'Oh yes.' I was surprised Ol's woes stemmed from his client and not his ten-year anniversary, or the threat of dating again he seemed unable to see through, but I was happy to give him space for a work moan. 'How did it go?' Judging by how downcast Ol looked, I imagined it must have been a dreadful meeting, something I'd had my fair share of recently. Perhaps we might compare notes.

'Their offices,' Ol said, concentrating on the floor between his knees, and his hands, which at this point, he was mashing together. 'I hadn't been there before.' Ol now sent his attention out of the front window of his living room, as though he could find whatever it was he needed to make him less uncomfortable outside. Then, he seemed to force himself to look at me. And that's when I began to understand there was no date; I was not there to babysit.

'His offices, Elle. I think you might know where they are. They're near the Southbank, by some disused railway arches.'

Chapter Twenty-Four

Day twenty-one, Saturday

The police officer on the scene in my hotel room, Thea, Flic's maid of honour, has just asked whether Dom has hurt me. My thoughts, which were already heading towards overload when I woke to see a dead man in my bed, then plunged into even darker chaos when Dom assaulted me, are now spinning out of control. How does Thea understand Dom's true nature? How did she ever come to be here, asking me questions I don't know how to answer? I feel as though my mind might explode.

If Dom has harmed me, raped me, it means I would have refused to consent. But I did consent, didn't I? When I asked him to help me make it look as though Anton harmed me, I told him yes. He warned me it was going to be rough; I shouldn't have been so shocked. But I feel spoilt. I feel pain everywhere and nowhere; I am both raw and numb. I can't find the words to say he didn't, but I don't know what happens to me next, in the following few moments, few days, weeks, and the rest of my life if I say my husband has hurt me. It all falls apart, my story that Anton harmed me, and that I acted violently in self-defence and if this version of events collapses, my chance to be with my baby again does too.

Thea is waiting for my answer. I realise I haven't said anything yet, though I can feel my mouth moving silently.

'It's OK. You take a moment. There's something I want to check.'

Thea scans about the room, peering at various shelves and surfaces, before zeroing in on the vase of dried flowers Dom had paused at earlier. Thea dips down to get a closer look. She extracts a clear plastic evidence bag from her pocket and plucks from the vase a dark, dried poppy, then tips the stem headfirst into the bag. Something small and black falls out, which Thea captures. She returns to me, holding it up ahead of her so I can see it.

'I don't know what that is.'

'A spy camera. I suspect these will be all over your house, in vases, air fresheners, digital devices, clocks.'

I gasp, then find the breath to speak. 'Just as he was about to leave, he wanted to come back into the room and check something without me seeing, while I was facing the door.'

Thea nods. 'And is that your handbag there?' She points to it, on the floor in the corner of the room.

'Yes,' I whisper. Thea drops the evidence bag with the spy camera in it onto the bedside table nearest to us, goes to my bag, feels along the sides, pinches the corners, finds what she was looking for and brings it to show me.

'It's an AirTag.' Thea holds out the outline of a small object somewhere between the cavity of the bag and the lining. 'Tracks your movements.'

241

'Dom,' I say and Thea nods almost apologetically, as if she is somehow to blame.

'Can you start by telling me your name?'

'Elle.'

'And can you tell me what you think's happened here tonight, Elle?'

'I . . . I really don't know.'

'It's OK. Perhaps you can tell me what you *do* know.'

Thea is momentarily distracted. Her fingers go to her camera, attached to her high-visibility jacket. She peers down at it, her fingers hovering near a button.

'I forgot to switch it on,' she says carefully. 'It was the shock of seeing him, seeing this,' she adds with greater certainty, gesturing at Anton's body under his red-white shroud. Then, she closes her eyes and takes a deep breath. She does not switch on her body-worn camera. She opens her eyes but addresses the floor, not me. 'I've never dealt with a murder. And facing *him* again after all this time. Anyone could appreciate why there might be some deviations from protocol. I'm pretty sure my supervisor would understand.' The latter part of this she says almost to herself.

'*Deviations.*' I croak. 'What are you talking about?'

'Sorry.' Thea scrunches up her eyes. 'Let me try again.' She breathes and then speaks with her eyes still closed once more, half to herself, half to me. 'I think I might have been brought here for a reason tonight.'

Brought here by what? By fate? By God? Who else? 'Did the night manager call you?'

Thea shakes her head. 'The police received a tip-off. The

242

caller didn't leave their number but said someone was in grave danger in this hotel. I found myself drawn to the area around the same time,' Thea says mysteriously. But what I need now is clarity.

'Am I . . .' I swallow. I can't say the words, but I need to know my fate. 'Are you going to arrest me?'

Thea eyes are wide open now. 'You're not the danger, Elle, but you are in danger.'

'In danger of going to jail?'

She moves to hold my hand, then stops herself, recalibrates to her more professional persona. She knows, I think, she needs to remain in control of her own emotions, in control of the situation.

'Elle, in your own words, please can you tell me what you understand of what's happened to you here?'

I hesitate. Where does it all begin?

'How about you start with last night,' Thea urges, reading my mind.

'Yes, OK.' I take a long breath. 'Well, I was at a work do; my friend Sal booked this room for us, but she went home. I . . . There's a colleague, a man, I've been getting close to him and I . . . I did want to be with him, but when I woke up, I couldn't remember coming here and it was my boss in my bed, not the man I've been . . . and there was blood, and he was obviously dead and I have . . . I just don't remember anything at all really and the window was open but the room was locked and he's been cut open with a smashed wine bottle and, the thing is, I did . . . I'm sorry to say that I thought I hated this person but I didn't want him to be harmed, not really, not like this. Anyway,

243

I've been trying to find out what happened, working out if it could have been me who did it. And then I called Dom, my husband, and . . . and he came right here and then he . . . then he . . .'

I can't speak anymore.

'And then, your husband came here to save you from all of it?'

'Yes.'

'And what did he say; what did he do when he got here?'

'He said that it didn't look like I'd been . . . I did wonder whether Anton had hurt me, you see, but Dom said it didn't look as though he had . . .' And when I say all of this out loud I feel utterly pathetic. How did it happen that Dom worked it so I don't trust my own body, my own mind? How have I let it get to this? 'And . . .' I whisper '. . . and he said he'd help me so it *would* look as though I had been attacked, so, I don't know, really, so it would look as though I'd only killed him in self-defence. So, I let him . . . I agreed *he* could hurt me.' I shake my head at myself and when I look at Thea, she is doing the same.

'Elle, listen to me. None of this was your fault.'

'How do you know that?'

Thea takes a moment. 'Tell me, did he seem quite prepared for what he found? Did he appear to know what to do when he saw what had happened?'

'Yes, yes, he did, but that's just what he's like, who he is.'

'*Who he is*,' Thea repeats. 'What have you learnt tonight about who he is? Tell me.'

'He's . . .' I think about it, try to locate the truth amongst all the confusion, the blur not only of tonight, but the last three

244

years of my life with him. 'He's a man who's been watching me when I didn't know. He's someone who's been tracking me when I wasn't with him. And that's not all,' I say, and it feels as though I am waking up from a very long sleep. 'He's been tracking my food, my periods, making it so I didn't want to see my family, couldn't see my friends anymore. He's made me feel as though if I didn't have him, I'd have nothing. *Be* nothing.'

Thea nods, but does not speak.

'He is a man who's made me doubt everything about myself, including whether . . .' I know I need to say this '. . . whether I've been raped . . .' Thea nods once, knows there's more I can say. 'Whether I've committed murder.'

'Yes, Elle. Yes.' Thea's smile speaks of pride and pain in equal measure. I am so grateful, so relieved to speak and be heard, to be seen as innocent of the situation I seemed to have no one else to blame for but myself. I would like to break down, disintegrate before this woman, my true saviour. But that's not what gets me back to my daughter.

'What happens now? What do I do? I need to get back to my daughter.'

Thea appears momentarily winded. Then, she resets. 'I understand.'

'Dom's tried to make me think I'm not capable of looking after her, but I am. I'm the only one who can keep her safe.'

Thea looks to be thinking for moment. 'Elle, may I ask you, would I be right in thinking your pregnancy with him was unexpected?'

'Yes. It was a total shock. I wasn't ready, but I love my daughter, I do.' And it feels so pure and sacred to say this, I do not want to wait a second more until I hold her again. My baby, my Agatha. 'Wait, how did you know my pregnancy was unexpected?'

'We'll get to that, I promise, but first, I want you to know it's OK, Elle. It's going to be OK now, alright? If we work together, you'll get back to your baby and he won't be able to harm you, or your daughter, or anybody else.'

'How? I don't see how we can do that.'

Thea nods, seems to be readying herself to tell me something on which everything depends. 'I'm going to have to switch on my body cam and my back–up's going to get here soon. They'll be sending a uniformed officer, someone with much more experience than me, but before all of that happens, I want to tell you some things that you can't forget and you can't tell anyone about. If you do, you and I could both find ourselves in trouble neither of us deserve.'

'OK.'

'I'm going to tell you some things, things that later on you are going to have to pretend that you don't know, including us having this conversation or having any influence over what happens next. I want to do this to because I'm worried if I *don't* help you as much as I can, you will be failed by a system that isn't designed to protect women. In my experience, we can only rely on each other for that.'

My mind goes back to the many case studies at work I've written up, women for whom our advisers had tried to get secure housing when they desperately needed it because of the dangers of men. I recall the women pestered by landlords for sex instead of rent, and the many women raped by their partner-perpetrators. And I remember the lawyer I interviewed who told me how single-digit conviction rates for reported rapes meant a de facto decriminalisation. I remember the women who were slaughtered. Their escapes did not come soon enough, but conversely, their husbands' and partners' often arrived far too rapidly. How many killers of women did I learn were living free after their foreshortened, caveated sentences, tempered by manslaughter and 'diminished responsibility' when their intent to kill was pure, and the responsibility entirely theirs?

'OK. I understand.'

'OK?'

'Yes. Please, tell me what we need to do.'

Thea takes a deep breath. I am not the only one facing their reckoning here tonight. 'Dominic Graham is my ex-fiancé. He caused me significant harm.'

'He did?'

My shock is clear. This strong, beautiful, vivacious woman, someone with a background apparently in medicine and law enforcement, is a victim too? She was engaged to Dom, had received Patience's apparent seal of approval. And yet, she was somehow just like me.

'He did, Elle. And I fought back. I brought charges against him, but I couldn't get the case to court in order to convict him.' Thea pauses at the pain of the memory, swallows before continuing. 'I believe you've been harmed by him too.'

'I have.'

'And that you're scared.'

'I am.'

'And that's why I would like to help you. Because I don't want you or any other woman to suffer as you and I have. So, do you think you'd like to do that, together?'

'Yes. Yes please.'

'I need to make you aware, if we're going to get the right outcome, we're going to need to work together. That's because I believe that man –' Thea glances towards the bathroom door once '– killed the man in that bed and is setting you up to take the blame.'

'But Thea, *Constable*,' I stumble. 'I need to tell you, before you do anything else, whoever investigates this, me, will find evidence I hated the man who's dead. He's my boss. There's evidence I wanted him to suffer; wanted him dead.'

'It's OK, Elle. Let's stay focused on Dom, if that's OK? Would he have any reason to believe you had plans to leave the relationship?'

'He would. I've been . . . I suppose you could say I've been having an affair.'

'I believe Dom would have known. I believe he's been monitoring you very closely. Knowing about your other relationship, that you weren't completely committed to him is what's made him even more controlling than usual, and it's made you more vulnerable than ever. That's why he's done what he's done.' Thea scans the room as she speaks. She seems to be rehearsing something in her mind as she does. 'OK, what we need to do now is make sure there's nothing in this room, nothing

248

significant that could put a shred of doubt in anyone's mind that he wasn't the one who did this. We want the right person to be punished here, not you, not your baby.'

'Thea?'

'Yes, Elle?'

'What you're talking about – is it . . . will we breaking the law?'

Thea pauses. 'Is what we're about to do legal?' she whispers, 'No. But I'm not so interested in the law as I am in justice. Elle, you can say no, ask me to stop and we'll sit tight and wait for my colleague to take over.'

I take a moment to really think about it. If I let Thea take control now, I may breach yet another point of no return. So, it comes down to this, who or what do I trust more: a criminal justice system that I've seen fail women every day, or a single, brave woman who's willing to put herself at considerable risk to protect me?

'If you are sure you're comfortable in us making our own justice, I want to help us do that.' I think of the potential footage on the camera – perhaps the truth about what happened to Anton, how and who killed him, but also of me being assaulted by him, or maybe not, depending on what the police or a judge and jury would be inclined to believe; followed by what Dom did to me. I can't have that played in court. I know how high the chances are I will be judged, perhaps more so than the men who did what they did to me.

'Thea, the camera. There will be footage of the murder, but also of me having sex with my boss and my husband. I don't know what it will look like. I don't know if anyone will believe me if I say I didn't want either to happen. But I didn't, not with my boss, not with my husband.'

'OK. OK.' Thea seems to understand immediately and then appears to start coaching herself again. 'The CPS, a jury, they won't need to see the footage to know who really killed your boss.' I'm not sure whether she's convincing herself or asking me.

'I don't know, will they? It could show what actually happened here tonight to Anton, as well as what happened to me.'

'But we know what really happened, don't we? You don't need to be violated all over again by having the police and a jury see that.'

'What if anyone finds out? Isn't that *destroying evidence*?'

Thea is undeterred. 'Patience will know how to do it properly.'

'Patience?' I whisper her name even more quietly than everything else I've said to Thea so far. 'I really don't—'

'Sorry, Elle, we're running out of time. Do you know what Dom used to kill the deceased?'

'Anton,' I say. 'The deceased. He's called Anton Bloch.'

Thea nods as though indulging me. 'Elle. Did Dom tell you how he'd killed Anton?'

It's extraordinary to hear Thea say it with such certainty. To hear my innocence being spoken of so emphatically, and by someone in some kind of authority, makes me feel more emotional than any of the horrific things that have happened to me since discovering Anton dead next to me. I have to embrace this certainty to get back to Agatha.

'He found a broken wine bottle under the bed, discovered

where it'd been smashed in the bathroom, but it wasn't like he acted like he knew it was there, I don't think. That's just Dom.'

'And the broken wine bottle, have you touched it?'

'I don't know. It's possible, last night, maybe.'

'You don't remember.'

'I don't. I didn't drink very much, I just . . .'

'Elle, it's quite possible he drugged you. He may have drugged the man he killed too, to make it easier for him to do what he did. It would not be the first time he's done this.'

'Dom drugged you?'

Thea shakes her head. 'You know about Flic? How she died?'

'She died very soon after being diagnosed with breast cancer. That's what I was told.'

'And you've been told who was one of the main people caring for her?'

My mouth has become very dry. 'Dom?'

'He killed Flic. I know he did. She was gravely ill, but she would have had more time with Cora if it hadn't had been for Dom.'

'How?' I drop my head in my hands.

'With GHB, gamma hydroxybutyrate, the same thing he's used to drug you, most likely, but it's fatal in the right dose. Fatal and hard to detect. I know he'd previously bought some, he may have been thinking about using it on me after . . . when . . .' Thea shakes the memory away. 'Anyway, he was on his own with Flic just before she died.'

'But why?'

'If you asked him, he'd probably say it was best for Ol if Flic didn't linger on as ill as she was, better for her. But the truth is,

251

it was about power and getting back at Flic because she wanted him out of their lives when she found out what he was really like after what he'd done to me. Ol, of course, wouldn't hear anything about how his heroic little brother might have decided the hour of his wife's death, but he knew, he *knows*, deep in his bones, he knows who his brother really is.'

'And Patience?'

'She knows what her son is like, but she's used to dancing a fine line with men like him.'

We both let the horror of all Thea has just said to seep into a short-lived silence. Thea is clearly on a mission, one that started long before me.

'Elle, if Dom drugged you and your colleague and killed him, I'm guessing he would have also associated you with the murder weapon when you were unconscious.'

'Oh god. If he has, then I'm going to prison; that's it, surely?'

'Even if your fingerprints are on that bottle, even if he put you right next to Anton when he killed him, it shouldn't be enough to introduce reasonable doubt that Dom *wasn't* the person who killed Anton.' A crackle on Thea's radio, then a voice advising more police are minutes away. Thea removes the camera from the evidence bag and gives it to me. 'Destroy this, destroy the footage.'

'But won't Dom tell the police about it anyway?'

'It will incriminate him, won't it?'

'Yes, of course,' I say. I don't want Thea to have any doubts in me, in our story. If she wavers now, there's a future for Agatha without me in it.

'That footage will prove to the police he's a rapist as well as a murderer, and the fact he put the camera there in the first place, the fact he was so insecure about not being able to keep his wife in love with him, under his control, that he felt he had to spy on her. I know Dom, so do you, his pathetic insecurity . . .'

'The humiliation. He wouldn't be able to live with it,' I say, and the idea I can use his debilitating need for total control against him is momentarily thrilling.

'He won't mention the camera if you don't. So, Elle, do you understand what you have to do?'

'I do.'

'Tell me.'

'I need to destroy the camera.'

Thea nods.

'I need to destroy the footage.'

'Go on.'

'I need to destroy my husband.'

Thea's eyes glisten with an electric emotion, a specific strength she's inviting me to share. I can't let myself think about how much of a risk she's taking. I only know that I am deeply grateful, and though she will never realise it, my daughter will be too.

Thea gestures to the spy camera. 'If you want my advice, don't watch what's on there. Don't watch anything of whatever he's got of you, not from tonight, not whatever he has of you from his house. You won't be able to unsee it. You can free yourself from that. You have a choice now.'

'I do.'

'I won't be able to speak to you again for a while, I can't jeopardise your case, but when this is all over, we will talk. Elle?'

'Yes?'

'You've got this.'

Thea stands to her full height, finally switches on her body-worn camera, takes a single long breath, walks to the bathroom and opens the door. I shove the spy camera into my handbag before Dom can see me doing so.

'Dominic Graham, I am arresting you on suspicion of the murder of Anton Bloch and the rape of Elle Graham.'

Chapter Twenty-Five

Day thirteen, Friday

Ol had just all but confirmed he'd seen me with Gabriel; witnessed me being intimate with someone who wasn't his brother.

'Ol, I . . .' My mind scrambled around for anything that didn't make me sound utterly squalid.

'You don't have to say anything.'

'We haven't . . . It's not serious but I'll stop; I'll leave my job,' I rushed.

'I'm not going to tell you what to do. Whatever you decide next is up to you,' Ol said gently. He he still couldn't look at me.

'I don't understand.'

Ol sighed, finally found it in him to view me directly. 'I don't want to know the details and I won't tell Dom about what I saw, or about this conversation.'

'OK, thank you, Ol.' I let my racing thoughts sink in a second. 'So, why bring me here tonight?'

'So, I could tell you to be careful, I suppose.'

I remained dumbstruck. 'I don't—'

'My brother, he's strong, isn't he?' Ol continued. 'He's cut

255

from the same cloth as Pa, which means he . . .' Ol took a deep breath in and exhaled the next thing he said. 'I recognise it might not always be easy for you. Because, well, because he's a lot like Pa.'

'What do you mean, Ol?'

Ol waited for a beat as though he needed to arrange his next words carefully. 'Like Pa, Dom has very high expectations of people and, well, I'm pretty sure I know how challenging that can be.' Ol winced. How he felt about himself, falling short of the kinds of men he thought Hugo and Dom were, as well as imagining my life with Dom and how that might drive me towards infidelity, all of it seemed to physically pain him. 'You should go now, Elle. We don't need to talk about any of this again. You can tell Dom I got cold feet about going out tonight because I found out something I didn't like about my date and thought better of it. He'll understand that. He knows how much I loved Flic. Somewhere he knows I'll never be able to move on, *shouldn't* ever move on. He really did love her like a sister,' Ol said the last statement to me, before frowning and speaking again, this time, as though trying to convince some invisible jury. 'He honestly did.' Ol focused on me once more. 'That's all I wanted to say.'

'OK.' I left my seat, steadying myself as I rose. 'Thank you again. I don't know what to say, only that I'll do the right thing by your brother, and I'm so sorry to have put you in this position.' I was about to leave the room when I stopped to say one more thing. 'I realise you're not ready to date anyone yet and you never will or could forget Flic, but I do hope one day in the not-too-distant future you'll find someone who makes you happy. You're a good man, Ol.'

He shook his head. 'Am I, Elle? You really believe that?'

'I do, of course. You're a great dad. And you've always been so good to me. You're being too good to me now.'

Ol grimaced and gave another faint shake of his head. 'I'm sure there's people who think I could be a whole lot better.' He paused for a moment before speaking again. 'Elle, I know he's no saint, but in his heart, Dom only wants the best; for me, for you, for all of us.' Ol turned his gaze once more to the window. 'I'll always be thankful for that.'

'I'll try to be the wife he deserves from now on.'

Ol nodded and gave a short, grateful sort of laugh. But as I turned to leave, I could see he was crying.

I walked to Patience's house, clutching my bottle of Amarone. I didn't call Dom to tell him the change of plan; my heart was speeding, my head ablaze with guilt, shame and fear. I didn't know how I would sound normal, even on a message.

Could I really trust Ol to keep my secret? I didn't understand why he'd do that. In the immediacy, I was also worried, as I wandered down Patience's road, if Dom would buy my story about what had happened to the food hamper he'd prepared for me. I was going to say I'd come across someone homeless and offered it to them. Giving people food or money if they seemed to need it was exactly the sort of thing I did, or I used to, until Dom made his dissatisfaction known. 'You know they'll only spend your money on drugs or alcohol,' he would say. 'And who could blame them if they did?' I might have replied, until I didn't, until I started doing not necessarily what I was told, but what I knew would not displease him.

I let myself into Patience's home, preparing to face my husband and pretend I hadn't arrived from his brother's house having been called out by him for my grubby workplace affair. Perhaps I could tell him I was serious about resigning from my job. Then, I thought maybe it really was time to go through with it, commit properly to being the baby's mum, dedicate my life to keeping her safe, discovering how to make her happy, learning how to make her into everything I was not and would never be. I gripped the neck of the bottle of my wine more tightly; I couldn't wait to drink a large glass very quickly.

When I entered the dark hall, I didn't call out. If the baby was still settling, the sound of my voice might have disturbed her. Instead, I headed up the stairs to Dom's office-bedroom where I knew he'd be working. When I reached the top of the stairs, I could hear something.

A woman.

A raised voice, speaking inaudible words.

Realising I still had the neck of the bottle in my hand, I found I was now holding it upside down, like a club.

I approached Dom's attic room door, bewildered and afraid of what I would see when I opened it. Damp, muffled sounds close to the other side of the door. The woman sounded as though she was sat at Dom's desk. My pulse thumped in my ears. I did not feel like knocking. I wanted to see whatever was happening without filter. I pushed the door open.

She was sat, red-faced, dishevelled and barefoot, on the office chair, which was pushed away from Dom's desk. He was not there. I had absolutely no idea what I had walked into.

'Sal?'

She gasped when she saw me. She went to speak, but her voice cracked in her throat. She swallowed; tried to speak again. I heard a toilet flush in the small shower room attached to the bedroom.

'Elle?'

Dom stood in the doorframe. He looked shocked, but why shouldn't he be? I wasn't supposed to be there.

'Ol wimp out of his date or something?' He spoke with an evenness that may have sounded a little mannered, but I was so confused by this point, I couldn't say if he sounded natural or not.

'No. He found out something he didn't like. What—'

'What's Sal doing here?' Dom went to finish my question, but he hadn't completed it.

What's Sal doing here, in your room with no shoes on? And is the odour in this room the usual mustiness from the overheated top of your mother's old house, or is there something else I can detect in the air?

'Yes. Sal?' I turned to her. 'What are you doing here?' I tried to say it with a laugh in my voice, but it did not come.

'Elle,' she said, then took a deep breath. 'I'm . . . I'm just . . .'

'I'm afraid Sal worked out who the boys' benefactor was. It's made her rather emotional, as you can see.' Dom walked towards where Sal sat and handed her some tissue from his pocket.

'Why didn't you call me?' I asked her.

'She wanted to have a go at me,' Dom said. 'She seemed rather cross with me – nothing new there, right?'

259

'I called him because I wanted to know what his game was. I mean, what is he about? Do you know, Elle? Do you really?' Sal's eyes seemed to shimmer with something: anger? Or perhaps she was feeling something of the humiliation Tim had experienced when he first knew about the boys' fees being covered. Given the spiky history between Sal and Dom, I supposed that made a kind of sense.

'Of course, she knows *what my game is*, old girl.' Dom dropped a palm onto Sal's shoulder from behind and gave it a chummy kind of shake. 'She's my wife.' Dom then left Sal and came to me, slipping his arm around my waist and bringing me to him for an emphatic kiss on the head. I found I did not want to inhale, didn't want my mind to start playing tricks on me over whether I could smell any trace of Sal on him. It wasn't because the idea of my husband betraying me would be devastating, it was the notion of Sal doing so.

'I don't want his money, Elle,' Sal said.

'Oh, come on,' said Dom. 'Why make it harder for yourself, Sally? Besides, it's not mine now, it's the school's; your sons'. It's done now, and there's nothing you can do about it.' Dom grinned like the tom cat who'd got the cream.

'Fuck you, Dom,' Sal said, shoving her feet back into her sliders, which were under the desk by the door. 'Just fuck you.' She pushed past Dom, who looked at first amused by Sal's outburst, then gave me a look to suggest I should say something to her to defend him.

'He was only trying to help!' I improvised in my state of confusion, calling down the stairs as Sal descended.

'Wake up, Elle!' she shouted without stopping or looking back. 'That's not why he does *anything*!'

Sal slammed the front door, and it was either this or the shouting that woke the baby.

'I'll resettle Agatha,' Dom told me as he moved to leave his room. 'I'm so glad you're here, darling. You'll have to tell me more about what's eating Ol.' He moved past me onto the landing before turning to speak again. 'Oh, and I'd really love to know a bit more about how your agency project is shaping up. I'd hate to think it's only me who gets to talk about work. You're clearly determined to make the most of your job so I want to hear all about it. Spare no detail.'

Was this Dom's guilt speaking, redressing how he never asked me how my professional life was going; or was he masking his guilt over whatever had passed between him and Sal before I entered his room? Either way, I didn't want to dance near the frontiers of any conversation that might skirt Gabriel territory.

'Oh, that's no fun,' I said as lightly as I could manage. 'Let's not talk about work at all. I'll open the wine and wait for you downstairs. We can talk about something much more interesting.'

The baby's cries grew louder, but Dom didn't move. He only watched me, his face blank. Another beat.

'Shall I go—' I tried to move ahead of him. By now, I really didn't want him near her.

Dom shook his head, his features apparently placid, but his eyes charged with a horrible intensity. Somewhere deep inside, Dom was raging.

'Don't you worry, darling.' A switch flipped again. My husband beamed at me, as though neither he nor I had any cares. 'You go ahead downstairs and start drinking your wine. I'm sure you're looking forward to it.'

Dom jogged down the stairs to Ol's old room where Patience keeps the ancient cot that Cora, then my baby slept in. 'Calm down, Agatha!' he called. 'Daddy's coming!'

At the sound of her father's voice, the baby seemed to howl.

Day fourteen, Saturday

Sal tried to call me a few times last night and again in the morning, but I ignored her. I didn't want to talk to her with Dom in the vicinity. He seemed to have been watching my every move since the evening at Patience's. In the end, we took ourselves home soon after the baby woke up. We both agreed she'd settle better at home, though, in truth I suspect neither of us wanted to risk Patience seeing the oddness burgeoning between Dom and me. It was as though he was constantly checking for signs of something. I began to wonder if maybe Dom was actually waiting to see if and when my jealousy might surface. But even though, by rights, Dom should have expected to face difficult questions after I'd seen him with Sal alone in his room, that wasn't going to happen. Knowing Ol had seen me with Gabriel meant it was me with loyalty to prove. Who was I to start grilling Dom when I was the one having an affair, one my husband's brother knew about?

In the morning, after I let Dom have sex with me (I cringed

inside the whole time, my mind unable to shut down the images of him and Sal together that kept springing up) I thought of something I hoped might put me on even safer footing than mere silence over seeing my best friend alone with him in what felt like highly suspicious circumstances.

'I'm going to tell Jordan I don't need his services anymore.'

'That's great!' said Dom. 'What made you finally see sense?'

'You.' That was all I had to say. Dom brought me in for another kiss I didn't want. I'd pleased him, but not enough that it stopped Dom from checking I didn't plan to call Sal in the bathroom later that day.

'Why are you taking your phone with you? If it's to call Sal, whatever you want to say to her, you know you can say in front of me.'

'I wasn't planning on calling anyone.'

'OK, but if you did want to speak to Sal, you don't have to do it in secret. I know, obviously, you'll be cutting ties with her now, especially after how she's treated me.'

'I'm not calling Sal,' I said, attempting to kick that particular can down the road.

By the afternoon, I felt caged. Then, I thought my luck had turned when I got a message saying baby swim was cancelled. I'd assumed Dom would leave me to go for his usual workout. The day was wearing on, and outside it had started to rain. I thought maybe while he was gone, I'd try to set up some kind of messy play for the baby, or perhaps hold her arms above her head while she walked the length of the living room and back, practising her walking. All without Dom either trying to stop me on the basis of whatever he probably knew about optimal toddler bone formation, or attempting to micromanage my every move with her.

'You not heading to the gym?' I asked as casually as I could, as I lay on the sofa observing the skin form on a hot chocolate Dom had made me that I hadn't wanted, while also watching the baby bashing her house of flames with her palms. She didn't seem to be finding it amusing anymore. I imagined she felt as captive as her mother.

'Thought I'd give it a miss today.' Dom reached over from his end of the sofa to pat my arse. 'Keep it cosy with you guys.'

At this, my frustration must have temporarily emboldened me. 'Why do you think Sal was so rattled when I opened your bedroom door yesterday?'

Dom barely missed a beat before shrugging. 'She wasn't *rattled*, she was raging. The second I answered the door, she immediately started ranting at me. So, I calmly walked away, headed up to my office, ignoring her until she'd calmed herself down, but she decided to follow me and give me what for.' Dom could tell I wasn't buying it. 'Wait, you don't think something untoward went on between me and Sal, do you?'

'No,' I lied. Though I couldn't really believe Sal would ever want to sleep with Dom, not in my heart, there was still a feeling I couldn't shake. I was out of step with her. Ever since she'd mystified me with her Marriage Rule talk, and perhaps even before that, I'd been getting the feeling she'd been holding things back from me and not just because she thought I might not be listening.

'You do, don't you?' Dom seemed delighted at the idea. 'Do I detect a little jealousy? Honestly, darling, she's not my type. I like my girls with meat on their bones.' He squeezed the butt cheek he'd just patted. It made me shudder. He noticed my reaction but interpreted it not as repulsion but somehow my need to know he desired only me.

'She's not attractive to me in any way whatsoever,' Dom continued, 'you know that, surely. Women like that . . .' Dom made a *yuck* face.

'That's not a kind thing to say.'

'It should make you happy,' Dom said, leaning over on to me, his hand now reaching up and around the back of my neck, a faint pressure.

'It doesn't,' I dared to say. I shook myself free of Dom's hold. 'I'd say it's time I opened some Amarone, let the air get to it before we drink it later.'

'Sounds great, darling,' Dom said, also leaving his seat, him to pick up the baby. From the kitchen, I watched him, putting her on his lap, then reaching for her hand with his mouth, his lips stretched over his teeth. I pulled the cork on my wine, but instead of setting the bottle aside for later, I took a glass, poured a large measure, and drank it.

'You know, your friend's outburst, her total absence of gratitude,' Dom called from the sofa, 'one way of looking at it is that it's come at a rather convenient time.' I let the tight, burning taste of the aged wine sour my cheeks and tongue and said nothing. Neither did I flinch when the acid from the alcohol began to burn my oesophagus. I poured Dom a short measure of wine, while gulping down more of my generous measure.

'I know she's been trying to speak to you. But I don't get

265

why you haven't answered,' Dom continued. 'What are you afraid of?'

'Nothing.' I returned to the sofa with two wine glasses.

Dom reached for my phone, which I'd left on the coffee table next to the abandoned hot chocolate. 'So, call her. Go on.' He held it out for me. 'Go ahead, call her back now.'

I took the phone from him, but only to put it down again on the far side of the table. 'I think she'll probably be watching the boys play rugby somewhere at this time on a Saturday.'

'Or not,' Dom said. 'Go on, call her. Call her while I'm right here to support you ending things.'

'I'm not in the mood right now, Dom.'

'Not in the mood to show your loyalty to me over a work colleague?'

'She's not just a colleague.'

'She's someone you think may have tried to sleep with me.'

'That's not what I said.'

'She's someone more important than me. Unless I'm mistaken?'

'Of course not.'

Dom put the baby back on her playmat next to the sofa and turned to me.

'Have I not done enough for you? Given you enough?' He gestured to the cavernous living space.

'Of course. It's just—'

'And have I not, repeatedly and emphatically, defended you against my mother; taken your side, prioritised you over her? Have I not showed you we're a team above all others, even her?'

'Yes. You have.'

266

'So, why don't I deserve *your* loyalty?' Dom had that familiar look about him, the wounded child. His voice had also edged towards the higher pitch that set my teeth on edge.

'You deserve my loyalty,' I told him, frightened of his reaction if I didn't fall into line. Me being disturbed by his volume and aggression I could handle, but him scaring the baby, if he became as angry as when he'd found out lawyers were scrutinising his supermarket deal, I couldn't tolerate.

'So, make the call.'

I kept my eyes on the baby as I stretched for my phone and dialled Sal's number. She picked up in one ring.

'Look, Elle, I know why you don't want to talk to me, but listen, please can we—'

'Sal. I'm here with Dom.'

'OK,' she said, and I could hear a kind of fear in those two syllables.

'Sal, we can't . . . I can't be your friend anymore. I'm sorry.' I turned to look Dom in the eye.

'And why would that be?' Sal asked me quietly.

'Because you can't speak to my husband the way you did. That's a red line for me.'

Silence.

'Elle, if you had red lines, he jumped over them long before what happened yesterday.' Sal ended the call.

'That wasn't so hard, was it?'

I didn't answer Dom. My mouth was full of wine again. I willed the alcohol into my veins, to deaden my mind so I need not think, into my limbs so I need not feel. I didn't know how I would ever stop drinking, that night and throughout the weekend that followed. And with my cancelled training session followed by the dinner we had scheduled with Ol and Cora, I barely did.

Day fifteen, Sunday

My Sunday dread was off the scale; I couldn't face Sal, or the big meeting at the ad agency that was scheduled for the morning, and I was supposed to be presenting alongside Gabriel. So, I got ahead of myself. In the afternoon, I drafted some final thoughts for Gabriel who'd have to lead on the meeting without me, which I planned to send in the morning, before sending Anton an email telling him I was sick and I didn't expect I'd be able to come in tomorrow. I should have known Anton had nothing better to do on Sunday afternoon than work. Teams must have notified him I was online. He took it upon himself to video call me. I felt duty-bound to answer the call.

'Hi, Anton.'

'Hello, Elle.' Anton's small eyes squinted at me through the screen. He'd clearly just come back from a run, his fine hair flat on a damp skull, still wearing a charity-sponsored electric blue vest, his exposed, pasty shoulders glaring at me. He was, on so many levels, the last thing I wanted to see. 'You look tired, but you don't look that ill. You seemed fine on Friday, so I just thought I'd check in.'

'OK. What did you need to check? That I'm ill enough not to come in?'

Anton tilted his head, as though trying to remain patient with an irksome child. 'It is my responsibility as a senior manager to care for both your wellbeing and also that of our organisation. It needs to be borne in mind that every absence is an expense.'

'Anton, you know I never take time off—'

'I understand that, but to be honest, I'll probably need to let HR know if I think you're planning an absence without a good enough reason.'

To be honest, Anton, everything that comes out of your mouth makes me want to punch you. 'HR? Why? Do I have track record of absenteeism? Is there a problem with my work?'

'Your *work* isn't something you can do if you're absent now, is it?'

'I really feel as though you're accusing me of something. Are you able to share your evidence for what's a very serious allegation?'

Anton took a breath with his eyes closed, ruffled at the idea of him potentially facing counter-accusation. He reset, saying in his most unctuous voice, 'Hey, let's dial this down a little. How about I turn a blind eye this time and log my concerns informally. I suggest we get some time together at the away day on Friday, discuss how we're going to manage your performance going forward. If challenges are being experienced, then they should be discussed.'

The away day. *Shit.* I'd totally forgotten about that. An unbearable day of 'team building' and 'thought showering' in some crappy hotel near City airport, all organised under Anton's auspices. I'd been dreading it so much I'd put it clean out of my mind, and now I had Anton's 'performance management' chat to throw into the mix. How could he be superior to me, I wondered. He didn't even know what a self-important idiot he sounded when he used the passive, both in his written and spoken word.

'*If **you** are experiencing **challenges**, not: If challenges are being experienced.* You can make me active in the sentence, give me ownership of the action. You don't need make me passive; have the action done to me.'

'I'm sorry, what?' He stared at me bewildered for a moment before his upper incisors came to rest on his damp lower lip in irritation.

'It doesn't matter. I'll be in tomorrow. You'll be seeing me, Anton. Dead, dying or injured.'

'There's no need to take that kind of—'

I'd jabbed at my keyboard to silence Anton and end of the Teams call.

'Thinking about calling in sick on Monday?' Dom had been listening to the whole thing from the corner of the kitchen. 'Don't you think the time's come for you to leave once and for all?'

I still wanted to resist falling into line with another one of Dom's big asks, on top of severing ties with Sal, no matter how shaky things may have been between us. I wanted to keep working not so I could keep on seeing Gabriel, not because I loved my job as much as I used to, but to have something that – unlike the house I lived in, the baby I'd had when I wasn't ready and was barely capable of parenting, the body I walked in – felt entirely my own. Between Dom's daily calls, endless messages, and his control over the way I got to and from my office, work was the only place where I had a modicum of freedom. If I didn't have that, then I would surely go mad; what use would I be to the baby then? I had to stay working. Anton could not be allowed to take that away from me. I hated him viscerally for that. Or maybe I was sending all of my hate, for myself, for my husband and what he'd done to my life, into a much easier target.

'I'm going into work this week,' I told Dom. 'After that, we'll see.'

Day sixteen, Monday

My hangover headache woke me very early. Dom was still asleep, so was the baby. Instead of trying to get back to sleep myself, I decided I was going to take control of my day. I slipped out of bed, showered in the bathroom downstairs and pulled out clean underwear and a creased dress from the tumble dryer. I wasn't desperate to be at work, I was dying not to be at home. I only messaged Dom once I was safely on the bus.

At the crunch meeting with the ad agency, we'd be sharing our copy ideas for their team's creative concepts. The meeting needed to go without a hitch, for the sake of the charity's next fundraising push and also, for my own sake. I had to prove I was an asset to the charity so Anton would have no case to 'performance manage' me out of the door.

I had to sharpen up; I knew I looked awful. My skin was dry and booze-sallow, the whites of my eyes, grey, and my hair refused to be coaxed into any semblance of neatness, the dull, lifeless arc of dirty tones fluffed and disorderly as new, postpartum growth was springing from my scalp. When I arrived at the office well before eight, my heart sank and rose almost in the same beat. Gabriel was already there. With no one else around, he didn't need to hide his delight at seeing me.

'You're here. I'm beyond happy.' Gabriel watched me as I dropped my bag to the floor and fired up my machine, smoothing down the outer layer of frizzy hair to my shoulders. 'I nearly called you, like about a thousand times over the weekend, but I don't know . . .' Gabriel ran his fingers through his own hair as he pushed past his embarrassment. It was delectable; within seconds of being around him, all my priorities and perspective shifted again. It would take all my will to stop myself from jumping into my abyss. I vowed to think of the baby, her face, her innocence, the image of her tolerance as Dom squeezed her fingers between his lips over and over the day before; how I couldn't do anything that meant I couldn't be near her, keep her safe, nudge her into being all she could be, not all I was not.

'I never want to be stalkerish,' Gabriel continued. 'Like, I promise I haven't even googled you or anything creepy like that.' He now looked stunned at his own candour and dropped his head into his hands. 'Shit, it's not even eight o'clock and I'm already acting like a total idiot around you. Right,' he said, looking about his desk, as though he might have found his self-control lying there, 'I must need a coffee. Please can I get one for you, by way of an apology for wholly unsolicited and inappropriate workplace comments?'

I laughed. It felt so wonderful, foreign too. My husband did not make me laugh. Surely, even worse than a life where sex was executed not out of desire but out of duty, was an existence where laughter was manufactured not from amusement but by obligation.

'You may buy me a coffee. But I'm coming with you.'

Gabriel and I were joined at the hip from then on in; in the coffee shop and throughout the first half of the day, when we went to Fitzrovia for what turned out to be a fantastic meeting with the agency. I left it feeling completely energised. The agency creatives loved the work; the whole campaign was shaping up brilliantly. We all had that feeling in the room: we were working on something that would connect with people, be remembered, win recognition, but more than this, refill the depleted coffers of the charity and maintain services to the women needing our support.

When we left the agency's offices, Gabriel was jubilant. We stood on the street just outside. He stopped in his tracks and beamed at me, holding his arms open in the air in front of me as though virtually hugging me. I knew he would not touch me without my consent. I moved forward into his space and brought him to me.

It began as a professional hug, the equivalent of a slap on the back, but neither of us wanted to it to end. We lingered. I could sense him drawing in the air around my neck, and I inhaled him; the utter, torturous bliss of the scent of him, being right next to his skin and his body, mine coming alive again in his presence. Gabriel's fingers found their way to the back of my neck, danced around the hairline at my nape, leaving me instantaneously tingling as though cold water was trickling down my neck to my spine, and also hot with the blood instantly flowing to my lips, to all the pieces of me that longed for him. His mouth was near my ear, the exquisite warmth of his breath on me.

'Oh, Elle. What am I going to do?' he said quietly.

'What do you want to do?'

'Do you really want to know?'

'Tell me.'

Gabriel pulled back from our embrace but only so he could view my face up close. 'I want to know absolutely all of you; every last bit.'

I closed my eyes, sighed with delight at the idea of letting him know all of my body, and sharing something of my soul with him; to know and to be known.

'What do you want, Elle? What do you really want? I mean, am I imagining things here, or do we have something? Because I really think we do.'

He kissed me with such deftness, such intense, meaningful, lingering tenderness, I did not know how I would ever stop that kiss, the whole thing. But stop I must. I made myself think of the baby, my guilt over her unwantedness, my lack of presence in her care so far, all the ways in which I was screwing her up by being here and not there. But didn't I do that already, when I put my need to feel as though I was moving forward with my life above being honest with Dom that I loved the progress he held the promise of enabling for my life more than I would ever love him?

Shouldn't I have imagined that one day I might be required to bring a child into that mess? I forced myself free of Gabriel.

'We do have something, but we can't do anything about it.'

'Because of work? Elle, my contract's up next month. I can wait that long for you. So, please, don't say *never*, just say *not now*.'

'Not now, then,' I said, happy he'd framed a reason to defer any definitive action on us. I kissed him one more time, fully on the mouth, then on the cheek. I wanted to kiss every millimetre of his face, all of him, but I couldn't then, I couldn't ever. 'We need to get back to the office,' was all I said.

When I got back to my desk, I found a jar of olives with a Post-it note on the lid:

It would have been a branch, but you can't eat a stick. I'll be at our table at 1.

I decided I would see Sal at Pret. I wanted to hear her side of the story. I needed to explain why I couldn't see her again outside of work, assuming I believed what she told me when I asked about what had happened between her and Dom on Friday. My stomach roiled. I needed her to make it easy for me to trust her now, facilitate her and I getting back into step with each other, so that I might still snatch an hour of release and something that felt adjacent to freedom with her over what would be secret lunchtime get-togethers.

Sal was already at our table when I arrived at one sharp. She wasn't crying, but I could tell that she had been, and that she was nervous.

'Hey,' Sal said, getting to her feet, almost moving to hold me, but pulling back at the last second. 'I didn't know how long I had you, so I got you a niçoise already.' Sal viewed the tuna salad in the cardboard-and-plastic tray in between us and shook her head dismissively. 'Anyway . . . yeah.'

I took my seat.

'Did you have sex with Dom?'

Sal was visibly taken aback by my boldness. She caught her breath and asked quietly, 'Is that what he said?'

'I'm not asking him. I'm asking you. Did you have sex with Dom?'

Sal swallowed, leant her elbows on the table. 'Listen, Elle, I . . .'

'Don't think about lying to me, Sal. I couldn't bear it. I know there's something going on with you, something you're not being honest about, something involving me and my marriage. I need you to tell me what it is. I need to know what I really walked into on Friday.'

'You walked into what you walked into: me angry at Dom for trying to control me and my family.' Her jaw hardened.

'I need you to be honest with me, Sal.'

'Your husband was trying to control me just like he tries to control a lot of things. That's why I was so angry.' She held my gaze as if willing her words into my mind once and for all. 'Elle, I understand why this whole situation with me, Tim, the money we don't want from Dom, has put you in a really tough position, and I get why you'd have to stick with your husband, but I was wondering, could we have one last bit of time together?'

'I can't, Sal.' I said, allowing myself to take some relief from her request. If Sal really had slept with Dom, it would be a pretty bold move to ask us to hang out alone. Why would she put herself through that if she was guilty of betraying me?

'Please, hear me out. The away day; let's make a night of it, and a morning. The hotel's a bit shit but according to Tripadvisor the breakfast's decent, and there's a pool.' Sal looked away from our table uncomfortably, then returned to me with tears in her eyes. 'Look, would you let me book us a room, or what? Tell Dom . . . I don't know, tell him whatever the fuck you need to, just let's try to have one last night. Please, Elle, do you reckon we could do that?'

Seeing my best friend, my rock, enfeebled and weeping was too much to bear. I told myself Sal was telling me the truth: she was angry at Dom's attempt to steer her life, just as she was raging at his moves to end our friendship. 'OK,' I said.

'Yeah?' she said, brightening, her relief palpable. 'You won't regret it.'

My phone's ringing halted any further conversation. I got up, turned away from the table to accept my lunchtime call from Dom, before leaving Sal and my lunch where they sat.

On the bus home, I worked out how I planned to tell Dom, deciding there was only one way I knew I could have any hope of him releasing me.

'I was thinking, as the away-day drinks are going to go on pretty late on Friday, I was wondering whether it was best to get a room at the hotel.'

Dom, who had been prepping food for the baby, paused chopping some red peppers. He rested his knife on the board.

'You want to go away for the night?'

'If that's OK?'

Dom sank his knife into the flesh of another bright vegetable so hard it made me startle. He remained silent, though by now I could hear the deep breaths he had begun to take through his nose. I could sense his rage from where I stood.

I held my nerve, stuck to the script I'd composed on the bus. 'I was thinking maybe I could get some spa treatments, take a swim, get a night of unbroken sleep, because, well, I was wondering whether it might be time to really focus on taking care of my body. Now I've stopped the weight training with Jordan, I want to get my body ready for another pregnancy.'

Dom's blade slowed again. He transferred his attention from the chopping board to me. His expression had that odd blank quality I'd started to see more of. I was afraid, but I didn't want to give up. Once Sal had planted the idea of getting away for the night, I realised how much I wanted that. I needed to get away from Dom, even if only for just one night with my friend, away from anyone who might hear us; somewhere that would give me some space to think, to regroup, to see if there was any way at all I might extract both myself and my baby from Dom safely.

'Because I was also thinking after I get this over with, this whole cycle of work out of my system with the agency project nearly finished, maybe we should go away for the weekend and really kick-start adding to our family.' As I spoke, my stomach contracted in repulsion.

'You really mean it, Elle? You want one night away before you'll focus fully on me and this family again? That's all you promise you need?' His voice was a slow, high-pitched whisper.

'It's not as serious as all that, Dom.' As I had done so many times, I invited some mirth into my tone that never quite managed to arrive.

'Because if you needed more than that, Elle. You know it would kill me? You know I couldn't live anymore if I thought you didn't really want me and the life I've given you?'

'I . . .' I began to speak but stopped when Dom abandoned his task, and walked to me quickly. He held my face in place to kiss me, before dropping his grip to my breasts. From here, one hand went to pinch the fold of my stomach, which is where it remained through the duration of the short-lived fuck that followed. I was free to spend one last night with Sal.

Chapter Twenty-Six

Day twenty-one, Saturday

'You're kidding, right? Whatever you imagine I did to you in the past, your wild ideas about my care for my sister-in-law; this is me, Thea,' Dom says in response to her putting him under arrest.

'You do not have to say anything,' Thea says unperturbed, 'but it may harm your defence if you do not mention, when questioned, something which you later rely on in court. Anything you do say may be given in evidence.'

'Are you fucking joking? Elle?' Dom gives me a furious and expectant glare. '*Elle*. Say *something*. I didn't do this. Tell her!'

I say nothing, but I can't look at him. He tries to step past Thea, but she doesn't shift, standing firm in front of Dom. In fact, before I can work out what's happening, she's overpowering him, using his own body against him, taking hold of the arm nearest her and thrusting forwards, placing her leg behind his, destabilising Dom so his own weight unsteadies him. When Thea puts her arm up to his chest, gravity does the rest. Dom twists as he falls, so he's chest-down. Thea bends one of his arms to her, joining it with the other behind his back. I'm agog at how easy she had made the whole process appear, though I realise straightaway, nothing about executing the manoeuvre has been easily won. I know everything she's done so far in this room has taken Thea's untold strength and self-belief.

'That's for resisting me,' Thea says slowly and quietly into Dom's ear, as though she had been waiting some time to say exactly this to him.

Two other uniformed police officers arrive soon after, another moment from a movie. Together with Thea, they bring Dom to his feet. I watch it all happen as though it is someone else's life.

'Suspect too?' one of the officers asks Thea. He's talking about me.

'Victim,' she tells them. 'We need a SOIT.'

The male police officer begins to shuffle Dom out of the room.

'Elle,' Dom says. 'I have a theory. Listen, Elle. *Elle*, you need to hear this, *please.*'

Some residual fear makes me look at him.

'Sal, Elle. Don't you see? It's *her*. She's involved in this somehow. I *know* she is!'

'I don't believe you.'

'You sure about that? Sure, you can trust her? You know she practically begged me to have sex with her that night. Yes, that's right. Don't look at me like that. I felt sorry for her, for fuck's sake.'

'Take him out of here, please,' I tell the police officers. They push Dom towards the door.

'She's the whole reason you're here, isn't she? The hotel room was all her idea, wasn't it?'

Thea helps the other officers shove Dom finally out of the

room. He could not look more like a murderer: the latex gloves, the overshoes, resisting arrest, spouting what would sound to anyone else like a desperate theory about his supposed innocence.

Thea follows Dom and the other police officers out of the room before stopping to turn back to me. 'It's going to be OK.'

'Is it? I don't know that it is,' I tell her. 'I feel so stupid, so weak; I don't trust anything about myself.'

Thea looks to the floor. 'You think men like Dom choose women they think are weak? Where's the sport, the sadistic pleasure in that? There's no game to win for them, no show of their power if there's none to take away to begin with. He chose me, he chose you, Elle, for your strength and then worked to take that away from you. And when he didn't manage that, he tried to punish you in the worst possible way.' Thea looks behind me to Anton's body and when she speaks again, she looks out of the corridor to check Dom and the other officers are out of earshot. 'But he won't win; we won't let him.'

I want to believe Thea; I feel as though the rest of my life and Agatha's might depend on it.

'Elle,' she begins again much more loudly, and it's clear that is the end of any 'deviations' from protocol, and any mention of them. 'One of my colleagues is going to take you away from this room and someone who'll you'll hear called a SOIT, a sexual offences investigation trained officer, is going to want to take you for a medical examination at one of our haven centres. They won't be in uniform, and the building is anonymous; it's a safe place, but you don't have to consent to anything you don't want to do, do you understand?'

'I think so. I want to do whatever I need to make sure there's justice.'

Thea blinks her thanks.

'What the hell are you doing here?' We both turn to listen to Dom, speaking at the far end of the corridor. Who is here? 'Mother, listen, you need to get me a lawyer, a good one, now . . . What . . . what are you doing with *her*?'

'Good evening, officers, I'm Elle's next of kin.' Patience ignores Dom.

'And I'm her best friend.'

Sal? Sal and Patience together?

'Can we see her?' Patience asks the other officers.

'She's coming out now!' Thea calls out to the pair of them, before speaking to me once more. 'I'll go and organise a clean room for you all to wait in for my colleague. Go ahead, Elle. You can leave now.'

Thea steps aside, leaving the path to the world outside of this hellish room, of Anton, of Dom, of the vestiges of all of my prisons, behind me.

I stumble over the threshold and into the corridor.

I am free.

Chapter Twenty-Seven

Day twenty, Friday

It was the last section of the away day before the drinks. Anton's team, including me, together with Sal's team were being forced to sit through another painful hour facilitated by Anton, this one entitled *Strategising the Future*. He's been grandstanding about this session all week, ever since my victory at the agency with Gabriel became common knowledge amongst the leadership team. This seemed to have spooked Anton greatly. He was even more odious and nit-picky about my 'performance' and prone to even more determined displays of power, telling Steve the agency reaction was 'all down to him hiring Gabriel'. This away day session was already showcasing classic Anton; starting with an introductory speech by him that went on far too long. It ended with him saying: 'So, guys, to maximise the session, I really want *no blame, no bad ideas* to be our mantra. OK? So, who wants to go first?' Anton prowled the stretch of carpet in front of a flip chart while gesticulating with a green Sharpie. He was determined to capture all the ideas for future impact from his colleagues, then present to the leadership team as his own.

Sal raised her hand.

'Yes, Sal?' Anton turned to face his flip chart, ready to write up her idea, his Sharpie poised.

'My suggestion for a more successful future for this organisation is to stop directing precious resources to corporate navel-gazing when most of us know exactly what we're here to do, today, tomorrow, every day.'

Anton's Sharpie remained hovering inches from his flip chart. 'Those sorts of perspectives aren't really in scope today, Sal, but thanks for sharing. Anyone else?'

Every time Anton turned to scribble someone's thoughts on his flip chart, Sal and I texted each other. It felt both juvenile and necessary.

Me: LW says no such thing as a bad idea unless it's one of yours.

Sal: Or, I don't know, the truth? Totally get why you hate him now. He can shove his Sharpie up his arse.

Me: Before someone rams it down his throat.

I was so glad to be messaging her like that, as horrible as I realised we were being. We were getting in sync again. Despite the weirdness I'd seen between her and Dom at Patience's house, she'd promised me nothing had happened between them, and I believed she would never lie to me. I was so happy we were going

285

to have some time together, chatting in our room, over breakfast and the early swim we'd plotted. When I was ready, I planned to tell her how unhappy I was with Dom. To share my growing fears over my future, and my baby's. I wanted to ask Sal's advice on how we might possibly get away from Dom. I wasn't ready to say words like 'divorce', but I knew I had to do something to change where my life was headed. I needed to imagine that a life with more freedom could be possible, one where we were liberated from the constant threat of Dom's neediness and anger.

Me: Jesus I need a drink.

Sal: You're in luck. I overheard LW talking to Steve about some corporate sponsor for the drinks reception.

Me: Really? Wow, we should be soooo grateful to Anton and Steve's private sector buddies. It's probably some disgusting private equity firm that fancies the margins on women's refuges.

Sal: Ha. I'd love to imagine you're wrong.

I'd been conscious to avoid speaking to Gabriel throughout the day. Attempting even normal conversation with him would risk others picking up on the energy between us. When the working sessions of the day were over and we were moved to the bar area where there were trays of sparkling English wine, courtesy of the corporate sponsor, I drank it almost without thinking as me and Sal bitched about Anton and talked over some ideas that might actually support the future of the charity. The evening wore on.

It was getting towards nine. I couldn't avoid Gabriel for much longer. Sal had gone to the bathroom. I was standing alone in the corner of our designated area, desperate to avoid chatting to Caleb, Steve or Anton, and trying to focus on building myself up for my big conversation about marriage with Sal. Gabriel spotted me on my own and seemed to take a deep breath before making a beeline. It was thrilling, the wine fizzing inside me, loosening my resolve; the sight of this beautiful man, not tall, not imposing, but self-contained and genuinely confident, not offering the world the arrogant, fragile proxy of self esteem Dom did.

'Hello,' he said.

'Hello.' Even a simple greeting was so loaded.

'I'm staying here tonight, Elle.'

'OK.' My heart rate kicked into another gear. 'I have a room too, but it's with Sal.'

'She did mention that. So, that means you have a choice. What do you want, Elle? Do you even know?'

'I'm . . .' *I'm what? I'm a wife, I'm a mother, I'm someone who needs to keep remembering what she needs to do so she can keep her baby safe.* 'I'm a person who's made some questionable decisions in my recent history that have made my life not what I thought it would be.'

'And you think being with me might be a *questionable* decision?'

At that moment, a waitress came by with a tray of drinks, the reserves of sparkling wine apparently exhausted.

287

'Excuse me, would you like to choose? The white wine is an Australian oaked Chardonnay, and the red here is an Amarone.'

I took the single large glass of red from the tray, so absorbed by Gabriel's presence that I didn't stop to wonder why there was only one, or how it was that the corporate sponsor had managed to supply my new favourite wine. Gabriel took a glass of the white.

'There's a lot I need to think about.'

'You can take your time processing whatever you need to; tonight, tomorrow, whatever you need, just don't write us off. Don't say never.'

At that, Gabriel walked away. I watched as he attached himself to a random clutch of colleagues while I downed almost a third of the glass of red in one full-cheeked swallow. The taste reminded me of being at home. I didn't want the Amarone anymore. I didn't want any of it: the booze, the house that wasn't ever mine, the stalled career, the shitty boss, the husband. I wanted my baby, and, in that moment, I wanted my lover, and I wanted to be free to be Elle Cotton again; to be moving forward in a future of my own making, with my own family, my mum and my brother and my stepdad there too; and with my best friend who was at that point coming back over to me. I was ready to tell her everything. But as she approached, Sal winced and rubbed her stomach.

'You alright?' I asked.

'Define *alright*.' Sal clasped her hand over her mouth before putting both hands on her hips and taking a deep breath. 'You spurned the filo prawns from the buffet at lunch?' Sal exhaled.

'Smart move. I'm fucked. Anyway, how was your deep and meaningful with the G-man?'

'Oh, it was neither.'

'He is *so* into you, mate.' Sal glanced over to Gabriel who couldn't disguise his longing from the opposite side of the room. 'Shit.' Sal clutched her stomach. 'I can't be here. I'm so sorry, Elle, we're going to have to try this again another time. I gotta go before I completely shame myself.'

'No, Sal, please don't go. Let me get you some water, sit with you a while.'

'What do you reckon the going rate for shitting yourself in the back of an Uber is these days?'

'Sal, please, if you go now, I don't know when I'll get to speak to you again properly.' I was scared I would never feel as brave as I did in that moment again. I was frightened I would end up returning to the house that wasn't mine, and the husband I didn't love, and prove too cowardly to leave either of them for any meaningful amount of time again.

'Sure you do.' Sal managed to get past the apparent spasms in her stomach long enough to calmly look me in the eye. 'You can't get rid of me that easily.'

'Oh, Sal, it's not—'

Sal's hand went to her mouth again. 'I have to go, like, now. Have a good night,' she said, turning to leave. 'Do me a favour. Make the most of the room, will you?'

I didn't have long to register what the glint in her eye meant as Sal left. My phone, which was in the pocket of my dress, buzzed. I knew it would be Dom.

Dom: Missing you very much. Wish I could be there. Do you miss me?

Me: Yes xx

Dom: Who have you been speaking to?

Me: The usual colleagues.

Dom: Which ones?

On and on the messages buzzed. More questions, requests for ever-more detail. My stomach turned and my pulse galloped. It was as though he was in the room. Meanwhile, Gabriel continued to watch me as I made small talk with some of Sal's team members, me catching his eye, sending a smile his way. Would my life be like this forever if I couldn't find some way of escaping my marriage? Without Sal's counsel, how could I make myself stay brave enough to make that happen? That night had to be when I'd make the break one way or another. It was then or never. I texted Dom:

My phone's nearly out of juice. Leaving it to charge in my room. Drinks will prob go on late, so I'll sign off now. Hope you have a settled night. Give the baby a kiss from me. Love you xxx

He sent me a string of further messages in the following minutes, as I nursed the glass of wine I knew I didn't want anymore, along with so much more. I did not open any of Dom's messages. I put my phone on 'Do Not Disturb' and walked across the room to the bar.

Gabriel was stood alone when I approached him.

'Sal's ill. I have the room to myself,' I said quietly. 'I'm going to leave shortly, and I would like you to leave soon after. It's room one-four-seven, on the ground floor, turn left at reception.'

Gabriel fiddled with the stem of his glass. 'I don't know, Elle. How can I be sure that's what you want?'

'It *is* what I want.'

'You send me such mixed messages. You're hot; you're cold; you want me; you think I could be a bad decision. Which is it?'

'It could be both. That's life. You don't always know until it's too late.'

Gabriel closed his eyes. 'I don't get you, Elle. I really want to, but I don't. I don't know what you really want.'

'I know what I want now, tonight: it's you. I want to spend the night with you, Gabriel. I don't care how it feels tomorrow.' I didn't care about my guilt the next day; in fact, I invited it. I needed to do something that would not wash passively over my life without impact.

'*I* do. I want you tonight, and I know I'll want you tomorrow. I think I need to think about it.' Gabriel looked back over his shoulder, aware our conversation would look unusually intense to anyone watching us. 'And so do you.'

'Please, Gabriel, I—'

'What are you two discussing? How you might wring a bit more out of Steve for the agency campaign?'

Anton had joined us. My heart sank.

'Something like that,' Gabriel said. 'I'll leave you to it.'

Anton watched Gabriel move to a pocket of people on the other side of the bar. 'Something I said?' Anton turned back to me. 'Where'd you manage to get that red from?' He gestured to the glass I'd been nursing. 'Our sponsors don't seem to have supplied this basic need. White gives me a migraine.'

I was still focused on Gabriel. 'Have what's left of this if you want. I don't want it anymore.' Anton viewed the glass, almost suspiciously. 'Take it or leave it, Anton. I don't care.'

'Alright, I don't mind if I do.' Anton took the glass off me, pulled a tissue from his pocket and wiped the rim before almost finishing the whole glass in two quick gulps as though if he drank it quickly he could achieve a wine buzz without catching whatever germs he imagined I harboured.

Meanwhile, I got my phone out of my pocket. 'I just need to check my messages a moment,' I said. But I didn't do that. I ignored all the further WhatsApps from Dom and instead activated my phone to record and dropped it into one of the front pockets of the dress I was wearing. If there was a chance Anton was about to incriminate himself on his campaign to manage me out, I wanted to make sure, this time, I gathered the evidence. We spoke for a bit, relatively normally, before I managed to steer the conversation around to his plot to oust me. It's at this point, I realised I felt quite drunk. Anton too was starting to show signs that the necked Amarone was taking its toll on him. Listening back to the recording, it sounds as though it was almost too easy to get him to reveal his hand. I couldn't get my mind to remember anything further from the 'night in question', but this is what I eventually heard on the voice memo on my phone:

Me: So, that's it, is it, Anton? There's going to be some kind of sham conshultation-thing, but there's only one conclusion? You're getting rid of me for no good reason.

Anton: Oh, I have my reasons. You've never respected me . . . you've never taken orders. Shit, my heads . . . my legs feel fucked. What the fuck. I need to hold onto you.

Me: Jesus, Anton, get off me. I'm feeling a bit woozy myself without you leaning on me.

Anton: Please, I'm not trying anything funny, I just need someone to . . .

Gabriel: You guys doing OK here?

Anton: Gabe! Don't mind ush. Elle 'n' I were just indulging in a spot of . . . colleague-to-colleague truth-telling. Weren't we, Elle? It's getting pretty . . . serious.

Gabriel: I can see that. Well, don't let me interrupt. I'll leave you two to it. Good night, Elle. Anton.

Me: Wait! Gabriel . . . I . . . Bloody hell, Anton, get away from me.

Anton: I can't. I feel like I can't stand. Shit, you need to help me.

Me: Why should I do anything for you?

Anton: Because . . . because I'm bloody begging you, fuck it, I am ordering you as your fucking boss: I feel weird, get me out of here before . . . before I crash out. The leadership team can't see me like dish.

Me: Yeah, you and me both. Jesus. What the hell was in that Amarone. I feel . . .

Anton: Elle, please. Help me.

Me: Why? You're trying to fuck me, Anton. You always have been, since they gave you the job and not me.

Anton: Don't jab at me like that, Elle. Jesus, calm down. You . . . you'll never be fucked. People love you and you've got everything: huzbund, house, kid. What have I got? I've got this fucking job. Help me, for fuck's sake, *please.*

Me: Alright, but . . . can you at least try to support your weight a bit more? . . . And remember, you'll owe me big time after this. You can't do . . . you can't do whatever the hell you want to me, OK?

Anton: OK. Alright. Whatever. We can talk again on Monday if you just . . .

Me: Come with me. I've got somewhere we can go. We'll be safe there.

Chapter Twenty-Eight

Day twenty-one, Saturday

Out in the hotel corridor, I'm greeted with the baffling sight of my mother-in-law waiting for me, Sal at her side.

'Patience, who has Agatha? Where is she?'

'She's with Ol. She's safe.'

'And now, you will be too,' says Sal.

Thea has left Patience, Sal and me in a family suite on the other side of the ground floor. We're waiting for a specially trained police officer to arrive and take me to what Thea described as a 'haven' centre where I'll have a medical examination. I've been given a fluffy hotel robe. Its softness and cleanliness are a dreadful contrast to how sullied my body feels, across its every surface, each fold and crevice. I can't wait to bathe. I can't wait to see my baby. And I can't wait another second to understand what secrets Patience and Sal have been hiding.

'Can we do or get anything else for you?' Sal asks, sat on one of the beds. I'm on an armchair, my feet on the seat, my legs before my chest. Patience stands, her back straight, her proper features tired, some stray hairs fallen from her 'Princess Anne'.

'I want the truth.'

Sal nods. 'OK, where would you like to start?'

I turn to my mother-in-law. 'Patience?'

'Yes, Elle?'

'You have been nothing but vile to me since the very start. And now, you're here to look after me, over and above your own son, apparently. I mean, god, you told me, *two days* before my own wedding . . .' I bring to mind that conversation at the pre-wedding dinner, when Patience had tried to pay me to not marry Dom, to get out of his life forever. Even as I finish the sentence mentally, dozens more memories flood my mind: Patience telling Dom the wedding was rushed; I wasn't ready to have a child. Patience must have left Ol and Flic's wedding album for me to find too, and put Thea's picture in my sight line. She wasn't doing all of this to keep me out of their family because I wasn't good enough for her son; she was breadcrumbing a path away from Dom so that I could leave safely. When that didn't work, Patience directed me towards the truth of my husband's monstrousness.

'You were protecting me?' I whisper.

'Trying to. And I failed, failed very badly. But I'm afraid there isn't a template for managing the harm a man like Dominic may wreak, though I'd had some preparation.'

'For what?'

'Dealing with a monster to whom I was indelibly attached.' Patience closes her eyes, takes a breath. 'Hugo was the father of my children and also a brute, an evil man who sought to control each and every aspect of our lives, mine in particular. I was so thankful when Oliver seemed to have escaped whatever void

Hugo had inside of him that made him who he was. Then, over the years I could see my younger son had inherited that darkness, that dreadful weakness that tries to assert itself as power.'

'Why didn't you tell me straight out? Why didn't you tell me about whatever he did to harm Thea? And what about Flic, for god's sake? Thea says Dom killed her.'

'We don't know about Flic, not really.' Patience folds her arms around herself, looks at the floor and I can see that she too knows, deep down. She knows Dom brought forward Flic's death, just like Thea said Ol does.

'*Don't* we know, Patience?'

Patience takes a sharper breath, this time in a bid to stop herself from crying, but when she speaks, it's no use. 'I . . . I couldn't live with myself if I allowed myself to believe I gave birth to a murderer, didn't do enough to shape my son so he didn't become even worse a man than his father. You're not so different to me. I've seen you falling into line with Dominic's demands, trying to pacify him, to keep the peace and a calm home for Agatha. I've watched you give up your family and, I should imagine, a great deal more to avoid displeasing him. He managed to do all of this by forcing you to take small steps, one by one, so you barely noticed he was pushing you into an existence you would have once believed unthinkable.'

There's silence for a moment. I let what Patience is saying sink in a little, reassess the game she's been playing with me, before thinking of the games I've played to keep Dom happy and calm. Having sex with him when I didn't want to was only the tip of a deep iceberg. I'd been so dishonest to myself, but what about

Patience? Couldn't she have done better by me if she knew what was happening to me within my marriage all along?

'Patience, the things you said when I was really struggling, when Agatha was born. You made me feel like I couldn't do a thing, not even breastfeed her.'

Patience shakes her head. 'I told you to give up and move her onto the bottle because I could see how much you were struggling. Dominic was obsessed with you giving her what he believed was optimal, no matter what it did to you. I was trying to let you know you had a choice, and I'd help you make that choice if that's what you wanted. I could see the whole thing was making you very ill.'

I rub my eyes, attempting to re-remember the various horrors it seemed Patience had inflicted on me over the years. Had everything she'd done to that point been about trying to shield me from the man she knew her son was?

'What about tonight? I saw you outside in the car park. Patience, I smelt your perfume in the room. What were you doing?'

'I know my son.' Patience's flushed features crumple into a sad smile. 'I knew he planned to come here, knew he was planning to harm you, though I wasn't sure how. I gathered he was feeling threatened; he knew you were not happy, that you were embarking on another relationship.'

'And you both knew all of this how?!'

'I've learnt to play my son at his own game.'

'And what game is that?'

'Surveillance. He had hidden cameras and AirTags and other

ways to track your life, your texts, calls. I monitor his life in the same way. I have access to his computer, his browsing history, documents.'

'I've been writing a diary. I thought it was hidden. It was in a folder within a folder on my personal laptop. He's read it? You've read it?'

Patience nods, pausing before speaking again. 'Somewhere, you knew what Dominic is; you've always known, I think. And when people ask you, *why did you stay*, why did you not detach yourself from him, you know the answers aren't always straightforward.' Patience closes her eyes. 'He is my son. He is the father of your child. He, like his father before him, dedicated the greater part of his emotional life to making it so that you don't trust yourself; no longer know what's normal or reasonable from what isn't; what's love and what's born of hate.' Patience swallows. She will not let herself cry again. 'You must hate women to do what men like Hugo and Dominic do, but maybe not so much as they must hate themselves. That's a prison of the mind's making. Men like them seek to incarcerate us too. The difference is, if we're fortunate, we can escape.'

'That's right,' Sal says, her head bowed to her lap.

'Sal?' I say. She raises her head, her chin pointing to the ceiling, her wet eyes closed at first before she makes them meet mine. '*Don't trust Sal.* That's what I emailed myself last night before I blacked out. Why? Why would I think that, Sal?'

'I knew,' she begins quietly, 'I *knew* from the very start he was no good. From the minute all those creepy bouquets started to arrive. A normal man doesn't feel the need to mark his territory like that. A sane guy doesn't send his wife fifty texts a day; doesn't stop her from cycling to work; doesn't stop her seeing her family or her friends; doesn't somehow force her into having a baby she doesn't want yet.' She sobs through the next words. 'Doesn't . . . doesn't . . . have sex with her best friend. Oh, Elle, I'm so ashamed. I'm so, so sorry.'

'You lied to me?' I must have discovered she lied last night at some point during the time I can't remember. '*Why*, Sal? You hate Dom. You've always hated him, haven't you? And what about me? Didn't you think about me at all?'

'The thing is, I did. Believe me, *a part of me* did, at the time, anyway. Elle, he'd done so many completely unacceptable things, and you just took it; that's what it looked like from the outside. I mean, what would it take for you to realise you needed to get away from him? So, when he came onto me up in his room after I gave him what-for over his covert strings-attached fee *donation*, I shook him off, told him to stop in no uncertain terms. And then, I don't know, he tried again, and it started to happen, and I'd be lying if I said that it being so long since anyone's touched me wasn't part of it, and I did think about stopping what was happening, I *did*. Then, I thought, *what's the one thing that'll make Elle realise what kind of a shit he is? And if I let **that** happen, she might never talk to me again, but, with any luck, she won't talk to him either.*' Sal shakes her head to herself. 'And then afterwards, straight afterwards, I realised how badly I'd fucked up. And that was even before Dom said if I tried to stay in your life, he'd tell you what'd happened. That's why he did it, you know. It wasn't about sex. It was about power.'

'She was vulnerable,' Patience says. 'He played on that. Like one of his machine-learning tools, he worked out how he might approach the matter to achieve the precise outcome he wanted.'

'You knew?' I turn to Patience. 'You knew because . . . you have cameras in his room?'

'I do.'

'He played me like a fucking fiddle,' Sal says. 'He thought paying the boys' fees was enough to buy me out of your life, but I didn't want his filthy money. Me doing *that* with him –' Sal shudders at the memory '– now *that* was one way he could keep my mouth shut and me away from you. Elle, I'm so, so sorry. I'll never forgive myself. I don't expect you to either.'

'You lied to me. After it happened. I asked you outright and you lied to my face.'

'How else would I be able to stay close to you?'

I pause a second to take in what I'm hearing, before my mind moves to the next thing I need to understand.

'The Marriage Rule. What was that all about? You were basically telling me I needed to shut up and put up.'

'No, I wasn't. The idea of the Marriage Rule was to force the issue, not force you to shut up and put out. I knew you were unhappy; you needed something to help you look that in the face. Don't you remember what I said to do if you're not happy about following the Marriage Rule?'

I think for a moment. '*If you're not happy following the Marriage Rule, you probably need to ask yourself why.*'

I remember my despair at the idea of having sex with Dom whenever he wanted.

301

'You tried to force the reality of what giving Dom what he wanted for the rest of my life would feel like. Why didn't you just ask me outright if you were worried I was in . . .' it's hard to say the words, words I've written and read as they applied to other women, but never to me '. . . in an abusive relationship?'

'Because it's not that easy, is it? You can barely say that's what it was now, when you're seeing everything clearly. You weren't ready to hear it. If I did go and say outright my worries about Dom, about your marriage, I was worried I'd see even less of you; you might be defensive, or ashamed, or you might even have been offended. You don't often help someone out of the situation you were in through a straight line of attack. You had to get there on your own. That's why I made up the Marriage Rule. I'd been thinking about me and Tim, and I'd come to the conclusion that marriages that last are about meeting in the middle on everything, the little stuff, the big stuff, money, work and, yeah, sex too. The Marriage Rule, it just came to me that day over lunch. It was outrageous, appalling, but it got you thinking, didn't it?'

'I started to question how I could live my life like that, obeying the rule, giving Dom what he wanted. I couldn't face it. It just made me feel . . . it made me want to not feel anything; made me want to drink it all away,' I say to myself, then turn back to Sal. 'I still wish you would have been more upfront with me.'

'If only it were that easy in reality,' Patience spoke out. 'If I had simply disowned Dominic, as I have wanted to do many times, he would do what he did to you and Thea to others without any checks and balances. I'd long suspected Dominic was his father's

302

son; there were incidents with girls when he was a boy, allegations he faced at work. What he did to Thea confirmed it.'

'Patience?' I ask quietly in case there are police in the vicinity. 'Do you know how Thea came to be here?'

Patience sighs and begins talking as though she has been thinking of the words that follow for some time. 'When my son escaped punishment for what he did to Thea, for a time I saw a bright and capable woman completely destroyed, which was, of course, his aim. It was the way his father ran his marriage to me.'

'OK.' I think of Ol's words: *Dom's a lot like Pa,* but can barely imagine Patience, of all people, falling victim to an abusive marriage. I want to know how she addressed Hugo's cruelty but that will have to wait.

'Thea found a new strength and a new purpose,' says Patience. 'Supporting other victims of abuse, doing what she might so they had more of what they needed in a time of crisis, so they might ensure they had the evidence they might require to convict perpetrators like my son, and, one day, if she could, perhaps see that justice found Dominic himself.'

'So, how did Thea get to me?'

'Ever since Hugo, I've struggled to sleep. I quite often use the small hours to catch up on Dom's activities. The night you were away, I was going through recent footage from his bedroom at my house. I realised he was planning an escalation of some kind. I think he was looking for more ways to control and punish you after he'd discovered your journal, sent a copy to himself; I believe that happened—'

'It was the day I went to babysit for Ol wasn't it? The day I left my laptop at home, when I saw Sal in Dom's attic bedroom at your house. He must have run back to the house after I'd left for Ol's and accessed it then. He must have been incandescent once he'd read it.'

Patience nods. 'And the week after, once he knew you planned a night away with Sal, I knew he'd booked a night nanny. He'd also paid a large sum to sponsor and staff your work's drinks reception. He explicitly asked the catering manager to make sure you and you alone would be offered the red wine I assume he used to drug you. He also insisted you had a ground-floor room, told the hotel that was your preference and that he'd like access to your room so that he might leave a *surprise*. He said that this was your *last night of freedom before you tried for another baby*, and you were to be the *secret guest of honour*. I knew you were in danger. I drove straight to the hotel and walked the perimeter, hoping I could work out which was yours. I saw the wide-open window and located your room. It was quiet. I managed to climb inside. And then, I saw you and that poor soul next to you and what Dominic had done to him.' Patience squeezes her eyes shut as if she might blank out the image in her mind. 'Thank god Thea was on her shift. I told her to get to the area, then tipped off the police anonymously. Then I called Sal, left a message for her, told her to get ready to help you.'

'I cannot believe . . . this?' I say, waving a weak finger in the air between Patience and Sal.

'We're an unholy alliance.' Sal's voice is so quiet, I can hardly hear her. 'Forged by guilt we couldn't do more to protect you and

304

get you the fuck out and away from him. I never thought he'd try to fit you up for killing someone. I mean, Jesus.'

'If I knew he was as dangerous as he's proved, I would have most certainly attempted a far straighter line of attack to make sure you were safe. I can't believe what he's done and what he was planning to do to escape the blame. But his plan isn't going to work out now, Elle,' says Patience.

My head throbs. 'It's not that straightforward, Patience. Dom got the wrong guy. It wasn't the man I've been . . . getting close to. It was my boss, who I despised. I'm not free yet. I'm not convinced a jury will believe me, the cheating wife who hated her boss. I need you to take this.' I get up and shove the spy camera into Patience's hand. She appears momentarily shocked before instantly burying her hand and the camera in her coat pocket. 'Don't watch the footage, but don't destroy it, OK?'

Patience's mouth moves as if she's about to ask me a question when the night manager calls the internal line to let me know the specially trained officer has arrived and will be with me shortly. I am more than ready to go with them.

Chapter Twenty-Nine

Day twenty-one, Saturday

I head back to the house after the examination; it was humiliating, dehumanising, but crucial to my case I'm sure. Sal and Patience waited with me throughout. The police say Dom will not be granted bail and while he might appeal, with all the evidence of coercive control against him, the manner in which he was found, the outerwear of someone most certainly looking to get away with murder, the rape I told them about, the injuries entirely consistent with this, he will remain in remand until his trial, which they say will happen within the next twelve to eighteen months. I say goodbye to Sal at the station without ceremony or promises. Patience drives us back to Dom's house. I tell her I do not want to talk about anything for now.

At the house, I find Agatha playing with Cora in the living area next to the kitchen. I rush to her. As much as I want to cry, to break down at the sight of her blameless perfection, her solid little limbs in her babygrow, the silk of her fine blonde hair translucent in the sunlight, I don't let myself. I want to show her my strength, to demonstrate that from now on, I will be the one looking after her, and I am more than up to the task.

'Good morning, Agatha; hello, Cora, are you helping look after your cousin for me?' Agatha immediately holds her arms out for me to take her. When I bring her up off the floor, I feel the most powerful surge of love for my child, a feeling I realise I've been required to temper, to manage sideways and down, so it could leave enough room for Dom's hate-fuelled dominance.

'She keeps on trying to walk,' Cora tells me with a terrific smile. 'I've been holding her hands to help her.'

'That's just what she needs, thank you, sweetheart.'

Ol stands, his arms crossed, staring out into Dom's garden. I go to him, Agatha on my hip. On seeing me, Ol immediately begins to cry. I glance over to Patience, who's in the kitchen about to make tea. She drops the kettle she was holding back down onto the worktop.

'Cora, come and help Grandma.' Patience emerges from behind the kitchen island, holding out her hand. 'You can pick out some clothes for Agatha after her bath.'

Cora leaves the room with Patience. Ol and I are alone.

'Ol?'

'I . . .' He pushes a clenched fist over his lips for a couple of seconds. 'I don't know . . . I didn't know he would ever, that he was ever capable of . . . I'm so sorry, Elle. Me and Mum, we're just so sorry.'

'I know,' I say.

'I have tried to help him, you know, over the years, I have. It's hard to ever accept your brother is so . . . so damaged.' Ol finally turns to face me. 'He hasn't always been all bad, Elle. I don't think I'd be here without him; don't know how I could have coped

307

with Flic without him. I—' Ol looks into the space ahead of him. I can't imagine how disappointed his wife would be with him, how furious Thea would be if she could hear him now. I see that Ol is a guilty man. That's perhaps why he'll never let himself find love again. He knows after what he's let Dom get away with, he simply doesn't deserve anything more than a life in his living purgatory.

'You know I spoke to Thea. About Dom. About Flic.'

'Elle, he didn't do what she thinks he did.' His eyes are wide and desperate. 'He wouldn't ever do that, not to her, not to me. I know why's Thea's angry and I know why you're entitled to think the absolute worst about who Dom is, but—'

'OK, Ol. Let's leave it there.' I'm so tired and I can see, when it comes to truly grasping who his little brother is, Ol is a lost cause. 'You should go now. Take Cora home, get some rest. I'm good now.'

'Yes,' he says, nodding vigorously, speaking from behind the clenched fist pressed across his chin and lips. 'Yes, I think I'll do that.'

After Ol leaves, Patience and I sit in silence for a few moments, absorbed in the sound of Agatha, who is making herself laugh by slapping down the flames emerging from her wooden house as she winds down before I take her to bed. I plan to nap next to her too. I intend to never leave her side and never to lose control of my ability to be her mother ever again.

'The thing I gave you before they took me to haven centre, Patience, I want to talk about it now.'

'The camera is somewhere safe. I know how to find the footage, wipe all traces.'

'Before you do, I need you to do something. Would you know how to download the footage onto a USB stick before you delete it?'

'Yes, but why do that?'

I pick Agatha up from her playmat and place her on my lap. Together, with the strength of her legs and the steady hold of my hands around hers, she rises to her feet. We both beam at each other, and she leans towards my face, where she promptly lands a wet, nuzzling kiss on my nose before pushing away to her full height again.

'Because I sleepwalked into what he tried to do to me, and I lost years of my life. A man died and he assaulted me; all of it when I wasn't conscious it was happening. I want control. I want the freedom to choose what I know. If I want to, if I have the strength or any reason to, I know I'll be able to fill in those hours from the night he killed Anton in high definition. The rest of the lost hours and months of my life these last three years, I'm going to have to refill, re-remember what was really happening; who he was; who you were; who I was.'

'I understand.'

'Thank you, Patience.'

We both watch Agatha once more. She reaches across to her grandma. Patience takes her fingers between her own, closing her eyes and letting out a sigh through her nostrils. I could see, in that small gesture, the relief, the loss of a great weight she had been bearing for far too long.

'We can't stay here,' I tell her.

'You must stay with me. In Ol's old room.'

'Thank you.'

'Once I've done what needs to be done, and then the police come through, we'll seal off the top of the house.'

I pack what I can into Patience's car. It's late afternoon and I'm sat outside her kitchen on a deck chair on a strip of herringbone brick paving. Agatha is playing at my feet amongst the pots of lavender and garden herbs before the labyrinth of Patience's back garden starts for real. I have just called my mum and told her all I could bear. She plans to get here tomorrow. I can't wait to see her and I cannot believe I have let a man try to break my connection with my own mother, as well as that with my best friend, but also with my own body, with my entire sense of self. But when it happens so slowly, and it arrives in your life in such a smart and persuasive package, I cannot blame myself or any other of the millions of women who find themselves undone by a man, and then trapped by the children we find ourselves making with them.

I'm drinking a glass of a concoction Patience had prepared for me: lemon, rosemary and verbena. It is an unusual blend, tart, fragrant and earthy. I could drink a gallon of it, sat, here, safe in the shade with my baby, careful to not let her wander off in the garden. Patience joins me. I can tell from her poised but nevertheless relaxed stance as she views Agatha from behind me, that she has indeed 'done what needed to be done' in dispensing of the footage Dom captured in the hotel room.

310

'I wanted you to know something,' she says.

'OK?' I reply, nervous about where this might go.

'The flowers, the ones in my hallway.'

'The fancy thistle things?'

'Not thistles, burdock.'

'As in, the weed?'

'The wildflower. On its first phase of growth, it remains relatively close to the ground. But after it dies, the second time it emerges, it grows taller than a man; I admire it enormously.'

'I see,' I say.

'It wasn't that I didn't want you in my family, Elle. It was that I didn't want my son invading what you might have otherwise made of yours.' Patience's features remain still, but there are tears tracking down her eye sockets to her fine cheekbones. 'I'm deeply sorry I did not do more to protect you. Admitting your own offspring is . . . whatever my son is . . .' Patience wipes away her tears. 'I would not wish that on any mother. I should have known earlier. He loved nothing more than sparring with his father. They were mentally the same person. As Dominic grew, he liked nothing more than to test his father, then defeat him. Oliver was little more than a pawn to pass between them. I didn't allow myself to entertain what Thea said Dominic did to Flic, but . . .' Patience's face stills.

'I suppose you were in an impossible situation. As was I.'

She turns her attention to Agatha, who had been making her bid for freedom into the darkness of the garden as Patience and I had been speaking.

'You should get to know the garden before she does.' Patience regards the dark puzzle of paths and optical illusions in our view. 'Searching for someone out there; someone you're desperate to find, for good reasons . . .' she looks to me '. . . or for bad, as Dominic noted that day you found me out here, it is indeed enough to give anyone a heart attack.' Patience eyes a patch of darkness somewhere in the middle distance. 'Eventually.'

Patience had designed her garden so she might hide from Hugo and hoped that perhaps one day, his rageful efforts to discover her might overwhelm him. For Patience, that day came.

'You . . . You really did that?'

Patience reaches into her trouser pocket, retrieves something from it and drops it into my hand: a USB stick. 'We women must do whatever it is we must.'

Chapter Thirty

One year later

I threw away Agatha's house of flames, and her musical mobile of compliant angels, the strains of 'London Bridge Is Falling Down' no longer the tinny sound of my sorrow, or hers. I work part-time, for now, in a different charity in a more senior position, a job share with another working mother, an old contact of Sal's. These days, I see Sal as regularly as I did before I ever met my soon-to-be-ex-husband.

Agatha's days at nursery leave her happily spent. By the time I take her to her cot next to my bed in Ol's old room, she settles quickly and sleeps soundly. Sometimes I wonder if it's down to her busy toddler days, other times I know it's because she no longer picks up on my depthless anxiety and the black spirit of her father about us. We'll be moving out shortly to a purpose-built flat near here. I'm ready for us to have our own space, but I will miss seeing Patience every day.

My new flat is small, paid for by me, but also with a little help from my mum and from Patience. We learnt that Dom's house was mortgaged and remortgaged up to the hilt and his supermarket deal had collapsed even before his arrest. The due diligence process by his prospective partners uncovered the caution he'd received for his crimes against Thea, and also allegations by former female employees of inappropriate conduct and sexual harassment that proved discoverable, though not necessarily punishable. That's the thing with men like him: they make their victims believe it's something about us, some specific and singular weakness that makes us the one woman stupid enough to leave themselves vulnerable to their assaults. But now I see that's not how it works. Men like Dom try to undermine, demoralise and manipulate as many women as they might to fill the void within, a black and terrible vacuum nothing can fill. These people have no right to live in the world, to walk amongst us as free men when their main purpose is to imprison women, though they do not use cages or bars to try to keep us where they would like us; they use the tiniest chink in our armour, and then they dismantle those things that kept us whole inside, piece by piece. And when they have done this, they use our own bodies against us.

Dom's disturbing predilections emerged in the trial: he had a fetish for feeding women. It was also confirmed he'd swapped my pill for placebos he'd bought online. And when he couldn't get me pregnant again, because I was secretly taking my own pills, he took to feeding me, indulging his fetish and trying to exert further control. The too-small dresses and the willingness to ply me with food and alcohol were all designed to weaken my self-esteem and my sense of self, to show how he could mould my flesh just as he wanted to shape every aspect of my life. It very nearly worked. It has been almost 345 days since my last drink, the GHB-laced Amarone the night Anton died, the night my husband tried to take ultimate control of how much I could ever need him by framing me for murder.

At the trial, Dom claimed his innocence throughout. The prosecution had compelling evidence, not only of the fact he had been there at the hotel, at the scene, but also of his purchase of GHB, the drug he'd put into the wine he had ensured that I, and unwittingly, Anton, drank. It was the prosecution's contention that Dom had drugged me, so he might kill Gabriel in a struggle and pin the blame on me. Instead, the dose I consumed debilitated me sufficiently that I had 'rough' but consensual sex with Anton before he and I blacked out and Dom killed Anton, assuming he was killing my lover.

There was an abundance of evidence to support how Dom had tried to assert coercive control as well as reproductive coercion over me. I'd been escorted through all the chapters of the controller's playbook. This is the narrative the prosecution shaped and that my testimony and much more besides confirmed; Dom's initial 'love-bombing' with gifts and flowers, the sweeping me off my feet that left me utterly destabilised and ultimately floored; how he worked to control my appearance and my body; my movements, my job. He tried to keep me homebound with pregnancies and babies, cut me off from my family and friends. He stopped me from properly parenting my child and made it so I barely trusted myself alone with her. The phone records showed he attempted to communicate on average thirty times every day in the run-up to the murder. The jury could see my marriage was not much more than an open prison.

I wanted to show them I was stronger than my story made me seem, while also aware I needed them to see I was utterly incapable of being the killer, despite what Dom's lawyers contested and some of the forensic evidence could be interpreted as pointing to. I managed not to look at the father of my child once. I showed the jury how even the sound of his voice still had the power to terrorise me, but like one of Patience's burdocks, I have grown stronger in my second phase than in my first.

My ex-husband has just been found not guilty of raping me. He has been found guilty of the murder of Anton and awaits his sentence.

'Thea would like to speak to you,' Patience tells me in her kitchen. We have just returned from court after the jury delivered their verdicts. 'She'll be here soon, if that's OK with you.'

'It is.' I have wanted to speak with Thea many times since that night a year ago, but I have been far too afraid. Our justice is delicate. I didn't want to risk shattering it.

Soon, Thea is sat in the front room where Patience had left Ol and Flic's wedding album, shortly after first her attempt to agitate the truth of who my husband was to the surface so I'd need to address it. Hanging Thea's portrait in her hallway was her first poke at my subconscious, to look again at things familiar.

'How are you bearing up?' Thea asks me. 'You did so well, with your testimony.'

'Thank you. I'm fine, or I will be.'

'Now the trial's over, I wanted to share my story and help you understand why I was ready to . . .' Thea struggles to find the words to describe her 'deviations' that helped secure our justice.

'Do what needed to be done?' I oblige.

Dom had tried to take Thea, a GP by day, through the same story as he had me, though with her, he did not get quite as far.

'Reproductive abuse is very much part of the playbook for men like Dom,' Thea says as our conversation progresses. 'As well as the spy cameras and all the tracking he subjected you to, Dom, *stealthed* me. He regularly took off his condom without my knowledge or consent. There were clues along the way, all the times I wanted to ask if he was sure it was on right, but just dismissed it. I finally put it together when I became pregnant. But it was his word against mine.' Though she is smiling, Thea has tears in her eyes. 'But even when I found out about and could prove the surveillance, apparently there wasn't enough evidence to convict him of any crime. What I had certainly wasn't enough to persuade Ol, apparently, that his brother was a rapist or posed any kind of danger to women.'

'Thea, I'm so sorry. What did you do next?'

'I only ever saw Flic alone from then on. I never wanted to see Ol again. Flic believed me. She begged Ol to cut ties with Dom. Dom knew about this. And then, she got sick, and I had to be civil to Ol and Dom too, who was always lurking around. In his grace, Dom informed Ol he forgave Flic for *choosing me over the family*.' Thea says sarcastically before shuddering.

'And your pregnancy?' I ask hesitantly.

317

'I had a termination; not something I ever wanted to be in a position to need, but it's what I had to do. When I was strong enough, I decided I'd join the Met as a Special, a volunteer police officer. There's an epidemic of domestic abuse and violence against women. I needed to do something about it, for me, for Flic, for all of us.'

'Poor Flic,' I say. 'I think about her a lot, especially when Patience brings Cora here.'

'She hated Dom being anywhere near Cora, ever since she knew what he did to me, even before he started offering to do some of the so-called *caring* to give Ol a break. That's when Flic started to get seriously scared of Dom. She said she felt like she was *losing time* whenever he was in the house and Ol was busy with Cora. Back when I started to suspect what he was doing to me, I uncovered his search and purchase history. GHB. I'm confident he's used it on other women before Flic, before you, maybe even me. I know he did it, Elle: he finished Flic's life for seeing what he really was and because she tried to show Ol too. I can't believe Ol is still so blind.'

'He's feels so indebted to Dom for standing up to Hugo for him. It's a blindness of his own choosing, but I agree with you, somewhere Ol knows Dom isn't who he'd like him to be. Looking back, he always refused to let him look after Cora on his own. Ol knows. He only chooses not to see it.' I take Thea's hand. 'I am so sorry about what happened to Flic. And to you. And I'm in awe at how you managed to channel all that pain and anger into helping other women.'

'I'm so glad I could help you, Elle.'

We sit for a moment with the enormity of what we've done, the risks we've taken.

I think very carefully about what I say next, 'I've been worried, petrified, quite honestly, about things falling apart. I've been waiting; I'm still waiting, in fact, should he move to appeal . . .'

'By referring to some *additional evidence*?' says Thea.

I hear movement behind me; the scent of *Je Reviens* in the room once more. 'And where would he find it? That *evidence* does not exist.' Patience lays a hand on my shoulder. 'He would have to somehow convince his solicitors, the police, the jury he had neglected to mention he had a hidden camera in that room, one forensics did not find, and that sent footage to some untold server. And if they were to retrieve said evidence, it would show my son committing a violent and perverted rape he has denied under oath after murdering a man while you, Elle, were in the vicinity but utterly oblivious, just as the forensics have indicated; wouldn't it?'

'Yes. Yes, it would,' I say.

'Elle.' Thea moves to take my hands together in hers. 'I won't worry if you don't. OK?'

'OK.' I close my eyes, not yet really believing my nightmare could soon be fully over.

'If the emotions you're having sit uneasily on you, or feel somehow unearned, trust me, you've earned them. This is what justice feels like,' Thea says.

'And if the experience of justice feels unusual,' adds Patience, 'that's because it is. So few women are ever in receipt of it.'

319

Thea leaves soon after Patience, who's off to one of her Propagators' houses nearby. Patience has intimated she's a good friend who, over the years, helped design her garden, supporting her as Patience devised, in a way not spoken of directly, the plan for how she might address her violent husband in some definitive but ultimately blameless way.

Now, I am alone, with my little girl soundly sleeping in her cot, and my new life all but here. I am ready to understand all that happened the night that changed my life, the night Anton died.

I put the USB stick into my laptop and begin to watch.

At first it's black. A blast of white light and Dom's face comes into focus, a room keycard in his teeth. Judging by the light, it's daytime. Dom would have felt confident neither Sal nor I would enter the room while he set up his camera. Dom places an unopened bottle of Amarone on my bedside table, the supposed 'surprise' he wanted to leave for me, before he crosses the room and opens the large window, then closes the curtains. He leaves.

Once it's dark, it's hard to see anything in the room. I can barely make out either myself or Anton as we bundle inside and fall onto the bed. Dom must have raged when he realised he should have left the light on, and couldn't see the exact moment it would be best to strike as he watched the footage live. But I, for one, am grateful I don't have to watch Anton do what he did to me. I fast forward through minutes of grainy black footage, my degradation unseen.

I skip forward until the moment Dom enters the room again, this time coming into view via the side of the lens near the window and on this occassion, in his overshoes and latex gloves. He hits the nearest light. Now, I can view the back of Dom watching Anton and I on the bed for a second. Dom stands over the two of us. He is visibly panting in rage, overcome by the sight of me lying next to another man. Then his breath appears to slow. Dom's hand goes to his face. He seems perplexed. As am I. Both Anton and I have our shoes on. In fact, we look to be fully clothed. Dom shakes his head in disbelief as if to say, **This** *is who she chooses over me*? Or perhaps it's, *This is the supposed 'young buck'?* I watch on, as confused as the version of my ex-husband on my laptop screen at the scene he's met with.

He moves to the side of the bed near the window and stands over Anton, then gives him a kick, hard enough to wake him.

'Rise and shine, you bastard,' I can hear him whisper.

When Anton doesn't respond, Dom gives him a rough shake, all the while, keeping an eye on me on the other side of the bed. Whatever Dom is planning, he hopes I'm drugged up enough not to see it.

'Wake the fuck up and fight me like a man, you little prick.' Still nothing from Anton. I can hear Dom gritting his teeth as he speaks. He knocks Anton's shoulder with his knee.

'Come on, let's finish this properly.' Dom's voice is louder, higher. He's desperate for the battle he needed to prove himself superior to the man I wanted to be with over him. 'Fight me!'

Anton remains out cold. Dom hovers over him for a moment. I expect this is the point Dom will turn around and head to the bathroom, returning with the smashed wine bottle, but I'm still confused as to how I'll come to end up naked next to Anton, with his marks on me, my hair between his fingers. On screen, Dom still appears to be deciding what to do next, his original plan to prove his dominance over my lover, apparently not working out.

'You . . .' He speaks to Anton now. 'You're nothing. You hear me? Nothing. You're not even worth killing.' Again, Dom sounds as though he's speaking through gritted teeth. He's still so angry, vengeful enough he'll change his mind about killing Anton.

Finally, Dom turns and walks past the camera to retrieve the bottle of wine from my bedside table before heading to the bathroom. Off-screen I can hear a cork pop. He returns with the bottle, but at this stage, while it looks emptied, it's still intact. He's holding something else, a sink-side tumbler. Dom puts it and the empty bottle of Amarone on the bedside table nearest me. What I'll see next will surely be sickening, but I need to watch it if I'm going to reclaim my life fully.

Dom goes to pull off my shoes before tugging the dress and underwear off my limp body roughly and without care, as though I'm not quite alive. Once I'm naked, he allows corpse-me to fall back onto the bed. Standing over me in total power, he drops his trousers and boxers and gets himself hard with his hand, seemingly already aroused by his total power.

Dom had already degraded me that night, only to return and do it all over again.

He looks to be running a condom onto himself before dragging my body towards him. I awaken. He wasn't expecting this; I did not have as much of his drug as he had wanted me to. I resist him as he pulls me towards him, turn on to my front and grab the covers of the bed. Dom takes a fistful of my hair, yanks my body right to him. I see only shadows of my body in front of his, grunting and squealing throughout the following seconds of violation. With all the fight I seem able to muster I turn onto my back, disengaging him.

'I've not finished with you yet,' he says, but I claw at his neck with the last traces of consciousness and all the strength I can find. He steps back and clutches his neck. 'Fucking bitch!' This is when my nails must have snapped, not fending off Anton. I'm back on the bed, still again. Dom appears to abandon his assault. I hear him apparently removing his condom, before heading to the bathroom. A toilet flushes.

When he returns to the bedroom, Dom goes to stand over Anton. He shakes his head.

'What's up, mate?' he says, unafraid of waking Anton now. 'Not man enough to have her?'

He removes Anton's clothes and underwear, roughly, piece by piece, throwing them aside so they join my pile of clothing on the second bed. Next, Dom prises open Anton's jaw, shoves his fingers in his mouth, making Anton gag. Then, Dom appears to poke the same fingers into me and throughout all of this, my pathetic ex-husband sounds like he's crying. From here, he grabs my head and thrusts me towards Anton's genitals. Dom stands back, as though proud of his grim handiwork. He webs his fingers with Anton's, grabs my head and moves it back and forth. But my degradation is still not sufficient for Dom. He wants more.

Dom pushes me off Anton, so I'm lying on my back. He kneels on the bed and drags Anton's limp body so it's across the top half of mine. He walks around to my side of the bed, grabs Anton by the hair and moves his face onto my collarbone. This is where he looks to be pulling Anton's jaw open and pressing it shut with my flesh caught between it, over and over until he is apparently satisfied with the impact. Anton grunts but is paralysed still.

Finally, Dom moves away from the bed. While he surveys the room, in the background, I am stirring once again. He removes his latex gloves and dons a fresh pair. He slips another condom from his pocket and returns to Anton. I can't see exactly what he does, but Dom is crouching with his back to the camera, and the next thing I can see is him walking back to my side of the bed where he tosses something on the floor. I assume it's the dry condom and its wrapper that Dom had managed to associate with Anton's DNA.

I watch myself stirring, this time more animatedly than before. Dom knows he has to go. It can't be long now until he takes the bottle back to the bathroom to smash it and sever Anton's neck. I'm already fighting nausea and palpations, but I need to see all of what Dom did that night, including Anton's murder.

'Bye, darling,' he says as he covers my body and Anton's with the bed sheets. 'I'm sure you'll come crawling back to me when you wake up, when you realise what you've done . . .' tears are creeping into Dom's voice again, as it climbs up an octave ' . . . when you don't quite know what's happened or why lover boy was so rough and nasty.' He stomps away, across the front of the camera.

That can't be it? My mind races for a moment, before he crosses the scene once more. This must be the moment he decides Anton is worth killing after all, that I don't deserve to be anywhere near our baby again, so he'll guarantee it by getting me put me away for murder. But, of course, Dom isn't as strong as he'd like to be. He is needy and weak. He couldn't go through with framing me. He'd rather see Anton's murder as something he might rescue me from, as a scenario where he becomes my self-styled all-powerful saviour once more.

Dom comes down to the level of my head and says into my ear, 'One more thing, darling. You know, you really can't trust a liar like Sal. Unlike you, your best mate was gagging for me to fuck her. She never did hate me, just needed to know I cared.' He strokes my hair. 'Thought I'd tell you while I had the chance.'

He leaves me once more, crosses the path of the camera, but doesn't return. Minutes pass. I mean to jump forward until I see movement on the screen again – the killer – if not Dom, arriving in the room. My thoughts fold into themselves again, eventualities I've not needed to think about since that awful night. Was it Patience who killed Anton? Sal? Because by this stage, I'm genuinely doubting it was Dom after all.

I see myself sitting up. I rub my head, cry out. I fumble around to find my phone. I fall back into unconsciousness for a moment. I come around again. This time, I bring my phone to my mouth and look to be trying to make a voice memo.

'Sal lied. Don't trust . . .' I'm asleep again before snapping conscious. 'Fuck!' I seem frustrated; I haven't managed my voice memo. 'Stay awake . . . stay awake . . .' I repeat and this time I'm thumbing a message to someone: me. 'Don't. Trust. Sal.' Satisfied I've sent it to myself, I drop my phone on the bedside table and flop back onto the bed. I still haven't seen Anton next to me. I fall

325

under again but wake soon after. This is when I swipe the hotel landline phone from its cradle. I speak where I lie.

'Wake-up call please, room . . . um, it's booked under Sally Porter . . . Time? I don't know . . . Need some time . . . three, no four hours to sleep, then I'll wake up, then I'll hear . . . Yeah, that's the earliest . . . four a.m. . . . give me a message . . . tell me at four o'clock, tell me, tell me it's time I woke up. Need to wake up as soon as . . . Thanks.'

When I drop the speaker back in the cradle, I lie back, exhausted.

That's when I notice I'm not alone. I see Anton naked next to me.

'*Whaaa*?' I breathe.

I manage to sit myself upright and half stagger, half fall off the bed, grabbing onto the bedside table as I do. I knock the empty bottle of Amarone over in the process, preventing it from falling by clumsily catching it. I look over at Anton, touch my skull, my collarbone, my lower abdomen.

I slur something.

'No. NO!'

I stumble past the camera and into the bathroom.

There's the sound of glass smashing.

I return to the bed, Anton's side, the wickedly sharp curve of the smashed bottle in my grasp. Anton stirs, see me over him, holding the weapon near his face.

'What! Please, I . . .'

But I don't hear him. I'm zombie-like, my head bowed. I push him onto his back, and he speaks through a breath, one of his last.

'No.'

I run the broken bottle raggedly, weakly across his neck, but it is enough. I stagger backwards and am sprayed with blood, though most of the flow hits the wall. My defence argued Dom held me in front of Anton, put his hand around mine when he performed this motion, but it was far simpler than that.

Anton's hands move to push me away, but only flail in the air. I drop the smashed bottle and my legs buckle. I stagger to the other side of the bed, my palm slapping against the wall, happening to find the light switch. Everything is black again. I don't see myself falling onto the bed next to Anton in our final, ghastly embrace, but I can hear him. He gurgles and moans, the sounds becoming less emphatic with every pump of his weakening pulse. Though I can't see him, I know Anton must be scrawling his final message.

EG

Elle Graham is my killer.

Mum

A cry for help? Or perhaps a goodbye to the one person who loved him. Finally, there is silence. I freeze the screen.

I killed Anton.

Why? Because I believed it was him who'd assaulted me in my confusion? Because in my altered state, neutralising him seemed just punishment not only for the harm he had inflicted in that room, but everything else I felt he'd put me through in the years leading up to that night?

I killed Anton.

Because I could? Because a man deserved to suffer even if it was not necessarily the right one? Perhaps I always knew what I did. I have seen how so many of us lie to ourselves. I am only one amongst many.

I killed Anton.

Perhaps my mother-in-law suspects this, but she has chosen to ignore it. Thea, too, I believe many have had her suspicions over my guilt but in an uneven, unfair, and cruel world, the outcome we've achieved together is as close an approximation to justice as it will allow.

But my husband, he knows he didn't do it, has been arguing that it must have been me, though he has not had the evidence to prove it.

A notification on my phone, a sound that, even a year after I received the last message from my husband, still makes me startle, prepare to fake my breeziness, my smile, my location, my food, my mood, the company I'm in.

The message is from the barrister leading the prosecution against Dom:

Dom is planning an appeal. Vital new evidence, apparently. His brother Ol claims to have access to secretly filmed footage from the night of the murder. Says he's held it back because Dom asked him to, but now he's got nothing to lose, Ol wants the evidence known.

Ol.

Ol, whom I no longer see. Not since that day in the kitchen after Dom's arrest. Now his brother is facing life in prison, he's seeking to finally repay the debt of care he feels he owes Dom for protecting him from Hugo. Ol was right when he said he could be a better man.

But I am not a good woman.

I imagine, for a moment, going to Agatha in her cot. I place a fresh bottle of water in there and an open tub of chopped fruit. She wakes as I try to leave; cries. She wants to be free of her cot; wants to come with me, wherever I am going. I tell her I love her. I tell her I am sorry. I leave her where she is and head downstairs alone. I'm in Patience's kitchen. At the back of the room, my destination, a dark door. I ignore the distant howls of my baby, swipe a bottle opener from the drawer, and walk down into the black of Hugo's wine cellar. There, I can do what must be done; all I am likely good for. I could choose now to drink myself into a stupor from which I may never return.

But I don't choose that.

I grab my passport and my daughter, and the keys to my mother-in-law's car.

Author's Note

In each of my books I've set out to write propulsive female-led stories readers can gulp down, but that also offer you something of an aftertaste that lingers in your thoughts after you've read the final twist. The contemporary themes of my books often arise from processing my own experiences, listening to other women or reading their stories.

I began developing the idea for the book you have just read perhaps six or more years ago. I was hearing and reading so much about mismatched libidos in long-term relationships increasingly defined by parental responsibilities. I wanted to write a character who found herself facing a central dilemma: keep her dream husband happy by having sex on demand, even if she's rarely if ever in the mood, or continue to say no to sex and risk her marriage in doing so. This all stayed little more than an untidy assembly of ideas for some years because it didn't feel enough on which to hang a book. Over the years, however, my attention has been increasingly captured by something else that is impacting the lives of millions of women and would shape this book.

UN Women reported, 'since the outbreak of COVID-19,

emerging data and reports [. . .] have shown that all types of violence against women and girls, particularly domestic violence, has intensified. This is the Shadow Pandemic [. . .] and we need a global collective effort to stop it.' The NGO also shared data on the hundreds of millions of women and girls worldwide who have been subject to domestic violence. This happens to every type of woman everywhere in the world every day. It may well be happening to someone you love. It may be happening to you.

Here in the UK, I have heard senior police representatives describing an 'epidemic' of domestic violence and coercive control mostly impacting women. During my edits, I read with fury the pitiful data on rape convictions (an offence of which women are more commonly victims than men – Office of National Statistics data in 2023 show more than one in four women had been raped or sexually assaulted, compared to one in eighteen men); and I read of cases where women were seriously wounded or murdered by their partners, sometimes in a 'sex game gone wrong', as though a woman can consent to her own death as part of a healthy erotic existence. Something is deeply wrong here.

Greater minds than mine continue to ponder what drives the widespread violence against women by intimate partners, and what exactly can be done to stop it. My tiny contribution here is to take you into a story where a relatively unexceptional woman living a solid lifestyle is brought into, and tries to get out of, a coercive relationship. I wanted to examine some elements of what I understand to be the abuser's playbook and how these are perceived by the victim and wider society: love-bombing, tracking and spying, reproductive abuse, cutting the victim off from friends and family, controlling movement and food, enabling addiction. In doing so, I hope to show how the kind of abusive marriage Elle finds herself in could happen to almost anyone, and to counter the question women suffering domestic abuse may too often face: *Why did you stay?*

It is an alliance of women and the awakened agency of the female lead's character that saves her. This does not mean I believe male violence and coercion are a problem women are responsible for solving. Nor do I blame mothers like Patience for the evil of sons like Dom. But the reality is, it is often women who provide the support networks that allow other women to escape these situations.

Some statistics to consider:

- In the UK, it's estimated a man kills a woman every three days.
- Of the 70,330 rapes reported to the UK police, fewer than two per cent led to a conviction.
- In the US, of the estimated 4,970 female victims of murder and nonnegligent manslaughter in 2021, more than one third were killed by an intimate partner.
- The percentage of women murdered by an intimate partner in the same reporting period was five times higher than for men.

While I hope men read my stories, the reader I imagine when I'm writing is invariably female. After all, according to one final statistic, men account for only twenty per cent of the fiction market in the US, Canada and Britain. In my previous books, I've ended my author's notes with something of an ask or aspiration from or for my female readers, a plea for empathy across female divides, a hope that more women will get to tell their stories. In this note, I ask nothing. Women have and always will help other women in need. If the global and persistent proliferation of violence against women by intimate partners is ever to stop, we need fundamental and profound action by men.

Helen Monks Takhar, January 2024

Acknowledgements

Thank you, Hellie Ogden, Clio Seraphim, Clare Gordon, Sabrina Taitz, Ma'suma Amiri, Grace Marshall, Leila Tejani, Madison Dettlinger, Stuart Gibbon.

Thank you, Kia Abdullah, Nadine Matheson, Anita Frank, Luan Goldie, Louise Hare.

Thank you, Victoria Lane, Chloe Leland, Sarah Fountain, Elizabeth Corrin, Frances Corrin, Charlotte Allam, Helen Nugent, Sandhya Shyam, Emma Guise.

Thank you, Mum and Dad Two.

Thank you, Mum, Dad, Jo, Mike, Chris, Caro, Dette.

Thank you, Ruth.

Thank you, Mohinder and Zora.

Thank you, Danny.

ONE PLACE. MANY STORIES

Bold, innovative and
empowering publishing.

FOLLOW US ON:

@HQStories